MW00934972

The Secret Gospel

DAN EATON

Copyright © 2015 Dan Eaton
All rights reserved.

ISBN: 150789130X
ISBN 13: 9781507891308

For Nicky, Sadie, Derek and Alice

Now there are also many other things that Jesus did. Were every one of them to be written, I suppose that the world itself could not contain the books.
—John 21:25

Convictions are more dangerous enemies of truth than lies.
—Friedrich Nietzsche

FACT

Fragments of a previously unknown account of the life of Jesus by the Apostle Mark were found in 1958 at an ancient monastery in the Judean desert. The account portrayed the Son of God as a mystic and a sexual libertine. Its discovery ignited a furious debate over its authenticity. That debate continues today.

The Muslim Brotherhood was founded in 1928 in Egypt. In 1941, a senior member traveled to Berlin, where he met Hitler and spent the remainder of the war.

The Carpocratians were a libertine Christian sect in second-century Egypt. The Communion, a California-based Eastern religious sect founded during the 1960s, carries on some of its traditions.

During the Second World War, Pope Pius XII failed to speak out against Hitler and his plans for the Jews. The Holocaust remains a historical thorn in the side of the Vatican.

1

Alexandria, Egypt
Saturday, 4 July 2009

In daylight, the last thing the old man would have seen was the nicotine stain of the North African coast on the horizon, but death came for him in the night, and he saw nothing, except perhaps blackness and stars, as he relieved himself through the ship's railing.

When the ferry berthed in the Port of Alexandria the next morning, his body lay sprawled on the wooden deck, neck twisted unnaturally, pants undone, shirt untucked.

Dust and sand swirled up from the sunburned coast, signaling the direction of land far out to sea. The *khamsin*, named after the Arabic word for "fifties" because it was said to come fifty days a year, was common between March and July. Tropical air moved up from the Sudan creating cyclones, sandblasting crops, and coating cities in grit along the North African desert belt.

Aubrey Bairstow surveyed the deck. His gaze settled on the corpse and he exhaled noisily. "Right, let's get this bloody thing over with."

The Egyptian police officer a few meters away threw him an inquiring glance, as if to say he hadn't quite caught the young diplomat's mutterings.

Sweat plastered Bairstow's blond hair to his fleshy temples, and damp rings spread in the armpits of his rather-too-tight but otherwise fashionable suit. This would mean paperwork, lots of it. Quite possibly, it would also mean canceling the remainder of his leave.

Bugger and shit. Shit, shit, shit. The thought made him even more irritable than usual.

A moment passed before he broke the silence again, this time to address the police officer. "Was anything taken?"

The man shrugged, uncomprehending, squinting in the bleached light. "English," he said unhelpfully, pointing at the corpse.

"Well, of course he is, or I wouldn't bloody be here," Bairstow said, cheeks flushed.

Roused at dawn by a call from the deputy ambassador in Cairo, his day went downhill from there. An elderly British tourist had been found dead on board a ferry from Haifa, Israel. He was to take care of the consular arrangements. It shouldn't take long, in and out, the deputy said.

Shit rolls downhill.

A uniformed policeman collected him at his hotel twenty minutes later, and they drove to the port. Diplomatic life was proving to have none of the glamour he dreamed of during his last term at Oxford. This was just the sort of business he hadn't imagined, yet callouts like this one were all too common. If it wasn't an accidental death, it was an arrest for disorderly behavior or a lost or stolen passport. He would make damned sure his room bill and train ticket went directly to the embassy, now that his weekend away from the hustle and bustle of the Egyptian capital was completely ruined.

A pale band of untanned skin peeked from below the frayed cuff of the dead man's shirt. Bairstow guessed a watch had recently been present. He eyed the policeman. Perhaps he was jumping to conclusions, but what else would you expect of a provincial cop on twenty quid a month? For many Egyptian men, a uniform simply served as license to profit.

No point in making a scene about it now, old boy.

"Thieving bastards," he muttered. The cop looked over again and smiled.

Bairstow pulled a pack of cigarettes from his jacket and tapped one loose as he stepped to the ship's railing. He flicked his lighter and drew in the smoke with a gulp of tangy salt air. On the larger deck below, a waiter flitted between couples lounging on wooden chairs around a plunge pool, and pampered children squabbled over a candy-striped life preserver. A man wearing the garb of a Roman Catholic priest sucked on a pipe at one of a dozen tables. All seemed oblivious to the body above.

"They will be allowed to disembark shortly. *Inshallah*, God willing."

Bairstow flinched, startled by the voice.

An unshaven detective in a black suit joined him at the railing. "The coroner thinks a heart attack. *Halas*, finished." He brushed his hands together, as if wiping dust from his palms, an expression and gesture that to an Arabic speaker meant the matter was decided, it was time to call it a day, to go home.

"Of course, there will be an autopsy."

"But of course." The Egyptian bowed his head a fraction in mock deference, and motioned Bairstow back toward the body and the cluster of policemen now standing idly around it, chatting and smoking.

"It appears he was drinking." The detective scratched his stubble and pointed to shards of broken glass with the toe of his shoe. He cleared his throat and expertly lobbed a glob of phlegm toward the railing.

"And urinating in a public place. Why?" He made a sucking sound behind his teeth. "I do not know, sir." That sucking sound again. "But I am a simple Muslim man and there is much I do not understand about Western ways."

The last thing Bairstow was in the mood for was a lecture, but he resisted an urge to glare at the man. In his year at Her Majesty's embassy in Cairo as a newly minted third secretary, his fourth year in the diplomatic service, he'd acquired a near permanent state of annoyance with the Egyptians, worn as a pinch-faced scowl, and born out of an almost complete inability to speak their language or adjust to their religion and customs. Most of his daily conversations were miscommunications that invariably left him irritable.

A dead Englishman was, in itself, of no particular concern. As a diplomat, he'd learned that people acted differently abroad than they would at home. Inhibitions were shed; often too much alcohol was drunk. More tourists died abroad each year than most people realized. The elderly succumbed to the heat, or got in the way of horse carts and buses. Younger men came undone in bars and brothels. Adventure seekers fell off pretty much anything that could be climbed. At worst, this poor sot's death would prove to be a mugging gone wrong, at best a heart attack.

The detective reached into his breast pocket, pulled out a distinctive red booklet embossed with a gold crest, and handed it to Bairstow.

"His British passport, sir."

Bairstow opened it to the photo page. A tanned face crowned with a cap of white hair stared back. Morton Smith. A quick bit of mental arithmetic put him at seventy-nine years old.

He closed the booklet and slipped it into his pocket. "Let's have a look at his cabin then, shall we?"

■ ■ ■

The policeman led him down clanking steel steps and along a narrow corridor, punctuated at regular intervals with wooden doors labeled with descending brass numbers.

It felt good to be out of the sun. Below deck, the light was dim, the air a little cooler. The steady thrum of the ship's engines drowned out the clamor of the port and mingled with the clack of leather soles on wood.

Cabin 58 was small and stuffy. The astringent odor of alcohol permeated the air, despite the open porthole. Sunlight filtered through the netted curtain, carrying with it the honking of horns from the quay. Jumbled books and papers shared the small desk with a half-empty bottle of single malt and a partially filled tumbler.

Bairstow frowned. Something brushed his subconscious and then was gone. A thin plastic raincoat lay over a vinyl suitcase on the neatly made bunk. He stepped over to the desk and examined the clutter. News clippings, some loose stationery, receipts, and travel documents. A plane ticket in its glossy sheath sat next to a fountain pen and an empty wallet. A heavy book lay open. He turned it over and read the title: *The One Who Knows God*, by Clement of Alexandria, from the Loeb Classical Library. He recognized it as a volume by an early Christian theologian.

In the vinyl suitcase on the bed were socks, neatly folded shirts, and underwear. He stared vacantly at the clothes for the best part of a minute. The edge of something poked out from under them. He pushed his hand down the side of the case and pulled out a slim velvet wallet. A heavy object slid from it and thudded onto the bed. It took him a moment to register what he was looking at, and he whistled softly.

The policeman at the door peered in, and then he returned to staring down the corridor and picking at his incisors with a matchstick.

The medal was a Maltese cross attached by a gold clasp to a wide, bloodred ribbon bordered with thin, black-and-white stripes. Four German eagles perched between the arms, each clutching a swastika, angular black crosses on a circular white background. It looked valuable.

Bairstow placed the medal back into its protective slip, returned it to the suitcase, and sat on the bed. He looked back at the scarred wooden desk, the whiskey bottle, and the tumbler. Something about the scene wasn't quite right. He replayed his conversation with the Egyptian detective a few minutes earlier.

What was it the officer said? *It appears he was drinking.*

No shit, Sherlock. He moved back to the desk and took a seat on the stool, sniffing the contents of the glass. A peaty single malt.

Then it struck him. The other glass, smashed to pieces on the upper deck. Why would the old man be using two glasses?

A scrap of paper lay on top of the clutter near the open bottle. He picked it up and took a closer look. Yellow and brittle between his fingers, it felt like the onionskin paper used in old typewriters. He stared at the scribble on the post office receipt: a name and a street address. Several seconds passed as he deciphered the handwriting.

The sudden realization of what he was looking at jolted him to his feet. The motion knocked the whiskey tumbler to the floor, where it bounced, rolled, and came to rest against the leg of the desk without breaking.

"Shit and damn." He brushed the splashes of whiskey from his pants and read the receipt again.

Mr. Alex Fisher, 5 Sharia Michele Lutfallah, Cairo. It was a name and an address he knew well: a close friend, perhaps his closest among the Cairo-based expat community, the Egypt correspondent for a British news agency.

Bairstow glanced toward the door, but the policeman had moved down the passageway. Despite the cool of the cabin, a bead of sweat found the corner of his eye. He blinked it away. *If you're going to do it, old chum, it's now or never.*

He slipped the receipt into his pocket, next to the dead man's passport.

2

Haifa, Israel
The previous day

Five floors above the quay, the air pressure changed; the atmosphere warped and then buckled, and a sudden breeze ruffled the grimy curtains. Professor Morton Smith looked up in surprise from the writing desk as a vein of lightning touched the darkening horizon. Within seconds, the first drops of rain spattered the windowsill, leaving circular prints in the dust on the ground below.

Winter could bring sudden rainstorms, even hail, but they were rare at this time of year and he felt unsettled. August, the hottest month in this part of coastal Israel, was just over three weeks away.

He returned his attention to the letter. The pen trembled in his liver-spotted hands.

I do not mean to be an alarmist, my dear Alex, but some very strange things have been happening. I sometimes feel that I am being watched…

He wrote rapidly, pausing occasionally to lift a cigarette from the ashtray on the desk littered with crumpled balls of writing paper. Time was running out to make the ferry for Alexandria. About an hour and he'd need to be leaving for the port.

His usual routines would have to be abandoned. Today, there would be no sipping cardamom-scented coffee the consistency of tar at a corner café. There would be no soothing *shisha*, with its bubbling bowl and apple-scented tobacco.

A vinyl suitcase rested on the floor near the door, and a thin raincoat lay on the bed beside a sleeping black-and-white cat. The tiny bellows of its lungs rose and fell in the sticky afternoon heat.

Smith read what he'd written so far. Dissatisfied, he balled up the letter.

My dear Alex...

Only a few weeks had passed since he made his discovery, quite by accident, in the writings of Ahmed El-Mestekawi. The reference was only passing, and it was clear the Arab army colonel-turned-explorer and part-time tour operator was ignorant of the full significance of what he'd seen in the Egyptian desert. But he was thorough, a man of military precision, and the notes from his expedition were blessedly detailed.

Smith lifted his gaze and stared out the window as a rusting passenger ferry and a few sailing boats made their slow passage across the ruffled surface of the sea. Voices rose from the road below through a profusion of flowers in the window box, mingling with the cries of gulls and hawkers selling pistachios and ice cream.

An hour passed. The rain stopped, no more lightning, and the sky brightened. He reviewed his latest draft. It would have to do.

With a heavy head, he ground out the remainder of a cigarette and lit another. The chair creaked under his weight as he ran a hand over the white stubble on his scalp and closed his eyes.

Fifty years ago. 1958.

He is in another room, walls the color of parchment, floor gritty beneath his boots. Dust motes drift in a shaft of honeyed light from a window somewhere high up. He is on the third-floor of a sandstone tower, in a small space. An oil lamp smokes on the wooden trestle, the cool air brittle and heavy with its scent.

As always in these wakeful dreams, the book is on the desktop; a seventeenth-century work of early Church history by Isaac Voss, missing its cover and title page. It is not, however, Voss's prose that have his attention, but the three pages of spidery handwriting on its endpapers. He steadies his camera. The phosphorous flash ignites with a pop. Shadows of bookshelves leap onto walls and dissolve.

Some days, and he knows they are becoming more frequent, reminiscences like this crowd in on him. The memories are like children pressing against his car in some chaotic third-world city street, grasping hands and brown faces against the dusty windows. When once he would have shooed them away, he now welcomes them, cracking the windows a little and letting in their tiny fingers.

An electrostatic crackle drifted through the window of the hotel room, interrupting his reverie, the sound of a throat clearing, and then the reedy voice of the muezzin beginning the *adhan*.

"Allah u Akbar, Allah u Akbar, Ash-hadu allā ilāha illallāh, Ash-hadu anna Muhammadan rasūlullāh." God is the greatest, God is the greatest. I bear witness that there is no deity except God. I bear witness that Muhammad is the messenger of God.

Men on the street below stopped to roll out mats, splashing water on their arms and necks in ritual cleansing before raising their hands and beginning one of the quintet of daily prayers compulsory in the Islamic faith. Sinking to their knees, palms splayed and pressed tightly to thighs, foreheads touched the pavement.

His hands shook a little as he folded the letter and slid it into an envelope from the small supply of hotel stationery. He pulled on the threadbare tweed jacket hanging from the back of the door and slid the raincoat over it, patting the letter nestled in the inside breast pocket. He lifted his suitcase, the cat scooted between his legs, and he stepped out of the room, pulling the door closed behind him.

An ancient wood-paneled elevator creaked and groaned its way up to the fifth floor, its tarnished brass gleaming dully in the light of the hallway's naked bulb. Waiting for the wire cage, his back to the landing, Smith did not see the young man in jeans and imitation-leather motorcycle jacket emerge from a doorway across the hall and slip quietly into the stairwell.

3

Tel Aviv, Israel

The email arrived on the secure system just before midday and played on Eli Zeira's mind for the rest of the afternoon. It came from the head of the psychological warfare unit, and it said there was a problem.

Problem my ass; the only problem here, Zvi Zamir, is you can't keep your dick in your pants. He sat back heavily in his folding chair, forcing a groan from its metal frame. One of these days, he was sure it would collapse, leaving him impaled and mortally wounded. There would be irony in that, and he appreciated irony, always had. To amuse himself, he sometimes imagined the headlines if the press ever got wind of such a thing. *Israel's avenger felled by camp chair,* or, more likely, *Secret servant takes it in the ass.* He chuckled. They'd have a field day, but you didn't become successful in this business by making friends.

Zeira had seen his fair share of action; some would say more. After the massacre of Israeli athletes at the 1972 Munich Olympics, he became something of a legend among the few who knew his identity. He'd been a member of the assassination squad directed to hunt down the murderers, a Palestinian terrorist outfit known as Black September, one by one. He personally dispatched four of them, and, regretfully, during one of the state-sanctioned hits, an innocent waiter who stumbled into his line of fire.

"Wrath of God" was his team's codename. Movies were made about them, the most recent by none other than the great man himself: Spielberg. He never watched those movies. Once asked why by a colleague, he explained that he had his own private screening most nights when he closed his eyes to sleep. In much of Israel, the Wrath of God team were still heroes. The rest of the world mostly saw them as murderers—a view increasingly shared domestically by those on the left of the political spectrum.

How quickly people forget the threats faced by Israel. The concentration camps, the gas chambers, the effort by madmen to wipe the Jews from the face of the earth, these things were not ancient history. They happened to real people.

He snorted and lit another cigarette. Sweat oozed from the weathered folds of skin at the nape of his neck. The air conditioning in the makeshift operations room was down, and he'd given up pestering maintenance. They would be busy with the renovations to his usual suite of offices on the top floor. He put down the file and absent-mindedly stroked the shaved dome of his head, exhaling a plume of smoke toward the ceiling. The room stank of cheap Arab cigarettes. A habit he'd picked up as a field operative, along with fluent Arabic in half a dozen dialects.

But that was a long time ago.

Now the director of *Metsada*, or Special Operations, he was responsible for orchestrating highly sensitive projects. As his long-suffering wife never tired of reminding him, these days he rarely left his room in the nondescript office block in downtown Tel Aviv—even to sleep. Those who worked within these walls called it the Institute. To its brother and sister services in other nations, it was the Institute for Intelligence and Special Operations, or Mossad, anointed by the state of Israel to ensure the survival of a Jewish homeland through the collection of information on its enemies and performance of special, covert tasks abroad.

At a knock on the door, he took a final drag on his cigarette and extinguished it in a Styrofoam cup atop the trestle table. There were no glass walls here, no polished marble and flat-panel displays. Kibbutz chic. The remains of the cigarette hissed, emitting a billow of yellow smoke that stank of burned coffee and plastic.

"Come."

The door opened and his secretary's head peered around the jam.

"Ah, Sara."

"Ephraim Halevy is here, Sir."

"Thank you. Please, show him in." *Enough reminiscing, the hour has arrived.* Zeira stood and ran his palms down the front of his rumpled shirt. He'd called the meeting immediately after the email from Zvi, one last chance to impress upon his team the importance of their mission. Pope Benedict's visit, his first to Israel, was fast approaching, and their assignment was critical to ensure it went off without a hitch.

"Yes, sir. By the way, Zvi called to say he's running a little late. He's bringing Hannah."

He grunted in acknowledgement.

Zvi Zamir was head of LAP, *Lohamah Psichologit* or psychological warfare, the Mossad unit responsible for propaganda and deception operations. Routinely late, Zeira wondered if it was intentional, part of an effort to always keep others on the back foot, off balance. He just found it annoying. Hannah Cohen, he had yet to meet; she was a young recruit, operational in the United States for several months, and under an assumed identity, some sort of Swedish or Nordic name, if he recalled correctly. He heard good things about her, but now Zvi was worried she was too young, too raw for what lay ahead. His email that morning requested a delay while another agent was found. Sure, Zeira was the first to admit that some of the groups Mossad infiltrated could be an exceedingly distasteful lot, even the ones that were pro-Israel. But he strongly suspected there was more to it. Zvi had a reputation for playing too close to home, getting romantically involved with his young prodigies, and it was becoming a problem. There was no room for sentiment.

The fact that Zamir was the same rank made the situation delicate. But time was of the essence, a soft approach wouldn't work.

A moment later, Halevy entered and closed the door. Zeira smiled broadly. Halevy he liked; he was dependable and damned good at his job. Out of uniform, a casual observer would not have picked him for a career officer in the IDF, the Israel Defense Force. Thin and pale with bad skin, he looked more like a computer technician, which in truth he was.

"Ephraim, good to see you. Thanks for coming." He strode around the table, palm extended. "How's life treating you?" They shook hands.

"I can't complain, Eli. Life is good, although I'm not sure Ruth and the kids would share that assessment."

"Tell me about it. No rest for the wicked, eh? I haven't slept in my own bed for a week." Zeira gestured at the camp cot pushed against the far wall of the operations room. "Anna has given up complaining. In fact, I think she may even be enjoying it this way." He chuckled. "How are things at 8200?" He pronounced it eight-two hundred.

The two men pulled folding chairs up to the table and got comfortable.

"Busy, as usual. We have no shortage of work, that's for sure."

Unit 8200 was the IDF's signals intelligence corps, responsible for eaves-dropping and code breaking, comparable in function to the United States' National Security Agency and Britain's GCHQ, Government Communications Headquarters. As a Jewish nation surrounded by enemies bent on its destruction, there was little in the way of telephone, email, fax, and radio traffic in the Middle East that Israel could not monitor. As an elite outfit, 8200 alumni were in high demand in the private sector, a real challenge for staff retention. Some had gone on to found Israel's most successful technology companies.

Zeira tapped the folder on the table in front of him. Its cover was red and bore a series of letters and numerals identifying it as signals product. "This makes interesting reading. The chatter has been increasing." (Chatter: the term used in intelligence circles to describe monitored conversations between known or suspected terror cells.) He extracted a cigarette from his shirt pocket.

Halevy winced when a cloud of tobacco smoke filled the space between them.

Zeira pressed on. "As you know, September's visit will be the first time Pope Benedict has set foot in the Holy Land, and the first papal visit since 2000. The prime minister is pulling out all the stops. Improving relations with the Vatican is among his highest priorities."

"I've noticed," Halevy said dryly.

"It is vital this visit goes well, so I think it's important we brief you more fully on this little operation of ours. You are our eyes and ears out there and it may help you sort the wheat from the chaff, so to speak."

A knock on the door and Zamir entered.

"Ah, Zvi, just in time." He was determined not to show his annoyance.

Zamir's physical presence never ceased to impress. A handsome face and im-posing physique that seemed to have matured rather than faded over the years. Zeira could appreciate why women were unable to resist his charms.

And more than a few men. He stubbed out his cigarette.

The LAP chief was followed by a blond woman in khaki shorts, hair tied back in a ponytail with an elastic band. She crossed the floor to the table. Her movements were functional, yet somehow graceful. While not conventionally beautiful, she was undeniably very attractive.

"And I take it you're Hannah."

The blonde nodded and offered a hand in greeting, but no smile. They shook.

"Pleased to meet you, sir."

Zeira said, "I was just filling Ephraim in. Perhaps you'd like to give us a rundown on the current state of play, Zvi. But first, I'd like to have a word, privately." He gestured to the door. "Then you'd better be on your way. We've pulled a few strings with the port authorities in Haifa, arranged for a delay to the ferry's departure to give us a bit more time."

Out in the hallway, he pulled the door shut. The building was quiet.

"I'll make this quick, and to the point. Don't shit where you eat, Zvi. It puts everyone at risk."

Zamir raised an eyebrow. "Excuse me?"

"Don't play dumb. You're fucking her, like you fuck all the others, the girls and the boys. I'm not here to argue. All I'm saying is these things have a way of getting out."

Zamir snorted. "This is 2009, not 1959, Eli. Men, women, nobody cares."

Technically he was right. Office relationships, while frowned upon, were not uncommon in this line of work. Life happened.

"Are you sure about that? And what about the *others* you're screwing, who knows about those? The boys with names like Mahmood, Bashir, Ali? A senior Israeli intelligence officer cavorting with young *Arabs* from the West Bank."

Now he had his colleague's full attention.

"No doubt the Institute will cover it up, brush it under the carpet. But it will be your legacy, what you're remembered for. Everything else you've achieved will mean nothing. Your entire career reduced to something tawdry, perverted. People will believe other bad things about you, things you've never done."

The blood drained from Zamir's handsome features. He opened his mouth to speak but thought better of it. The conversation was over.

Back in the operations room, Zamir took a seat at the table, composure regained. His briefing took forty-five minutes. When it was over, he and Hannah left. They took an elevator to the roof of the building, where an IDF Blackhawk helicopter was waiting, blades turning.

Within seconds, they were airborne.

4

Haifa, Israel

A chime sounded and the elevator shuddered to a halt. Smith hauled open the concertinaed metal grille and shuffled into the cramped compartment. The gate closed with a clatter and the elevator jerked into motion, beginning its slow descent to the hotel lobby.

Reception was deserted and he rapped on the counter, knuckles loud on the cheap wood veneer. Several seconds passed, and a sleepy-eyed boy emerged from a darkened back room. He stifled a yawn, rubbed his face hard with the palms of his hands, and turned back to yell through the doorway.

"Papa!"

A light flicked on out back and the guesthouse owner appeared, roused from his afternoon nap.

"Ah, good afternoon, professor. You are checking out?"

"Yes indeed, I've a boat to catch."

"It is always a pleasure to see you. I hope you have enjoyed your stay in Efa." Like many Hebrew speakers, particularly those native to this port city, the proprietor used the Arab pronunciation for Haifa. "Would you like me to arrange a taxi to the port?"

"That would be most kind, thank you."

The bill settled, he emerged blinking into the noisy sunlight on the busy street. The boy from reception materialized to lift his suitcase into the trunk of the old Mercedes taxi and then stood by, waiting for a tip. Smith pushed a wad of notes into his hand.

"You'll look after that cat, won't you?"

The boy looked down at the worn notes and his eyes widened. Smith ruffled his hair.

"Not all of it on sweets, young man. The cat, remember."

The youngster's head bobbed rapidly.

The taxi pulled away, and Smith made himself comfortable in its backseat. He took out a handkerchief and mopped his brow, brushing away a fly that landed on his cheek. The driver steered into the stream of traffic moving toward the old harbor district but was forced to an abrupt halt by a speeding bus. It was a close call, and the taxi driver leaned on his horn and swore in rapid-fire Arabic. Then he floored the accelerator, narrowly making a gap behind a truck.

Disaster averted, Smith settled and allowed his mind to wander back through the city's turbulent past. It was a place he came to know well. In the early years after the war, before the British gave up their mandate in Palestine and Israel was created, Haifa was the point where thousands of Jews tried to enter against British orders. Many were fleeing Europe, where the Nazis had slaughtered six million of their brethren. Some succeeded in running the British blockade, but others were caught and sent away. Smith recalled with sadness the days he spent waiting at the waterfront as each new vessel arrived, examining each face.

The waiting was in vain but this city's history was now part of him.

As the Mercedes gained speed, a high-powered motorcycle emerged from the alley beside the guesthouse. It accelerated into a gap in the traffic. Immersed in his thoughts, Smith did not notice the bike ease into a space a few vehicles behind. Even farther back, a late model Ford Fiesta with a Hertz logo on its windshield pulled into the traffic from outside the guesthouse, where it had been parked for much of the day.

The ride to the port took fifteen minutes. At the terminal, there was chaos. A bomb threat had closed the check-in counters, and Israeli police, with their dogs, were everywhere. But the travelers remained calm. This sort of disruption had become normal, and people built it into their routines. Smith used the time to find a post office, where he sent his letter using the Express International Mail Service.

Finally, hours later, boarding was complete and the decks of the ship crowded. He stood at the railing in the evening light as the crew cast away the ropes, and the ferry slipped out of the harbor. Hands thrust into the pockets of his jacket, he stood on the lower level, where there was a small swimming pool and a café. Passengers waved and shouted to friends and relatives on the pier.

The city's skyline was almost close enough to touch, dominated by a large government building housing the Ministry of Interior and the Ministry of Immigrant Absorption. It shone like a bloated disco ball in the evening sun, testament to Israeli modernity. His gaze skimmed the rooftops, over the equally large but nondescript building housing the Shabak, the Israeli domestic security service. Not far from the waterfront, the historic Arab neighborhood of Wadi Salib squatted in the evening heat.

Smith turned to examine the faces of his fellow passengers. *If they are watching me, I can't see them.*

A young woman with a backpack caught his glance and smiled. He smiled back and she moved up to the rail next to him, sliding off her pack and clamping it securely between her long, suntanned legs. Shoulder-length blond hair whipped across her face and she pulled it back, fastening it in a ponytail with an elastic band. They struck up a conversation, and Smith soon learned she was a student of archaeology, from Finland, and she would spend the next few months studying in Cairo. He felt himself relax, pleased to meet a fellow scholar. The tension of the past few months slipped away, and they remained on the deck chatting until the coast of Israel was a brown smear on the horizon. The ship's wake curved back toward land, widening and eventually disappearing into the chop of the ocean.

5

Sinai Peninsula, Egypt
Sunday, 5 July 2009

The thermometer on the dashboard edged toward forty degrees Celsius as Alex Fisher waited for his taxi at the edge of the Black Zone. Barely midmorning and the hood of the white armored Toyota Land Cruiser was too hot to touch. Heat off the tarmac played games with his vision, causing the road ahead to shimmer and dissolve into a watery horizon.

For the umpteenth time, he pushed in the dashboard cigarette lighter and waited for it to click out. It was a habit he knew others found more than a little annoying, but this morning he felt too crappy to care. He would be firing up his third or fourth cigarette of the day if he hadn't chosen this month to quit. His foul mood wasn't helped by the mysterious phone call last night from Bairstow, or the hangover that sat like a steel band around his head, just below the brim of his Kevlar helmet. The weight of the bulletproof vest was the final insult, its crotch flap pressing cruelly on a full bladder struggling to cope with the large bottle of water he'd drained at 5:00 a.m. in an effort to flush out the booze, an effort he now very much regretted.

The soldier in the driver's seat next to him, a plump but not unattractive New Zealand private named Jemma Harris, snatched the lighter and applied it to the tip of a Marlboro Light.

"Cheers, mate."

Alex groaned.

The delicious smoke curled out Private Harris's short, sunburned nose and pooled on the ceiling before drifting out the open window into the stifling desert air. Somewhere out there were about six thousand weary Palestinians stranded at the closed Rafah crossing into the Gaza Strip, a host of terrorist outfits, roving bands of angry Bedouin tribesmen, hundreds of suspicious Egyptian police, and a multinational peacekeeping force.

Alex was glad to be leaving.

A camel ambled across the tarmac in front of the vehicle, chewing a torn piece of a cardboard box. There weren't any Lawrence of Arabia-style sand dunes here but just a flat, monotonous landscape of hard-packed sand and sun-baked rock. He was tired of it.

Parked on the shoulder, the Land Cruiser idled beside a barbed wire and concrete-ringed checkpoint, manned by Fijian soldiers in the bright-orange helmets of the Multinational Force & Observers in the Sinai, known colloquially as the MFO. For a bunch of Pacific island-dwelling seafarers, they were a long way from home. Filthy, barefooted local kids milled around the gate calling out in Arabic. A soldier climbed down slowly from his watchtower and disappeared inside a bunker. He emerged a minute later with two cartons of juice and lobbed them over the wire to eager little hands.

Yesterday's drive up from Cairo for his rendezvous at Checkpoint One Bravo had taken just three and a half hours, including a stop for scalding black tea in El-Arish, a once-thriving tourist town on the Mediterranean coast now inundated with refugees and deemed too dangerous for foreign troops to enter. Alex left his driver and taxi at the checkpoint, with strict instructions to return for him at 10:00 a.m. the next morning.

Now, he shielded his eyes as he stared into the distance, willing the taxi to appear.

Since a series of suicide bombings targeting MFO vehicles eighteen months ago, the area along the Egypt-Israel border where it touched the turquoise edge of the Mediterranean was known as the Black Zone. The MFO operated under US Department of Defense threat conditions. The threat level was now "Charlie," Private Harris told him with a hint of pride. There was only one higher: "Delta," which meant an attack was in progress. Alex looked over at his chaperone and wondered idly how old she was. He would put money on her not being long out of high school.

On the trip up, his driver, Emad, pushed the car to speeds in excess of 150 kilometers per hour, a white-knuckle ride even by Egyptian standards. The effort obviously exhausted him, and Alex guessed he must have overslept at a hostel in El-Arish.

He stared at the road ahead and wished Emad would hurry up.

Things had been slow in the newsroom for the past month, and, for want of anything better to do, he arranged the visit to the MFO base at El Gorah, a former Israeli redoubt vacated after the last Arab-Israeli war. Tensions were rising in the Sinai, and his editors in London liked his idea. A series of hotel bombings along the Red Sea a few years back left dozens dead and even more maimed, capturing international headlines. Despite the surface calm of recent months, Israeli intelligence sources assured Alex that the Sinai, with its local tribes and impenetrable mountains, was at risk of turning into the next Afghanistan. News of Hamas's takeover of the Gaza Strip was the clincher, and he'd decided to make the trip. Getting the appropriate permission from Egypt's foreign press minders and the MFO headquarters in Rome proved more problematic than anticipated. It had finally come through two days ago with a little pushing from a mate at the American embassy.

But it was Bairstow, his friend at the British mission who called last night, urging him to come to Alexandria. Something about a dead English tourist on a ship. Much to Alex's annoyance, he seemed intent on stringing the whole thing out, refusing to go into detail on the phone, all the while hinting at deeper mysteries. Typical. Bairstow had a habit of playing the drama queen.

Frankly, it hadn't sounded like much of a story to Alex, and he'd been eager to get back to the "couple of beers" that turned into a heavy drinking session with his hosts, a rowdy contingent of Kiwi and Canadian Army drivers. Surrounded by hostile desert, their base at El Gorah did not want for creature comforts, a veritable Club Med with its air-conditioned barracks and large swimming pool. To Alex's delight, it also boasted a Base Exchange with the best liquor store he had seen since arriving in the Middle East. He now thoroughly regretted his enthusiasm for the discovery.

Eventually he'd hung up on Bairstow but not before agreeing to meet him in Alexandria. Just one more regret to add to the morning's list.

He leaned forward to push in the cigarette lighter again, but froze midmotion. A speck appeared on the horizon, moving in and out of focus in the heat haze. It grew larger until an aging black-and-white Peugeot station wagon pulled up next to the Land Cruiser in a fine cloud of sand.

As Alex shrugged off the bulletproof vest, the relief was immediate.

"God I need a piss. I've heard wearing these vests is as close as us guys can get to the feeling of being pregnant."

Private Harris snorted, expelling a plume of smoke.

"Be thankful you don't have boobs, then." She grinned, leaning over to haul the body armor onto the seat next to her.

She ran a critical eye over her charge as he straightened out his rumpled shirt. Beneath several days of beard, Alex's face was deeply tanned, but there were dark half circles under his bloodshot eyes. His light-brown hair was matted with sweat and stuck up at odd angles as he hauled the helmet off and placed it on the dashboard.

"Hey, thanks for everything." He pushed the armor-plated door, which swung shut with a heavy thud.

"Send us the story," she said through the open window. "I'm expecting to be famous."

Alex opened his mouth to speak, but the Land Cruiser was already moving, and he watched it until it disappeared in the liquid haze rising off the macadam.

Unshaven and unapologetic, Emad spilled out of the driver's door of the Peugeot, offering a string of excuses in broken English and rapid-fire Arabic.

Swallowing his annoyance, Alex forced a smile.

"Ma'alesh." No harm done, he assured the agitated driver, reminding himself he needed this man's cooperation for a rather large detour on their way back to Cairo.

6

The traffic slowed almost to a halt as the Peugeot entered the suburbs of Alexandria. A horse-drawn cart flipped on its side blocked the road, carpeting one lane with fruit and vegetables. Smashed watermelons littered their path, the bright-red flesh attracting thick swarms of flies. Emad steered the taxi into the opposite lane, partially mounting the curb. The maneuver elicited honks of protest from the oncoming vehicles.

Dozing in the backseat, Alex was wakened by the commotion. He yawned and stretched, hangover finally gone, the world now a much kinder place. The drive to Alexandria from the fortified checkpoint at the edge of the Black Zone took just three hours. After he explained to Emad his desire to return to Cairo via the ancient port city on Egypt's northern coast, they haggled over the price. As usual, the bargaining started with the driver saying he was not at all interested in financial gain, pointing out that he was a proud man and they were friends. Alex could pay what he felt the service was worth. It was a typical opening gambit, an appeal to honor in a culture where bargaining was in the blood. Not to engage good-naturedly would be interpreted as an insult.

When Alex suggested the princely sum of five hundred Egyptian pounds, Emad looked mortified. He sniffed and made a sour face, twisting his lips. But the expression was fleeting and his eyes now twinkled with mischief.

"Five hundred American dollars! Okay, it's a deal." He began to chuckle at his own joke, holding out a cracked and leathery palm for Alex to shake on it. The laughter started as distant thunder in his chest, and morphed into a wet sound, the kind that only years of tobacco smoking or severe asthma can produce. The air hissed and gurgled up from his lungs, making Alex wince.

He first met Emad three years ago, almost as soon as he stepped off the plane in Cairo to begin his Middle East posting, and quickly grew to trust him. There was no doubt the man severely overcharged for his services, but in all other respects he was honest. They had a symbiotic relationship that Alex valued immensely.

"Not dollars, my friend, pounds."

"You are taking food from the mouths of my children," the driver complained.

"Okay, seven hundred. That is my best offer."

"Make it one thousand, but I swear my wife will kill me."

They sealed the deal with a handshake, and Alex slumped into the cracked vinyl upholstery of the Peugeot's backseat. He closed his eyes, allowing the rocking motion of the road and drone of the car's engine to lull him into a meditative state.

As they sped west through the desert, his thoughts returned to last night's phone call. Aubrey Bairstow's price had never been more than company. Two years ago, when they'd met, he had suspected there might be more to it. There was something extremely socially awkward about the young diplomat. But while Bairstow made no secret of his homosexuality, the advances Alex initially suspected would come never eventuated. It made him feel foolish to think about it now. It wasn't that he didn't like the young Brit. In fact, he had grown rather fond of him. But he seemed to take an enormous amount of pleasure in making people flinch. For someone with so few social graces, Alex often found himself wondering how the chubby, blond-haired Englishman carved out a niche in the field of diplomacy.

After meeting at an embassy function at the grand British Residence on the Corniche el-Nile in Cairo, they bumped into each other again in the cramped alleys of Khan el-Khalili, a district known as the Turkish bazaar during the Ottoman period and now usually just referred to as the Khan.

The next week, Alex invited him for a drink at the bar in the Windsor Hotel, and, as the months went by, they met more often. Alex sensed a deep loneliness in Bairstow, concealed beneath the bluster and irritability. He appeared to have few close friends and had taken to passing on snippets of diplomatic gossip and the occasional useful tip-off.

A blast of the car horn jolted Alex back to the present.

Emad cursed and shook his fist at the windshield as a truck swerved in front of his taxi. The sudden motion caused the driver's sleeve to ride up, revealing a crudely drawn cross on the underside of his wrist. The faded green tattoo signified that Emad was a Copt, from Egypt's ancient Christian minority.

Alex's phone chirped in his pocket. He pulled it out and examined the caller ID. Bairstow. The conversation was brief and he hung up.

"Emad, you know where the police hospital is?"

■ ■ ■

When they met at the morgue in the basement of Alexandria's police hospital on Alfy Bey Street, they greeted with a hug. It was an acknowledgement of friendship that Alex noticed was becoming increasingly common among Western men these days. He liked it, the real human contact. Of course men in Egypt and a number of Asian countries he lived in were not shy of such physical contact. He'd seen prime ministers and presidents strolling hand in hand with their generals as they discussed affairs of state. Alex had few truly close friends but many acquaintances. Close relationships had become a casualty of his itinerant lifestyle, so the ones he had, he cherished. They were handpicked.

The two men separated with a handshake.

Bairstow looked more disheveled than usual. He'd neglected to shave, and his suit jacket and pants were rumpled.

"Jesus, Aubrey! You sleep in those?"

"Good to see you too, Alex."

An eerie quiet pervaded the green-painted corridors. Chilled air and formaldehyde masked whatever scent of death there might have been outside the examination rooms. The two men chatted in hushed tones for a few minutes, as if fearful of waking the building's expired occupants. They turned to Bairstow's phone call the night before and the subject at hand.

"You didn't hear it from me, old man, but it turns out this fellow had quite a colorful past. Professor at Cambridge for three decades, a leading authority on religious ritual in the ancient world..."

Alex was exhausted. Bairstow's tone irked him as much as his insistence on drawing this whole affair out. The night before, after explaining the circumstances of the man's death, he refused to give a name for the deceased on the phone. *For Christ's sake, the guy died of a heart attack. No big deal. That sort of thing happens all the time.* "Fell from grace after discovering a manuscript in 1958. Caused quite a stir in the bookish world of New Testament scholarship..."

Alex's head snapped around. Bairstow had his attention.

"...when he discovered a previously unknown account of the life..."

Alex reached out and steadied himself against the wall. The words coming out of his friend's mouth had literally taken his breath away. His lungs seemed to have shut down for the space of several breaths, as if his body somehow forgot how to draw in and expel air.

Bairstow noticed the blood drain from his friend's face.

"Alex, what's wrong?" He took hold of his elbow.

Alex pulled away. His skin felt cold. Finally he managed a deep gulp of air, like a diver returning to the surface.

When they came, the words were whispered. "Jesus, Aubrey...Ahh, shit."

7

"Christ, Aubrey," Alex gasped. "I know this guy."

"I haven't even told you his name, or the strange bit." Bairstow looked deflated. "What do you mean, know him?"

"It's Morton. Professor Morton Smith. He discovered an ancient manuscript. It quoted from an unknown text written by one of Jesus's disciples, the Apostle Mark."

"How the devil did you know that?" Thunder stolen, Bairstow appeared positively crestfallen.

They stood outside the double doors of the viewing room. A janitor, eyeing them suspiciously, wrung his mop over a metal bucket and returned his full attention to the grubby floor. Bairstow pushed the swing doors open and an unshaven, dark-eyed attendant looked up from behind a desk where he was reading a newspaper.

The body lay on a metal gurney in the middle of the room, draped with a pale-green shroud. Alex braced himself for what was to come, unsure he was ready for this. An aromatic candle burned in a bracket on the wall. Its sweet scent did little to mask the odor of disinfectant and the cloying smell of death it attempted to banish. Tiers of stainless-steel doors, human-sized filing cabinets, lined the far wall of the room. Two other trolleys bearing draped forms sat next to a row of hand basins along the wall to their right. This was not a place any self-respecting Egyptian would linger. The Islamic custom was to bury bodies within the first twelve hours of death, unless they were foreigners, or foul play was suspected. The indigenous Coptic Christian community observed the same custom.

Newspaper abandoned, the attendant moved to the corpse in the center of the room. Without warning, he peeled back the sheet with a single, practiced movement.

Alex gasped. The old man's body was thoroughly cleaned, skin a bluish hue, blotchy and marbled. An ugly y-shaped incision ran from belly to shoulder blades, crudely stitched up with what looked like fishing line. Deep purple bruising covered the side of the skull. Alex gritted his teeth. "God Aubrey, I thought you said it was a heart attack."

"It was, according to the coroner. They think he landed pretty hard on the railing as he went down. Police reckon he was probably dead before he landed."

Alex swayed, vision blurring. He blinked rapidly. It took several moments to remember what he was about to ask before they entered the room. He turned to face Bairstow, who'd begun apologizing.

"What do you mean you haven't told me the strange bit?"

Bairstow inhaled deeply. "There were some odd things, but the reason I called you was that I found your address among his stuff, on a post office receipt, on the desk in his cabin. Look Alex, I'm really sorry. Really I am. I had no idea you actually knew him. I thought…" His voice trailed off.

Alex stared at the body on the table. The physical form was familiar, but somehow, with the life gone from those limbs, the man before him was a stranger. Yet there was no doubt it was him.

He cleared his throat, hoping his voice sounded steadier than he felt.

"We met in Cambodia a few years ago. I was based there before Cairo. You said there were several odd things. What else?"

"Uh? Oh yes, he had Nazi memorabilia in his suitcase."

"What do you mean Nazi memorabilia?"

"I searched his stuff, part of the job. There was a velvet wallet down the side of his suitcase. Inside it was a medal of some kind, a white cross with swastikas. It looked valuable."

Alex struggled to process what he was hearing. "It's hardly odd. The bazaars are full of it. A lot of people collect that kind of stuff," he mumbled, sounding unconvinced by his own argument.

"There was something else interesting." Bairstow paused for effect.

Alex's temper flared. He noisily expelled air through his nose. "Just spit it out, Aubrey, please. The suspense is killing me."

"Okay, okay, give me a chance." Bairstow raised his hands, palms out in a defensive gesture. "There were two glasses, Alex. He was drinking in his cabin. It stank of booze. There was a bottle and a partly full glass on the desk. Yet he had taken his glass with him to the deck. It was lying next to him, smashed to pieces. I mean, it's not conclusive proof or anything, but I'd say he had a guest."

Alex wasn't listening anymore. He was miles away, in another time and another place.

8

Phnom Penh, Cambodia
20 November 2000

He was late. Motorcycles and trucks careened past as he stood at the roadside. The smell of woodsmoke mingled with the faint odor of unwashed bodies and sewerage. Alex felt in his shirt pocket for the invitation. He squinted in the gloom at the hand-drawn map. The nearest lamppost thirty meters up the street weakly illuminated an intersection jammed with evening traffic. Horns honked in the hot air as trucks, motorbikes, and rickshaws nosed like schooling fish into the main flow. Where the street turned right on the map, a peeling wall topped with coils of rusty barbed wire blocked his path. Alex peered down the street, looking for a break in the grimy expanse. Then he balled up the printout in disgust and dropped it in the gutter.

Trotting forward, he saw that the alley was almost invisible. Easy to miss, a darker patch in the deepening gloom angling toward the river. Voices and rowdy music drifted over tin roofs from local cafés along the main drag. A full minute passed while his eyes adjusted to the blackness.

Soon the sounds of the busy road gave way to the scuff of his feet on baked earth. A wet stench infused the air with the taste and smell of stale rubbish and rotting vegetation. Alex was reminded of something he learned in science class at school. To smell something required tiny particles of that substance to enter the nose. He put a sleeve to his face and breathed through the fabric. He recalled his last visit to the Alligator Ski Club a month earlier, soon after arriving in the city. Moored to the bank on a pontoon of oil drums, it was a popular watering hole where hacks from the international wire agencies mingled with diplomats and aid workers. The owner, who claimed to have served in the French Foreign Legion, offered water skiing to those drunk enough to brave the latte-colored waters. On most evenings he had no shortage of takers.

That visit nearly ended in a fistfight and provided Alex with his first closeup view of a Glock 9mm. He'd arrived on the back of a friend's motorbike, and they were well into their third round when a drunk Russian embassy official, who he later learned went by the name Vassili, rolled in with a large entourage and insisted they join his table. When Alex politely declined, the man withdrew hurt and then became bellicose. He stormed over, tossed their drinks into the Mekong, and proceeded to order a round of vodka shots for the entire bar.

Just drunk enough to care, Alex jumped to his feet. It was then that he felt a firm hand on his shoulder. The hairy paw was attached to the man from Moscow's bodyguard, a sullen fellow who gently laid a well-oiled automatic pistol on the bar with his other hand and stared meaningfully into Alex's eyes. No words were exchanged, but he understood perfectly. Suitably chastened, the inexperienced foreign correspondent was quickly persuaded to accept the Russian's hospitality.

Now, at night and alone, the neighborhood seemed menacing, and he cursed himself for turning down a ride to the party. In a bustling city of a million people, it was hard to believe there could be such a complete absence of illumination. Once the sun sank below the outlying bush, only the quay around the main hotels and a few of the wealthier suburbs in Phnom Penh had streetlights. Alex remembered reading somewhere that most people still cooked on charcoal and lit their modest homes with kerosene. Death was never far away, fires from spilled lamps killed whole families as they slept.

■ ■ ■

The sound of voices grew stronger and the dirt beneath Alex's feet turned to cracked cement. He emerged at the water's edge, an expanse strewn with plastic shopping bags, used condoms, and drink bottles. It was obvious he was in completely the wrong place. He softly cursed himself for being alone after dark.

Poverty was the city's defining character, and most of Alex's expat acquaintances could tell stories of being robbed, usually for money and almost always at gunpoint. A few foreigners, invariably drunk, sometimes to the point of belligerence, had been shot and wounded for refusing to hand over their possessions. But most cooperated and escaped unscathed.

A week after arriving, Alex awoke in the night to see shadows projected like a silent film across his living room wall, six floors up from Sisowath Quay. All the windows were barred, but he'd left the balcony door open to let in the river breeze. He was initially unsure of what he had seen and not immediately convinced it was real. But dawn revealed blood and scraps of clothing in the razor wire separating his roof from the one next door. The final proof: a pair of his Levis and a backpack dropped in haste along the escape route.

Returning to the present, Alex realized he was lost. Time to return to the main road and hail a motorcycle taxi, spend what remained of the evening propping up the bar at the Foreign Correspondents Club, a block down river from his apartment.

As he turned, a light flicked on in a nearby riverfront home. A white-haired European man peered out into the darkness from the ground-floor window, staring almost straight at him through the wrought-iron grille.

The man spoke to someone unseen behind him before closing the window and drawing the curtains, leaving a wide strip of light where they failed to meet. Curiosity piqued, Alex moved closer. It was rare for a Westerner to live in this part of the city, and he briefly considered knocking on the door and asking for directions. Through the gap, he could still see a good portion of the room.

There were at least a dozen people, dark-skinned locals and several foreigners. Men and women were taking places on the floor and on stools. The man from the window was among them, perched on a simple wooden bed pushed up against the far wall. In the light afforded by a single bulb hanging from the ceiling, bowed faces were obscured in shadow.

The scene had taken on the air of a religious ritual, and Alex found it impossible to turn away.

A different European man stood in the center of the room, now with a white sheet wrapped around his shoulders. He seemed younger than the man Alex had seen at the window, dark hair neatly trimmed over deep-set eyes. The sheet dropped to his waist, revealing a well-muscled chest covered in a sprinkling of hair. He motioned in the direction of the gathering.

A pretty young Khmer woman wearing an identical white robe rose to her feet, her dark skin contrasting with the cloth that draped her slim, boyish figure. She smiled shyly at the group. Somebody just out of Alex's line of sight began to sing, and, one by one, the others joined in. Alex didn't recognize the words or the language, but the tune seemed vaguely familiar.

The young woman's robe slid to the floor and she was naked, hands clasped in front of a dark thatch of hair below her stomach. She stepped forward, closer to the man. Alex's throat tightened.

For the first time, he noticed a large plastic tub in the center of the tiled floor. The girl stepped into it and the man bent down, retrieving a plastic scoop, the kind commonly used by locals to bathe. He dipped it in the water around the girl's feet and sluiced it over her head as the singing continued. The water ran over her breasts and down her stomach and hips, which Alex could see were scarred with the pale marks of childbirth. The man repeated the action several times before reaching out and touching the girl's face.

Someone produced her robe and she stepped from the tub and quickly wrapped it around herself. She did not flinch as the man took her arm, and the others filed out of the room.

Alex's heart was beating wildly. He felt an uncomfortable mixture of disgust and arousal. Looking away from the window and down the darkened alley, he let his eyes adjust again to the gloom. Whatever was going on inside was none of his business. He knew all the stories of the city's notorious sex industry, had even written a few in the weeks since his arrival. Western men, picked up in regular sweeps of the less reputable neighborhoods, arrested for failing to pay the right bribes. Few remained locked up for long, securing release for the appropriate fee. They learned quickly that kicking up a fuss attracted attention and put Cambodian judges in the awkward position of having to keep them locked up for longer.

Alex peered back into the room. It was empty, and he wondered fleetingly if he had imagined the whole thing. Stepping carefully away from the wall, he turned and threaded his way up the alley to the road.

9

Secret Gospel Scholar Dies in Middle East
by Alex Fisher
Alexandria, Egypt (5 July 2009)
A British scholar made famous by the discovery of an ancient
and previously unknown account of the life of Jesus has been
found dead aboard a ship in the Mediterranean.

A professor at Cambridge University for many years and an expert on religious rituals in the ancient world, Dr. Morton Smith,
seventy-nine, was found lying on the deck of a passenger ferry
on the morning of 4 July.

Egyptian police believe Smith died of a heart attack. The ship
was traveling from the Israeli city of Haifa to Alexandria on
Egypt's Mediterranean coast.

The coroner at Alexandria's central police hospital said Smith
sustained a head injury that probably resulted from striking the
ship's railing after a massive heart attack.

British embassy officials said local authorities promised a thorough investigation, and preparations were underway for Smith's body to be flown back to the United Kingdom.

Smith was best known for his discovery in 1958 of fragments of a previously unknown account of Jesus's life, attributed to the Apostle Mark and later dubbed the Secret Gospel.

He reported finding it while cataloguing the monastery library at Mar Saba, a 1,500-year-old Greek Orthodox hermitage in the Judean desert, about twelve kilometers south of Jerusalem.

"If authentic, the discovery would raise serious questions for the study of the New Testament and the history of early Christianity," said Tarb Herman, lecturer in Ancient History and Biblical Studies at Cairo's prestigious American University.

"The new passages were open to interpretation, and their implicitly sexual nature upset many people. The professor believed they justified a reevaluation of the historical Jesus as more of a mystical or guru-type figure.

Smith's early work established his reputation as an intellectual cut above most other academics in the field of biblical scholarship. But his sharp wit and unwillingness to suffer fools won him few friends," said Herman.

The newly discovered passages from the Gospel of Mark were contained in a letter by the third-century church father Clement of Alexandria.

Clement's letter, written in ancient Greek, was copied by a later scribe onto three pages used in the binding for a seventeenth-century book. Smith photographed the pages, but left the book at the monastery, from where it has long since disappeared.

In 1960, he announced his find in a report to the Society of Biblical Literature. The story was reported in newspapers around the world and caused an outcry from religious groups.

The same year, a list of the seventy-five other manuscripts Smith catalogued at Mar Saba appeared in the journal *Archaeology*, as well as the Greek Orthodox Patriarchate journal, *Nea Sion*.

Many biblical scholars remain skeptical, questioning whether the excerpts from Clement's letter were in fact genuine quotations from Mark. Others openly accused Smith of an elaborate hoax, forging the Clementine letter and the excerpts attributed to Jesus's disciple.

Debate around the professor's findings, and in particular the interpretation he placed on them, saw him gradually ostracized from the academic community.

Although he continued to teach until the late 1990s, he became a recluse and eventually retired, moving to Cambodia, where he continued his study of religious ritual and cults.

Smith received his bachelor's degree from Cambridge, a doctorate in philosophy from the Hebrew University in Jerusalem, and a second doctorate, in theology, from Harvard Divinity School.

He had no surviving family.

10

Cairo, Egypt
Monday, 6 July 2009

Alex was not an early riser at the best of times, and the past few days left him exhausted.

After leaving the morgue, he hammered out his story on Smith at the coffee table in Bairstow's hotel room in Alexandria. Much of the story he already knew. Google, and a call to an academic at the American University in Cairo, provided the rest.

Knowing some of Smith's past put Alex well ahead of the competition. Most of the other Cairo-based correspondents hadn't bothered to leave their offices, covering the story with briefs cobbled together from calls to the police and the British embassy. It wasn't a huge deal, but it had enough intriguing elements to make it a good yarn and was picked up by half a dozen papers, including *The New York Times* and *The Guardian*. More important, it earned Alex praise from his editors during what had been a lean month for news.

He left Alexandria and wrote up his Sinai story that night at his flat in Cairo, in the leafy inner-city residential district of Zamalek. It was after midnight when he finally lay on his bed under the whirling blades of the electric ceiling fan.

He did not surface until after 11:00 a.m. the next day.

Without showering, he dressed and stumbled down five flights of concrete stairs to the street, collecting his mail from the letterbox in the lobby on the way past. A beeline for the news agent outside the Marriott Hotel for a copy of *Al-Ahram*, an English-language weekly, and by quarter past he was seated at his favorite café on the corner of Twenty-sixth of July Street and Sharia Yehia Ibrahim.

A boy wearing a grubby T-shirt that read "Never Underestimate the Power of Stupid People in Large Groups" tried to sell him a used copy of the *International Herald Tribune* as he ordered a *mashut*, sweet Arabic coffee, and a slice of *baklava*, flaky pastry filled with honey and nuts. None of the other tables were occupied, and the boy persisted until a fair-haired man with a scarred face took a seat close to the shop front and ordered a Coke. Alex watched as the man pressed a few coins into the boy's hand and patted his bottom.

Fucking sicko. He returned his attention to *Al-Ahram*.

There was not much hard news in the paper. He read a story about the Middle East peace process and a short feature on the refugee situation on the border with Israel. An Associated Press article headlined "Vatican, Israel End Spat Over Terrorism" caught his attention. The Vatican and Israel were agreeing to end a public feud over terrorism, with the Israeli prime minister calling the Pope "a true friend of Israel." The dispute erupted when the Pope in one of his sermons failed to include Israel on a list of countries that were victims of terrorism. The Vatican initially rejected the Israeli complaints and suggested Israel routinely broke international law by cracking down on Palestinian militants. The public spat, the writer of the story explained, threatened to damage improving relations between Israel and the Holy Roman Church.

Alex turned the page but found little of interest. He scanned the rest of the paper. There was a fifty-word brief reporting the death of British academic Morton Smith, which was being investigated by the Alexandrian police. The reporter quoted the lead detective, who said the cause of death was believed to be natural. It wasn't until he had finished a second cup of coffee and was preparing to leave that Alex remembered his mail.

The first two letters were pay slips forwarded from the head office in London, and he slid them unopened into the pocket of his khaki shirt before turning to the third. The envelope was stationery from the Port Inn Guesthouse in the Israeli city of Haifa. It bore an Express International Mail Service stamp.

The address was written in a familiar spidery hand. Alex swallowed. He recalled his conversation with Bairstow in the morgue…*a post office receipt, on the desk in his cabin*…He'd completely forgotten.

Damn, this is too weird. But it makes perfect sense.

Inside was a single sheet of hotel stationery covered in the same familiar script. Alex's hands trembled slightly. He breathed deeply and looked around at the other tables. The blond man was still there, but otherwise the place was empty.

He began to read.

11

My dear Alex,

Before I say anything else, let me apologize profusely for being such a poor correspondent.

It has been years since we last saw each other, and I hope this letter finds you in good health. I have read your many excellent dispatches from Cairo in various publications and see you have done rather well for yourself.

I have been engaged in some very interesting research in Egypt and Israel for the past three months. Please do not be upset that I have not contacted you. I shall explain more in the fullness of time. For now, I'll cut to the chase, as a younger man might say.

Do you remember the story I told you in Phnom Penh about my discovery of Mark's Secret Gospel and the pious outrage it stirred up among my academic colleagues and the lay community? Of course, you will not have forgotten! As I'm sure a fellow with such a finely tuned nose for a story quickly surmised, there is more to it. I rather think it is something you will find interesting in your line of work.

I will be eighty in a few months and sadly there may not be many years left. I do miss those dinners we used to have on my verandah by the river. Ah, how I love to talk! I shall be in Cairo later in July. There is a gentleman I want to visit, one of the country's finest modern-day explorers. Many would say the finest.

I would be pleased if you would dine with me then, for old time's sake. I shall explain all when I see you. Your head office in London has been kind enough to furnish me with your telephone number.

I do not mean to be an alarmist, my dear Alex, but some very strange things have been happening. I sometimes feel that I am being watched, but perhaps that is just the foolishness of an old man. Now I'm rambling! I am tired and I will lay down my pen.

Please take very good care of yourself.

Yours as ever,

M. S.

3 July '09

12

"Shukran gazilan. Thanks very much. Keep the change." Alex slammed the door and raised a hand in salutation.

"Afwan, al-'affu. Tisbah 'ala kher. You are welcome. Goodnight."

It was dark when the taxi pulled away from the curb below his fifth-floor apartment. A couple of stray cats scurried hissing from a stinking pile of household rubbish waiting for the *Zabbaleen*, the city's garbage collectors, on their early morning rounds.

Everything thrown away in Cairo, every soiled rag, old newspaper, or hunk of stale bread, began an unseen journey from the moment it was thrown in the trash. The *Zabbaleen* were a community made up mainly of Coptic Christians who eked out a meager existence collecting and disposing of the city's waste. They generally performed this service for free, making a living through recycling. Invisible to mostCairenes, they lived on vast garbage dumps on the city fringe. Researching a story, Alex visited one of their settlements. He was shocked by what he saw. Moqattam sat in a quarry on the far side of a large hill that essentially hid it from the city. It was home to nearly thirty thousand people who spent their days picking through the detritus of one of the world's biggest urban sprawls. They combed it for food scraps, which they fed to their livestock. The rest was carefully sorted, washed, resold, reworked, or simply used again. Many of the garbage collectors suffered terribly from disease. Authorities in Egypt tried for years to replace the *Zabbaleen* with a modern waste collection and disposal system, contracting large foreign companies. The process attracted a good deal of controversy. Alex had written about that too. Cairo's wealthier inhabitants naturally objected to higher fees for the modern disposal service, which, as it turned out, was far less efficient.

The smell of the refuse forced him to breathe through his mouth as, limbs heavy, he climbed the stairs to the darkened lobby of his apartment block.

The letter had unsettled him. The inky shadows now gave him the creeps, his imagination working in overdrive, creating sinister shapes in the blackness.

You're behaving like a little girl. Calm down.

He increased his pace, taking the steps two at a time despite his exhaustion. The events of the last few days were hard to digest: Smith dead, and then the letter, his old acquaintance seemingly reaching out from the grave.

It all felt so unreal, the full force of it only hitting him now. In the absence of anyone else to do the job, he identified the body for the Alexandrian police. The physical features were familiar, but with the life gone from his limbs, somehow Smith seemed diminished, just a body, a shell rather than the larger-than-life man Alex knew.

The double glass doors to the tiled lobby on Sharia Michel Lutfalah were slightly ajar and he pushed them open, making a mental note to tell the building management the lock was broken again. The lift was already on the fifth floor so he took the stairs, two at a time. Lit weakly by naked bulbs on each landing, they smelled of damp. He could afford to live in a much nicer building, right on the river, but he liked the location and being among the locals rather than in one of Cairo's many expatriate enclaves. The fact that the rent was about half what it would be in a swankier apartment block didn't hurt either.

Alex sensed something was different before he saw it.

He rounded the final curve of the stairwell. The door to his apartment was wide open. Arab voices drifted through the gap. Adrenaline prickled the back of his neck and scalp. Leaden legs momentarily refused to take his body forward.

Approaching the door, he peered through and then stepped into the foyer. From the kitchen to the left came the sounds of drawers opening and closing.

The foyer light was off. A moment's hesitation, he reached out and flicked the switch.

A shadow moved on the kitchen door.

"Hello, is somebody there?" Fear overrode any feeling of foolishness. *Of course, there is someone bloody well there.* The sound of shoeless feet on the hardwood floor emanated from his study, across the hall from the open-plan living and dining area. Someone was going through the papers on his desk.

"Hey, who's there?" This time more forcefully, fear replaced by anger. He stepped into the kitchen.

■ ■ ■

A chime sounded and Sadie removed three steaming mugs of coffee from the microwave oven. An Arabic sitcom blared from the TV on the bench.

She turned.

"Oh, there you are, darling. What's wrong? You look like you've seen a ghost."

"What's the door doing open?" Alex's anger evaporated, replaced by sheepishness and something approximating relief. He'd been seeing Sadie Cooper for about six months, and she'd had a key for most of that time. They met in the library of the American University on Kasr El Aini Street, where she was in her second year at the Arabic Language Institute. Alex was instantly attracted to her, one of the most beautiful women he had ever seen. Her purposefully modest clothing did little to hide a lithe frame and pretty legs. Catching his eye as he stared across the library desks, she rewarded him with a look that said she knew this.

"I saw you get out of the taxi and opened it, silly. I was on the balcony. I'm cooking, by the way. Late dinner. Here, you're shattered." Sadie handed him one of the mugs.

"Aubrey, coffee's ready! Alex's here."

13

Bairstow's bulky frame, clad in rumpled linen pants and white cotton business shirt, appeared in the doorway. He reached over and took a mug from Sadie without looking up.

"Thanks, doll. I say, old boy, I rather like this bit about 'spooky parallels' between Christian right-wingers and Islamic fundamentalists."

He was reading the first draft of an opinion piece Alex was toying with submitting to a European magazine.

He quoted: "'They both divvy up the world between the saved and the damned. Both have declared a holy war on secular culture and liberal democracy. They reject the separation of religion and state and seek to establish a new order based on their own interpretation of divine laws...'"

Alex sighed, and, catching a worried glance from Sadie, rolled his eyes. Aubrey's limited social graces did not extend to a respect for privacy, and he had a frustrating habit of picking up and examining anything within reach.

"He was waiting at the door when I arrived," Sadie mouthed silently with a theatrical shrug.

Oblivious to their exchange, Bairstow plowed on.

"'But perhaps the spookiest parallels come in their views of the end of the world. A common scenario is a colossal confrontation in the desert in which the armies of God destroy the armies of Satan. Radical Muslims, of course, identify Israel and the United States as the forces of evil. Christian fundamentalists see

Islam as the ultimate enemy…' Hang on, that's crap, that is." Bairstow paused and looked up. "A bit simplistic, to say the least."

For fuck's sake. Alex hated others reading his unfinished work. He stared daggers at his friend who'd returned his attention to the draft.

"'The terrifying implication is that the ordinary followers of the three monotheistic religions of the region—the Jews, Muslims, and Christians—will be the primary victims of this Holocaust.'"

Alex had enough. "What's crap? Neocons like George W. Bush are definitely on the Christian Right and trying to paint Islam as the ultimate enemy."

"Yes, but when you get down to brass tacks, I'm not sure Israel and the United States are really the ultimate target for a lot of these Muslim zealots, or that the Muslims are at heart the enemy truly motivating the Christian Right."

Alex snatched the draft and threw it on the kitchen bench. "That'll do. It's not finished."

"Sorry. You're angry, I can tell." His friend looked sheepish.

"Nope, anger would be too simple." He glared at Bairstow. It was impossible to stay annoyed at him for long, and besides, he had a point. "Now, how about a real drink?"

He opened the fridge and pulled out a large bottle of Stella beer. Sadie put three glasses on the bench and Alex filled them carefully, ensuring the froth didn't spill over onto the counter.

"It's something I've been mulling over, just ideas really. I'd be interested in your professional opinion as a diplomat, Aubrey. It seems to be a polar view of the world that most Western governments are doing little to combat."

Bairstow was thoughtful as they moved out onto the balcony, the doors pushed wide. Sadie washed salad vegetables with filtered water in the sink, her back to the two men. Her T-shirt stuck to her skin, damp with sweat.

"You know there has been a hell of a lot of loose talk, not to mention millions and millions of words written, especially since 9/11, about a 'clash of civilizations.' A confrontation between musty, old, backward-looking, repressive Islam and the innovative and freedom-loving West," said Bairstow. "People are always throwing that theory around, as if it's a given."

Alex took a gulp of his beer before replying. Bubbles tickled his throat and he stifled a belch.

"I read in *The Boston Globe* the other day that it was a 'clash between positivism and a reactionary, negative world view.'" He used his index and forefingers to draw quote marks in the air. His ability to repeat passages verbatim from things he'd read or heard rarely failed to impress.

"Another article in the *Washington Post* said, 'While the West used the last two centuries to advance the cause of human freedom, the Islamic world, by contrast, was content to remain in its torpor, locked in rigid orthodoxy, fearful of freedom.'"

Bairstow grimaced. "You know Samuel Huntington himself actually entertained an analogy between the Islamic fundamentalist movement and the Protestant Reformation, saying both are reactions to the stagnation and corruption of existing institutions. They advocate a return to a purer form of their religion. They preach hard work, discipline..."

"Whoa! Hang on a minute." Alex threw his hands up. "Weren't the Protestants supposed to be the good guys? An emerging progressive force compared to the musty old Catholics. We were supposed to cheer for the Protestants in our high school history texts, right? So shouldn't we be applauding the Islamic extremists now?"

"Well done, top marks! But not necessarily a view Her Majesty's government would want to hear a trusty Cairo envoy espousing in the current climate." Bairstow smiled archly, reaching over and carefully refilling both their beer glasses.

The soothing effects of the alcohol began to chip away at the day's rough edges.

Bairstow's cell phone chirped in his pocket. He extracted it and flipped it open with a groan before covering the mouthpiece.

"Won't be a tick, old man. Anyway, Huntington doesn't really entertain the analogy for very long. Shame he didn't extrapolate a little."

Sadie emerged onto the balcony and leaned against the metal railing, her back to the street. Her long dark hair was piled in a topknot and skewered with a ballpoint pen. Music drifted from the stereo in the living room, the voice of Natasha Atlas from her debut album *Diaspora*. The multilingual, half-Jewish Egyptian-Palestinian diva was one of Sadie's favorite recording artists, and she found the blend of traditional Arabic music and techno beats almost trance inducing.

"What do you reckon, Sadie? You're the smart one here. You've been studying this stuff," Alex said.

Sadie wrinkled her nose and frowned. Despite the darkness, Alex could see the startling green of her eyes.

"I think he's got a point. No disrespect, but it's something the mainstream media seem to be ignoring. Let's extend Huntington's little flirtation with that theory a bit."

"I'm happy to extend any flirtation you might suggest." Alex grinned.

"It challenges the notion that we are dealing with two hugely different, opposed civilizations. For a start, it could easily be argued that Islam is actually clashing with itself," Sadie said.

"Exactly, and that supports your earlier assertion that there are big similarities between the fundamentalists on both sides of the fence." Aubrey closed his phone and returned to the conversation.

Sadie paused to muster her thoughts.

"Like the Protestants of the sixteenth century, the Muslim fundamentalists are a relatively new force on the wider Islamic scene. Wahhabism—the dour, repressive creed espoused by the Saudis and the Osama bin Ladens of this world—only dates from the mid-eighteenth century. The strain of Islam that inspired the Taliban, which has become pretty much indistinguishable from Wahhabism, cropped up in India just a little over a century ago. So when we talk about Islamic fundamentalism, we are not talking about some ancient essence of Islam, we're talking about something relatively modern.

"You see the same thing in churches and mosques back in England. The appeal of fundamentalism is to younger people searching for something different, modern."

Alex leaned forward, brain clicking into gear. "In other words, Islamic fundamentalism isn't necessarily a response to the West. Rather it is a response to earlier allegedly corrupted strands of Islam."

"Yep, that's how they'd see it. Just like Protestantism was a response to Catholicism. Wahhabism grew out of opposition to the Ottoman Empire and to the homegrown Sufism of Arabia." Sadie took a sip of her beer, licking the foam from her upper lip.

"We admire Sufism in the West for its tolerance, mysticism, and poetry, its ecstatic rituals, its music, even. But it's also, especially in rural parts, a religion that bears more than a casual resemblance to late medieval Catholicism. It encourages the veneration of saint-like figures at special shrines and their celebration at festivities. It's something the fundamentalist mullahs abhor. Just as the Protestants smashed icons, prohibited carnivals, and defaced cathedrals, the Wahhabists insist on a reformed style of Islam, purged of all that. Remember all the TV footage from 1996. When the Taliban took over in Afghanistan, their first task was stamping that stuff out."

Alex stretched, his brain felt overloaded. But the conversation took him away from the confusing thoughts that crowded his mind earlier in the day, and he was grateful for it. His stomach rumbled. Preoccupied after receiving the letter from Smith, he'd not eaten since breakfast.

"Let's eat. Aubrey, fancy picking the top off that bottle of Omar Khayam white in the fridge?"

"It'd be rude not to." Bairstow grinned and shuffled into the kitchen. Alex stood and gave Sadie a peck on the cheek.

"Clever girl."

Sadie smiled and winked. "I'm ravenous after all that."

14

Phnom Penh, Cambodia
24 November 2000

The sound of gunfire is relatively common on the streets of the Cambodian capital at night. A sharp crack, sometimes two, and then silence, broken only by the barking of stray dogs.

The sustained rattle of machine guns occurring now was far less common, yet it was not what actually woke Alex just after 2:00 a.m. With the ancient air conditioner cranked to high, and the bedroom door firmly closed against the hot night air, it took a full minute before the angry vibrations of his cell phone phone on the nightstand penetrated his slumber. Alex flailed in its general direction, knocking a half-full glass of water onto the tiled floor, where it bounced once and then shattered.

Fuck. He flailed some more.

Finally his fingers closed around the offending device. He flipped it open and heard the excited voice of his young Cambodian assistant, Kimseng.

"It's the coup, Boss."

Loud popping noises, punctuated by the rhythmic crump of rocket-propelled grenades, filtered down the line. Alex was suddenly wide-awake, sitting bolt upright, despite having only recently gone to bed. The alcohol-fueled dinner at Happy Herb's, a hole-in-the-wall serving pizzas garnished with marijuana just below his apartment on Sisowath Quay, had ended barely an hour ago. *Christ,*

Murphy's law. Big stories happened at the most inconvenient times. He'd done some of his best work hung over.

A couple of seconds and the room stopped spinning. He tried to think clearly. "Get the car from the office and pick me up in ten minutes."

"Already there, Boss. I can be at your place in five."

■ ■ ■

Kimseng drove while Alex stared anxiously out into the muggy darkness. They drove slowly, deliberately, the interior light on, illuminating their faces in yellow, windows wound down. There was nothing to be gained by alarming the already jumpy security forces converging on the city.

Their black Russian-built Volga sedan had already crawled through several road blocks manned by nervous soldiers. Alex held up his foreign press card to sleepy-eyed officers who waved them through. Painted-faced men in full jungle camouflage crouched behind the garden walls of apartment blocks and the city's crumbling French-colonial mansions, as the car turned onto the main road to the airport. Ahead, the night sky flashed, each illumination followed by the whump of a mortar, a lesson in the physics of light and sound. The crackle and pop of small arms fire drifted through the window, and Alex found himself wishing the head office had shown more urgency with that consignment of flak jackets and helmets, the ones reassuringly emblazoned with PRESS in big letters. After weeks of rumors and mounting tension in Phnom Penh, the moment had apparently arrived.

"Where are we heading?" Alex said, turning to Kimseng as he lit his second Marlboro Light since getting in the car.

His local reporter's face appeared jaundiced in the light of the car's interior. It was a mask of calm. Alex thought about the differences between them. It was more than age and the color of their skin. Kimseng's mother, father, and two siblings died under the Khmer Rouge's brutal reign in the late 1970s. Death was a fact of life, and to him Phnom Penh's rough streets were ordinary. Born half a world away in New Zealand, Alex spent the best part of his working life borrowing other people's misery in a desperate effort to escape his homeland's mundane confines.

"Ministry of Defense, Boss. Radio says the rebels came off the last train into the station just across the road from there."

■ ■ ■

Weeks later, much of what happened that night would remain a blur. It was Alex's first experience of combat reporting, although, to his knowledge, he was never shot at directly. Truth be told, he hadn't left the car, something he would omit when recounting the story to his editors safely behind their desks in London. He would remember the bodies as they drove by in slow motion, the blood in the gutters, and phoning in the story to the World Desk. But, as coups go, it was a fizzer. Troops loyal to the battle-hardened Cambodian prime minister, a one-eyed former Khmer Rouge rebel named Hun Sen, quashed it easily and mercilessly.

A little-known group calling itself the Cambodian Freedom Fighters, a ragtag band of about seventy men financed by wealthy expatriate Khmers in Long Beach, California, slipped into the center of Phnom Penh. Armed with B-40 rockets and AK-47 assault rifles, they'd attacked government buildings, peppering them with fire, and then they turned their weapons on a radio station and a nearby army barracks. State security forces engaged the group in a fierce gun battle that lasted several hours, leaving bullet holes in the peeling facades of office blocks and blood staining the footpaths.

By daybreak, eight people lay dead, all of them rebels.

In the days that followed, more than two hundred people were rounded up. The city swirled with rumors, as government soldiers marched into its slums and markets arresting sympathizers. As is often the case amid the confusion of such events, the expatriate community huddled together in its bars, restaurants, and massage parlors. Complete strangers exchanged theories and bought each other rounds of drinks. They bragged about close calls—a bullet hole discovered in the garden wall, a servant's father, husband, or brother taken in by the police in the night for questioning, returning home bloody and bruised, or, worse still, not returning at all.

It was during that period Alex first met the man he'd seen standing at the window of the old riverfront mansion. The world's attention quickly moved on.

A man named Vicente Fox was sworn in as president of Mexico, ending seventy-five years of control by the Institutional Revolutionary Party. Across the border, the United States Supreme Court released its landmark decision in *Bush v. Gore*, deciding the 2000 presidential election and ensuring the term "hanging chad" took its place permanently in the English lexicon. Leninist guerrillas launched an attack in Istanbul, and a series of bombs exploded in downtown Manila, killing twenty-two people and injuring dozens more. Cambodia's failed coup slipped from network news bulletins, and the country returned once more to relative international obscurity.

Having finished work early one evening at his small office on 214 Street behind the Royal Palace, he was at the Foreign Correspondents' Club. Despite its exclusive- sounding name, the establishment was a restaurant and a bar, run as a commercial operation, one of the city's most successful. It boasted large balconies overlooking the riverfront, commanding a sweeping view of the point where the Tonle Sap joined the much larger Mekong. During the summer rainy season, the Mekong would rise to a point where it caused the current in the Tonle Sap to reverse and flow back toward the thousand-year-old temples of Angkor, several hundred kilometers to the north, making it the only river in the world to flow in two directions. Cambodians marked the change with a huge festival called Bon Om Touk, ushering in the fishing season and involving rowdy water fights and boat races. But that was still months away, and the river was far down the garbage-strewn banks.

Alex took his beer to the balcony and slumped onto one of the high stools lining the plaster balustrade. He squeezed his eyes shut and rubbed his temples.

"Mind if I join you?"

An elderly gentleman stood at his shoulder, full glass of red wine in one hand. The voice was old-school English, but beneath the thinning cap of cropped white hair, his complexion was olive. Alex recognized him immediately as the man in the window the night he'd been searching for the Alligator Ski Club.

"Sure, be my guest." He gestured to the next stool and proffered a hand. "I'm Alex." They shook.

"Morton Smith. Lovely view, isn't it? I can't get enough of it."

15

Cairo
Tuesday, 7 July 2009

"It would be one of the most significant discoveries in the history of biblical scholarship, period, if it were authentic."

Professor Tarb Herman sat in a lounge chair in his spacious third-floor office.

"The purported age of Professor Smith's find was as important as its content. Possibly as early as AD 58. That's years before any of the Gospels now in the New Testament are believed to have been written and closer to the time the historical Jesus actually lived."

The professor was surprisingly young, casually dressed in jeans and a button-down shirt. At a guess, Alex would have put him in his early forties. They sat across from each other sipping syrupy black coffee from small glass cups. A tray of Egyptian sweets sat between them on an intricately carved *mashrabiya* coffee table.

"So is it? Authentic, I mean," Alex asked. He took a notebook from his shoulder bag and rummaged in the front pocket for a pen.

"That's the million-dollar question. It depends who you talk to. Smith certainly came in for a lot of criticism from others in the field. But the problem with academics, particularly in biblical scholarship, is that they have a propensity to work backward, making the evidence fit their own preconceived notions."

"You mean some scholars concluded it couldn't be true, so therefore Smith must have invented it?"

"Precisely, but others have put forward more reasoned arguments as to why they think it a hoax. That said, Professor Smith's manuscript does help explain one of the most puzzling mysteries, or narrative glitches you might say, in the New Testament."

Sunlight filtered in golden rays through the partially shuttered windows. Outside, the American University's new campus on the outskirts of the city looked more like a building site than the hallowed halls of one of the Middle East's most famous institutions of higher learning.

A hissing sprinkler system fought a losing battle against the fine red dust suspended in the stifling morning air. Armies of workers clad in dirty *galabayas* and white turbans planted gardens among the palm groves surrounding the History faculty complex. The professor's office was in a low-slung white structure, connected to a series of semicircular lecture halls by a covered walkway lined with flowering blue lotus and papyrus plants.

After dinner the previous evening, Alex had fired up a shisha pipe and taken turns with Aubrey and Sadie drawing in the rich, water-cooled tobacco smoke laced with apple and molasses. To hell with quitting smoking; he could add that last effort to a dozen or more failed attempts in the last couple of years.

He showed them the letter from Smith, and they talked into the wee hours. All three were intrigued by the professor's discovery of the ancient manuscript and his sudden, unexpected reappearance in Alex's life. There was also the mystery of who the professor was drinking with before he died. By the time he and Sadie finally went to bed, Alex had resolved to do some digging.

■ ■ ■

Professor Herman stood and walked over to a bookshelf behind his expansive glass-topped desk. Running a finger meditatively along the spines of a series of files, he pulled one out and returned to his seat before opening it. Alex leaned forward. The beige folder contained a selection of articles from scholarly journals as well as newspaper clippings, some yellowed with age, and printouts from a library microfiche.

"I toyed with a book on early Christian Gnostic writings and their interpretation during a sabbatical a few years back. It never quite eventuated, but I've kept most of my research. I'll return to it one of these days."

Herman flicked through the articles as he talked. "Smith wrote two books about his find that were published about fifteen years after the initial announcement to the Society of Biblical Literature. One was a scholarly tome with detailed linguistic and historical analysis. The other was a beautifully written but somewhat racier text for the layman. These are some of the reviews."

He began reading from the papers in front of him.

"Patrick Skehan: 'A morbid concatenation of fancies.' Joseph Fitzmyer: 'Venal popularization…replete with innuendos and eisegesis.' Helmut Merkel: 'Once again total warfare has been declared on New Testament scholarship…'"

Alex was taken aback by the harsh tone of the comments.

"Here's one by Pierson Parker from the *New York Times Book Review*: 'Dear reader, do not be alarmed by the parallels between…magic and ancient Christianity. Christianity never claimed to be original. It claimed…to be true.'"

As they talked, it became clear that Smith's manuscript discovery caused quite an uproar, not only in the cloistered world of New Testament scholarship but in the popular press also.

Alex was curious. "What exactly was it that was so objectionable? To judge by some of these reactions, Smith's discovery threatened to call down the Apocalypse."

Herman examined at his watch, apparently deciding whether to give him the long or the short version.

"I think we had better start at the beginning."

■ ■ ■

Herman explained that in 1941 Smith had gone to the Holy Land on a traveling scholarship. With war raging, the Mediterranean was eventually closed to civilian passenger traffic, leaving him stranded in Jerusalem, unable to return home. By a stroke of good luck, he found a cheap hostel next door to the Church of the

Holy Sepulchre, and, with little else to do began a doctorate in philosophy at the Hebrew University. He soon befriended the superior at the hostel, a man by the name of Father Kyriakos Spyridonides, who, it turned out, was also custodian of the Holy Sepulchre, and one of the highest-ranking officials in the Greek Orthodox Patriarchate of Jerusalem.

Father Kyriakos took the young scholar under his wing and eventually invited him to visit the monastery of Mar Saba, a full day's journey on horseback from the city. Established in the fifth century, like St. Catherine's at the foot of Mt. Sinai, where the Codex Sinaiticus—the oldest complete text of the Bible—was discovered, Mar Saba had been inhabited for more than fifteen hundred years. Such uninterrupted occupancy was a rarity. Most of the region's ancient hermitages were, at some point, sacked by invading armies, their libraries looted or destroyed.

Herman paused, ordering his thoughts before proceeding. After a month at Mar Saba enjoying the solitude, Smith returned to Jerusalem, where he spent the rest of the war writing his doctoral dissertation in modern Hebrew. When the war ended in 1945, he found passage home to England, before traveling to the United States and Harvard University, where he did another PhD on ancient Palestine. During that time in America, he apparently developed an interest in Greek manuscripts, their discovery and decipherment, and, after several lecture-ships, he took up a position at Cambridge back in his native Britain, as professor of ancient history.

When in 1958 he was owed a sabbatical, Smith gained permission from his old friend Father Kyriakos to return to Mar Saba in the Judean desert, where he planned to conduct research and set about cataloguing the monastery's neglected library, housed in a tall sandstone tower.

During the weeks at the hermitage, he discovered some previously unknown commentaries on the works of the Greek playwright Sophocles and dozens of other manuscripts, beautifully preserved by the dry desert air. But, as he later reported in his book, Smith eventually resigned himself to the likelihood he would find nothing of major significance in the ancient tower.

Herman paused again in his tale, refilling their coffee cups from a long-handled brass pot. Once again, Alex had the impression of a man marshaling his thoughts about him. The professor stood and returned to the bookshelf, where he removed two volumes and laid them on the table. One was a handsome, ox-blood, leather-bound copy of the Bible, the other a slim paperback bearing the title *The Secret Gospel: The discovery and interpretation of the secret Gospel according to Mark*. It was the shorter, racier of the two volumes written by Smith, for the layman.

The professor picked it up and flipped through the pages until he found what he was looking for.

"Ah, now here we are, page eleven." He stabbed at the book with his forefinger and began to read. Alex sat back and closed his eyes. It was not difficult to imagine the voice he was hearing was that of his old friend.

"It was late one afternoon, close to the time I was due to return to Jerusalem, that I found myself staring in disbelief at a handwritten text. I had not even noticed it when I first picked out the book containing it. But now that I sought to decipher the tiny scrawl, it began, 'From the letters of the most holy Clement, the author of the *Stromateis*...' If I was to take this at face value, I had a previously unknown text by a writer of huge significance to early church history."

Smith recounted that he set about photographing the manuscript, which appeared as a three-page handwritten addition to the endpapers of a seventeenth-century copy of a work by another early church father, St. Ignatius of Antioch. He took three sets of shots, just to be sure. It was not until sometime later, however, in his stark monastic cell at Mar Saba, that he began working on a rough translation.

He became more excited as he read.

The text was a letter addressed by Clement to someone called Theodore, evidently a Church elder of some sort, written in response to questions about a troublesome and blasphemous early Christian sect known as the Carpocratians.

Professor Herman turned the page of Smith's book and cleared his throat.

"Much was already known about this particular offshoot of the church. It was named after its founder, a so-called heretic named Carpocrates.

"A number of other ancient writers mention him. They paint a picture of him and his followers as a sordid breakaway group. One even claimed they had invented an entire theology to justify their immoral practices, arguing that because God made all things, all things were to be enjoyed as common property among God's people. That included spouses. They also reportedly believed in a kind of reincarnation in which the soul would be trapped in the human body until it experienced everything it could experience, after which it was released. Their typical worship service consequently bore a closer resemblance to a Roman orgy than a prayer meeting." Herman allowed himself a wry smile and returned to the text.

In his letter, Clement congratulated this person called Theodore for his success in dealing with the Carpocratians, who, in their dispute with him, apparently appealed to the Gospel of Mark.

"Now this is where it gets interesting," said Herman. Alex shifted in his seat. He had heard much of this before, directly from Smith during those long, humid nights in Cambodia, but the story lost none of its appeal in the intervening years.

"In his letter, Clement explained to Theodore that there were three versions of Mark's Gospel in circulation in ancient Alexandria, and, in the process, recounted a previously unknown story about the Apostle Mark. After the Apostle Peter's death, Mark brought his original account of the life of Jesus to Alexandria from Rome. There he penned a 'more spiritual version for the use of those who were being perfected,'" Herman said, quoting Clement's letter.

"This second text was apparently kept in great secrecy by the Alexandrian Church for use in initiating those more spiritually advanced into 'the great mysteries.' But, after Mark's death, Carpocrates somehow obtained a copy and adapted it for his own use, essentially creating a third version of the Gospel."

Herman explained that because this third version was polluted with "shameless lies," as Clement put it, he ordered Theodore to deny the Secret Gospel's existence and its authorship by Mark, even under oath.

Herman looked up at Alex, fixing him with a meaningful stare, indicating he had reached the crucial stage in the narrative.

From Clement's letter, it was apparent to Alex that Theodore had asked questions about specific passages quoted by the Carpocratians and whether they were true to the secret version Mark had penned. By way of reply, Clement transcribed two sections of Mark's text that appeared to be ancient accounts of Jesus's life not known from any other source. The first fragment of the so-called Secret Gospel of Mark would have been inserted between Mark 10: 34–35, in the Gospel we know today.

Herman read the translation from Smith's book.

"'They came to Bethany. There was one woman there whose brother had died. She came and prostrated herself before Jesus and spoke to him. Son of David, pity me! But the disciples rebuked her. Jesus was angry and went with her into the garden where the tomb was. Immediately a great cry was heard from the tomb. And going up to it, Jesus rolled the stone away from the door of the tomb, and immediately went in where the young man was. Stretching out his hand, he lifted him up, taking hold his hand. And the youth, looking intently at him, loved him and started begging him to let him remain with him.'"

Herman again looked up from the page. "Similar miracle stories are readily found in the New Testament, such as the raising of Lazarus in the book of John, or, indeed, the story of the rich young man in Mark. But there was, of course, a significant difference. The passage did not end there."

He began reading again.

"'And going out of the tomb, they went into the house of the youth, for he was rich. And after six days Jesus gave him an order and, at evening, the young man came to him naked beneath a linen cloth. And he stayed with him for the night, because Jesus taught him the mystery of the Kingdom of God. When he left, he went back to the other side of the Jordan.'"

Herman explained it was this part of the discovery that caused the most outrage. It was hard to miss the homoerotic overtones.

The second fragment of the Secret Gospel transcribed by Clement would have been inserted into Mark 10:46. Herman picked up the oxblood Bible on the coffee table between them and flicked through to the appropriate chapter and verse. He handed it to Alex.

"Notice anything?"

Alex searched the page and spotted it immediately.

"It seems like there is a break in the narrative, something missing."

"Exactly! It awkwardly reads, 'Then they came to Jericho. As he was leaving Jericho with his disciples...' Why mention arriving in Jericho if you don't say what happened there? This has long been recognized as a narrative snag in Mark's Gospel. If Smith's discovery is to be believed, this strange construction did not occur in the Secret Gospel," said Herman.

He laid Smith's book out on the table between them for Alex to follow and ran his forefinger along the line of text.

"In the Secret Gospel, this bit was inserted between the sentences 'Then they came to Jericho' and 'As he was leaving…' So then it would read, 'Then they came to Jericho. And the sister of the young man whom Jesus loved was there with his mother and Salome, but Jesus would not receive them. As he was leaving Jericho with his disciples…'"

After Clement quoted this second excerpt, he went on to explain that certain other passages Theodore had inquired about were Carpocratian inventions and not true to Mark's version.

"And it appears that just as Clement prepared to give Theodore the true interpretation of the story about the young man who loved Jesus and spent the night with him, the person who was copying Clement's letter into the back of the book by St. Ignatius stopped, and the manuscript was cut short."

■ ■ ■

They talked for over an hour. Herman sat back and looked at his watch again.

"I've got to be at a lecture in fifteen minutes," he said, the regret evident in his voice.

Alex's mind boiled with questions, but they would have to wait. He thanked the professor and stood to leave.

"Before I go, may I ask one more question?"

"Certainly."

"Do scholars of the Bible actually believe there is any historical foundation for the miracle stories? I mean such stories would rely on the supernatural, wouldn't they? And scholars, in my experience at least, almost always seek to understand the world in realistic terms. I mean, surely it's more plausible for the modern critic to propose reasons for which an early Christian community might have come to understand Jesus as a miracle worker and subsequently produce mythologies depicting him in that way."

Herman smiled, thoroughly pleased to find someone so interested in his specialist field.

"Now there is a topic we could easily spend the rest of the day on. But that was, indeed, another thing that irked some scholars about Professor Smith and his interpretation of the manuscript. He refused to place an artificial barrier between the stories and their literal meanings, holding that the best explanation for the literary and historical evidence was that Jesus himself actually meant to perform—and was understood by his followers to have performed—magical feats. Among these was a baptismal rite in which he was able to induce hallucinations, a technique actually quite common in ancient Jewish mystical texts. It is that rite Smith believed was referred to in the Secret Gospel when Jesus taught his followers "the mystery of the Kingdom of God."

"Here," said the professor opening Smith's book again and leafing through it, apparently having forgotten his rush. "This is how he describes it: 'Piecing together indications in the canonical Gospels and the Secret Gospel of Mark, we can build a picture of the baptism ritual Jesus performed in order to induct disciples into the mystery of the Kingdom of God. It was a water baptism administered to a chosen few, alone and in the dark of night. The outfit for the disciple was a linen robe worn over naked flesh. This covering was removed for the immersion. Then, by unknown ritual, the disciple was possessed by Jesus's spirit and thus united with him. He participated by hallucination in Jesus's ascent into heaven, entered the Kingdom of God, and was set free from the laws of this world. That freedom probably resulted in the completion of the spiritual union by a physical one. Such coupling is known to have occurred in many forms of Gnostic Christianity and some ancient forms of Jewish mysticism.'"

Alex drew a sharp breath. He could see how thoroughly shocking to the established Church such an interpretation might be; to suggest that Jesus engaged in sex with converts, both male and female, as a rite of passage.

The professor closed the book. "Smith evidently knew how controversial he was being and relished it," he said with a chuckle. "In an interview with *The New York Times*, just before his books hit the shelves in '73, he was quoted as saying, 'Thank God I have tenure.'"

Alex grinned. He could imagine his old friend saying it. It was just his sense of humor.

The meeting over, he accompanied the professor down the stairs to the lobby, where they parted with a handshake. Herman took one of the covered walkways to the lecture theaters.

16

The library at the American University was the tallest building on campus, and Alex had no trouble finding it. An old-fashioned card index in wooden cabinets occupied much of the ground floor, looking out of place next to banks of sleek flat-panel computer terminals. Seven stories of book-lined balconies rose from the central atrium to a domed skylight high in the ceiling. Alex located the volumes he was looking for in the card file, before riding an elevator to the fourth floor, where the history and religion collections were housed.

After the meeting with Professor Herman, he'd stopped at one of the student cafés for a cup of coffee. It left his mouth scalded and bitter tasting but provided a chance to put his thoughts in order. His conversation with the professor raised more questions than it answered, and he realized they'd barely touched on the authenticity of Smith's find. He soon found himself scribbling questions in his notepad.

Who wrote the letter scrawled into the back of the seventeenth-century edition of Saint Ignatius's work, and when? Did the scribe actually have a fragmentary copy of Clement's letter at his disposal? If so, was the letter actually written by Clement, or could it have been forged? If Smith was the scribe, the perpetrator of an elaborate hoax, why would he do it? Would anyone decades later really care enough to kill him?

The questions seemed hopelessly difficult. With Smith dead, perhaps the truth was now beyond reach.

■ ■ ■

He found an empty reading desk on the fourth floor. Students, mostly in Western dress but some of the women wearing Muslim head scarves, were scattered around the other tables or browsed between the stacks. The chilled, dry air smelled of books.

Alex was a bibliophile. He loved libraries and their particular aroma. But it was not just the smell of books and the paper they were printed on, the leather, ink, dust, and hand sweat, tobacco even, or coffee, depending on where the last borrower liked to read. It was what the smell sometimes did to him. He could pick up a book and, in an instant, be transported back to his childhood by its smell, remembering rainy mornings spent in bed, reading his favorite stories. He could lift a book to his face and inhale, imagine the journey it had taken to where it now lay in his hands. Different kinds of books had different smells, too, from the cheap newspapery tang of an airport bookstore thriller, to the classy, sweet-gloss scent of a coffee-table tome.

He allowed his mind to wander. *Perhaps people choose books like they choose other people.* Wasn't there a theory that people chose their life partners, their husbands and wives, largely on smell? If you liked their smell, then your immune systems were compatible and your children would be healthier, or something like that.

Focus, Alex. His notes stared back at him from the desk. He needed a cigarette. Making his way to an outside balcony, he pulled a crumpled pack of Marlboro Lights from the pocket of his cargo pants and tapped one loose. The air outside was hot and heavy. The sudden change in temperature made his sinuses ache and he stifled a sneeze. Keeping an eye on his bag through the window, he patted his shirt pocket for a lighter.

"Can I help?"

A young blond woman stepped from the railing. She held out a plastic lighter. Alex put the tip of his cigarette to the flame and drew in deeply. He exhaled a satisfying stream of smoke.

"Cheers. Must have dropped mine somewhere."

"No problem." Their eyes met. She held his gaze and then smiled broadly.

From her accent, she sounded European, perhaps from one of the Scandinavian countries. There was also no denying that, although modestly dressed in faded jeans and a loose-fitting blouse, she was very attractive.

"Alex Fisher," he said, offering his hand.

"Noora. You are a student here?" Her grip was firm.

"Journalist, actually. Visiting one of the professors and decided on a bit of research. This, however, is called procrastination," he said, flashing what he hoped was his best boyish grin and holding up the half-smoked cigarette.

Noora laughed and something tightened in the pit of his stomach. This girl really was gorgeous. *Don't stare like an idiot.* He moved his gaze out over the campus. They stepped to the railing and leaned against it.

"I have the same problem." She nodded at her own cigarette. Her words were clipped, clearly pronounced, as is often the way with people who have acquired English as a second language.

Noora peered over the edge, and Alex took the opportunity to look at her again. She had the kind of face and figure that wasn't quite beautiful in the classical sense. He felt sure most men nonetheless paid her plenty of attention.

"I simply can't stand this weather."

"It's called the khamsin," Alex explained, "a hot, dry southerly that blows from the African interior over Egypt and into the eastern Mediterranean. The dust devastates crops. Locals hate it, but we're at the tail end of the season now."

Noora rewarded him with another smile.

"You should experience the *simoom*," she said, pausing to take a drag of her cigarette. "In the desert it can get so hot and oppressive that the body overheats, unable to perspire quickly enough. Sand from it has been known to blow as far north as the coast of England. Ancient writers called it the red wind and sailors referred to it as the sea of blood."

Alex laughed out loud. He'd underestimated the girl completely.

"You're quoting Herodotus, so you are a classics scholar?"

"I spent several months in Lebanon on an archaeological dig last year. Or perhaps I should say spent several months stripped off in my tent trying to stay hydrated."

Alex chuckled.

"So what brings you to Cairo? Been here long?"

"Not long. I'm not sure what I think of it yet. I'm doing my doctoral thesis under Professor Tarb Herman."

"No way! I was just in his office. He seems like a pretty switched-on kind of guy."

"One of the very best, they say. Anyway, nice to meet you Alex, but I've got to run or I'll be late for class." She offered her hand and they shook again.

Alex hurriedly dug in his pocket for his wallet and pulled out a dog-eared business card. Without thinking, he scribbled his home address and phone number on the back.

"Here. Call if you are in town, and we can get a coffee or something."

"I'd like that."

Noora examined the card and a frown spread across her face.

"This is actually quite close to where I live, I think."

"Really?"

"I share a house with several other postgrads, not far from that bridge. I forget its name. It goes over from the island to the Egyptian Museum. We are all doing research there."

She turned and stepped through the door.

"It has been nice meeting you."

Alex was about to say the same, but she was gone, making her way between the stacks. He stared after her, taking a final drag on his cigarette before grinding it out under foot and heading back inside.

■ ■ ■

Please God, no.

Could he have the wrong desk? His bag wasn't there, neither was his notebook. Desperately, he cast around at the other tables.

Nothing, shit.

He approached a group of students seated nearby. They hadn't seen anything.

Craning over the railing, he peered down to the atrium four floors below. Dozens of people were browsing through the card catalogues. Whoever had his bag must be long gone.

How could I be so stupid? He was about to turn toward the lifts when a flash of movement caught his attention. A blond-haired man strode past the card index and computer area toward the sliding glass doors. Alex experienced an odd sensation, a flicker of recognition. He certainly recognized the familiar canvas bag slung casually over the man's shoulder.

Without thinking, he raced for the stairs, taking them five at a time. His feet thumped loudly, and students turned to stare or flattened themselves against the banister.

The blond man had disappeared through the library doors by the time he reached the ground floor. He charged through and was momentarily blinded by the bright sunlight. He looked around wildly before making for the western corner of the building. Rounding it, the way ahead was deserted.

He jogged back to the other corner. Again, nothing.

Fuck, fuck, fuck. Doubled over, hands on knees, gasping for breath.

After a couple of minutes, he collapsed onto a bench beside the path and checked his pockets. At least he still had his cell phone and wallet. But everything else was gone; notes, digital recorder, house keys, contact book, and, worst of all, Smith's letter.

Hands trembling from the adrenaline, he wiped them on his shirt and pulled out his phone. He scrolled through recently dialed numbers and hit Sadie's.

"Hey, it's me."

"What's wrong? You sound terrible."

"You'll never believe what just happened. Some fucker nicked my bag…"

"Damn!"

"Thing is, he was a foreigner. It's weird too…He looked familiar. I think I've seen him somewhere before, but I can't put my finger on it or figure out where. Where are you?"

"Still at your place, using the computer. I haven't checked my email forever. What do you mean you think you've seen him before?"

"I'm not sure. I'm so pissed off there aren't words for it. See you in an hour, babe. I was going to do some research here, but I think I'll just get the books and come home."

17

Phnom Penh, Cambodia
15 December 2000

The crumbling villa on the Mekong looked as if it had once been among the city's grander mansions. Built in the French-colonial style, it had its own pier jutting out into the river's muddy flow. But there was no boat and probably had not been for many years. Weeds and rotting vegetation clung to the rusting steel piles of the landing area. Alex had not visited this part of the city before, but Phnom Penh was littered with places like it, run down and redolent of a more illustrious past.

Peeling ochre walls and cracked red roofing tiles bleached almost pink by the sun emanated an air of dilapidated grandeur. Standing in the alley outside, he rang the buzzer. The evening was stifling and sweat ran down his back, making his shirt cling uncomfortably.

Inside, bare feet slapped on tiles. It was still early and the sun had yet to slip past the city's low skyline across the river, plunging the city into a blackness that would be barely distinguishable from the surrounding bush.

The door opened and a round brown face peered out from the gloom of the interior.

"Hi, is Dr. Smith home?"

The young girl smiled shyly and stood aside as Alex stepped into a long hallway. Books and framed photographs lined most of its length. Brass pots and delicate stone figurines jostled for space with a flower-filled vase on a narrow side table. The air was heavy with the sweet fragrance of white blossoms. It was like he'd stepped into another world after the pungent odors of the alley.

"That you, Alex?" a voice bellowed from somewhere in the interior. "Come in, come in. Glad you could make it. I hope it wasn't too difficult to find."

"Not at all," Alex yelled in return.

He followed the girl down the hall into the main living area. The floor-to-ceiling shutters were pulled back. The room opened directly onto a broad riverside terrace, and the boat landing Alex had seen earlier. A warm breeze filtered through the large space, stirred by the slowly turning blades of two ceiling fans.

Still no Smith.

"In here, Alex."

The voice came from down another, shorter hallway to the left. Alex stepped through into a tiled kitchen.

"Ah, there you are! Now, how about this?" Smith wore a baggy linen shirt. Its ivory color matched that of a loose pair of linen drawstring pants. Bare feet were tucked into a pair of black rubber flip-flops. He handed Alex a tall ice-filled glass. A sip revealed it to be a stiff gin and tonic.

"Thanks. This is an incredible place you've got here. Do you live alone?" Alex said. He took another gulp.

"Just me and Vary here," Smith said, indicating the young woman who showed Alex in, "plus her husband and their two small children. He manages the garden, she cooks and keeps house."

The two men moved out onto the terrace, Smith limping just a little, favoring his right leg. They sat in cane armchairs facing the river. Vary had been busy. A low wooden table supported an array of snacks. Nuts, dried fruit, and several dishes he didn't recognize.

Music played somewhere in the distance, the nasal sound of a Cambodian folk ballad drifting downriver.

The sun was now low over the buildings on the far bank, framing the golden spires of the Royal Palace, national museum, and, farther upstream, Wat Phnom. The girl had fired up two kerosene lamps, which smoked in the torpid air. Their sharp fuel smell mingled with the astringent odor of insect repellent.

A deep orange glow began to spread over the surface of the water. Without warning, a thin black plume rose from the arched roof of the museum, curling up toward the darkening sky.

Alex blinked and looked again. The plume darkened and undulated. He turned abruptly to his host and pointed toward the old building. "Is that smoke billowing from under the eaves?"

Smith laughed. "Bats, man, millions of tiny bats."

Alex frowned, but, turning back to the river, he could now make out the tiny creatures as they swooped low over the water, scooping up insects and leaving tiny ripples on its slow-moving surface.

"They've been roosting under the leaking roofs and eaves of the museum for years, the most dangerous threat to the preservation of its ancient treasures, yet also one of their chief benefactors."

"Really, how so?"

Smith explained that in the days of the Khmer Rouge, more than two decades ago, the museum was abandoned as Cambodia's hard-line Communist regime drove people onto collective farms in the countryside. The bat population exploded.

"Ever since then, the museum's curators have struggled to drive the creatures out. Their droppings badly corrode the priceless artifacts. In recent years, however, they've changed their minds.

"The museum needs the bats, you see. It receives virtually no government funding. Frankly, it's broke. Employees barely get paid. Yet bat guano sells as fertilizer at the central market for eighteen cents a pound. Can you believe it? For years, the museum has been subsidized by the shit trade!"

■ ■ ■

Dinner was a mix of spicy Cambodian dishes and basic French fare, and they ate mostly in companionable silence. Alex thought back to their first meeting at the Foreign Correspondents' Club on the far bank of the river, a stone's throw from the palace, just days after the failed coup. They drank together for most of the night, enjoying each other's company. Alex eventually confided that he'd spotted Smith through the window of a house while searching for the Alligator Ski Club. The first time he'd laid eyes on the professor, he had assumed it was his residence he was crouching outside of. That was not the case, and the story Smith subsequently told him as they sipped their drinks and watched the river traffic left Alex thinking about little else for days.

Alex hoped to raise the topic of the ancient manuscript again this evening with his new acquaintance.

He had at first suspected the old man of being a little crazy. It was amazing the characters a lawless backwater like Cambodia attracted, life's flotsam; and his fleeting encounter with the aging professor while looking for the floating bar had done little for first impressions. But after Googling Smith and running his name through various newspaper archives online, he realized the man was perfectly sane and indeed discovered what came to be known as the Secret Gospel of Mark some years earlier.

Smith was now one of the world's leading experts on Christian cults, and it was the general state of lawlessness that attracted some of the world's more bizarre sects to the strife-torn Southeast Asian nation of Cambodia. That included the one the professor was currently documenting, a California-based group planting new "churches" in the Third World.

At the age Alex now was, his parents were missionaries in the Middle East. Some of his earliest memories were of family holidays tracing the stories of the Bible through the region's ancient ruins. He'd gone on to study Greek and Roman history at university, dreaming of becoming an archaeologist until he found he was more gifted with modern than ancient languages, and, when it came down to it, not particularly talented at them either.

He had a basic understanding of ancient texts and their transmission down through the centuries. He also knew that strange Gospels appeared with some regularity, and there were plenty of people out there who were not beyond pawning off what purported to be a firsthand account of the life of Jesus as authentic. Often they recorded the "lost years," accounts of the Savior as a young man. Some even had him traveling to India to learn the wisdom of the Brahmins. Mostly of it was total horseshit. It was a well-trodden genre that went all the way back to the second century. Nowadays, such accounts were usually the stuff of supermarket tabloids, not above printing the discovery of alien spaceships or London buses on the North Pole.

But what about forgery by serious academics in modern times? It seemed farfetched, but Alex decided to be direct.

"Morton, that story you told me about the Secret Gospel. I've been thinking a lot about it," he said, turning briefly to look at the man next to him before focusing his attention back on the river. Smith's pleasure was obvious.

"You said some scholars accepted it as genuine, while others were less inclined to do so. But do scholars really ever fake documents to suit their own ends? Surely they would never get away with it."

Smith did not reply immediately. He stared out at the river, and Alex wondered if he had offended the old man. Yet when the reply came, it was evident from the tone of his voice that he was enjoying himself.

"May I tell you an amusing story?"

"Sure, go ahead."

"Do you know what an *agraphon* is?"

Alex thought back to his Greek classes at university. The word was familiar.

"It means something not written or unwritten, doesn't it?"

"Bravo! Indeed it does. But it's also a technical term used by scholars to refer to sayings of Jesus recorded in sources other than canonical Gospels of the New Testament."

It was dark now, the world reduced to tiny circles of light cast by the smoky lamps. There was no breeze and the flames rose straight upward, burning steadily in the languid air. The river was just visible, a shimmering silver plane suspended somewhere in the middle distance between them and the lights of Sisowath Quay on the river's far bank.

"You mean like in the book of Acts in the New Testament, I'm not sure of the chapter and verse, where the Apostle Paul records Jesus saying that it is better to give than to receive? If my memory serves me, that doesn't appear in any of the four Gospels, does it?"

"You know your Scriptures," said Smith, his voice betraying surprise and pleasure. "A rarity in the younger generations these days."

"A misspent youth." Alex chuckled, refreshing both their glasses from a chilled bottle of German Riesling resting in a melting bucket of ice at the end of the table.

"Thank you." Smith dabbed his lips with a napkin. "Let me tell you about an article which appeared in the *Catholic Biblical Journal* in 1950, written by the respected scholar Paul Coleman-North of Princeton, who, during World War II, served in the US Army in North Africa. French Morocco, to be precise.

"As he recounted in his article, *An Amusing Agraphon*, while visiting a mosque in 1943, the good professor came across a book filled, as one might expect, with Arabic writings. But, pressed between its pages, he was surprised to find a single loose leaf of parchment in ancient Greek, a set of sermons on Matthew 1:13 and 19:25.

"Of course, there was a war on and Coleman-North had no camera, but he was able to make a careful transcription of the letter and later study it, finding to his surprise that it contained a previously unheard-of agraphon. You will know of course Matthew 24:51, where Jesus tells the disciples that in hell 'there will be weeping and gnashing of teeth.'

"Well this manuscript goes on to recount one of the disciples asking the obvious question: 'But Rabbi, how can this happen for those who have no teeth?' Jesus is said to have replied: 'Oh ye of little faith. If some have no teeth, then teeth will be provided,'"

Smith was laughing now, his whole body rocking, eyes shining with tears.

"It's a great story and a lovely little agraphon. But, alas, it was too good to be true," he said, wiping his eyes.

"I was a student of Coleman-North just before the war and he used to joke that dentures would be provided in the afterlife so those who were toothless would be able to wail and gnash their teeth! Nobody, of course, has ever seen the manuscript he claimed to have discovered in the Moroccan mosque, but no scholar worth his salt now doubts that the professor simply made the story up. A kind of scholarly practical joke."

"But why bother? Publish or perish, is that it?"

"You'd have to ask him, although he passed away several years ago. Perhaps it was arrogance, a way of thumbing his nose at the scholarly community. He was a very clever man and possibly wanted to see what he could get away with. He did, after all, get it published, with erudite philological analysis, in a respected academic journal."

They sat quietly contemplating the story for a few minutes, before Smith said, "Perhaps too, he was fed up with those who try to interpret the Scriptures too literally and wanted to have some fun at their expense."

18

Tuesday, 7 July 2009

Alex ended the call, slid the cell phone back into his pocket, and wiped his face with a damp sleeve. The shock of having his bag stolen was replaced by anger and a healthy dose of disgust at his own stupidity. He lived here, yet most tourists were smarter than he'd been. Being in the university library was no excuse for letting his guard down.

He looked down at his hands. They were steady now, and he consoled himself by imagining the disappointment on the thief's face at finding no wallet in the satchel. Then he winced at the memory of the brand-new Sony digital voice recorder, bought duty- free just last month. It cost a small fortune. He'd have to go back to his clunky old tape recorder for the time being. He groaned.

But other than Smith's letter, the rest was no big deal. Like all good journalists, he kept two copies of his address book, containing three years' worth of scrawled contacts, recorded in a near-illegible hand.

Alex thought about the letter, trying to remember exactly what it said. There was a warning, wasn't there? Something about Smith being followed, and an admonition for Alex to take care. *The ramblings of an old man, surely.*

Then why do I feel so rattled? The thief was a foreigner. One that somehow he was sure he had seen before. He had a good memory for faces, although the high angle made it difficult to gain a clear view. *I'd love a few minutes alone with the fucker.*

Alex trudged up the library steps and took the lift to the fourth floor, where he found the books he was looking for.

By a small miracle, he also found his notebook under a nearby desk, where the thief must have dropped it in his rush for the exit. He flicked though his notes from the meeting with Professor Herman and the list of questions he wrote down for further research. At least the day hadn't been a complete waste. After a few minutes at the checkout, and a frustrating half hour trying to report the theft to campus security, he was on the street hailing a cab.

Exhausted, he flopped into the ripped upholstery of an ancient Mercedes and wound down the window. Hot air blasted his face. The driver struck up a friendly banter, pointing out landmarks in broken English as they sped into the city. Lost in thought, Alex filtered most of it out, feigning interest with the occasional grunt or nod.

Finding his way around Cairo's vast sprawl seemed impossibly difficult when he'd first arrived, but he quickly found the city wasn't an unfathomable mystery. It was divided into a series of distinct and easily recognizable districts. Midan Tahrir, not far from where he had found his apartment, was its heart. The downtown area surrounding the square was a profusion of broad streets and narrow alleys crammed with cheap eateries, jewellery shops, and budget accommodation. To the west, just past the dilapidated Egyptian Museum, the Nile flowed around the island of Gezira, where he lived in the inner-city suburb of Zamalek.

The northern extent of the central city was marked by Ramses Square and the central train station, under a vast glass and plaster dome. Farther south, Garden City, the diplomatic district with its broad well-swept streets and numerous police checkpoints, separated downtown from the beige, crumbling expanse of Old Cairo. Farther south still was the walled enclave of the ancient Coptic quarter, home to the world's oldest Christian community. And in the distance, between the Midan Tahrir and the looming desert massif, sat the working-class suburbs, cluttered apartment blocks festooned with drying laundry, which made up the true soul of the modern metropolis.

The taxi skirted a traffic island, barely missing a group of pedestrians, and flew up onto an expressway above the Islamic district. Unchanged for centuries, its spiky of minarets and dun-colored dwellings with exquisitely carved shutters were built so close they gave the illusion of touching above the rutted, narrow alleys where motorbikes and delivery vans fought for right of way with pedestrians, donkey carts, and livestock. In the distance, framed against the rocky, sandstone ridge that marked the start of the desert, Alex caught a glimpse of the dark walls and domes of the old Citadel, before his taxi found an exit and plunged back into the chaos below.

The trip was quicker than he anticipated, and the driver soon wheeled the cab onto the 6 October Bridge, named after one of Egypt's several wars with Israel and known locally as Cairo's "spinal cord." A glimpse of the lateen sails of dozens of feluccas moored along the river's edge, and his taxi descended again onto Gezira Island and Zamalek.

The garish pink walls of the Marriott Hotel loomed in the windshield. He was nearly home.

19

Sadie pocketed her cell phone and padded through to the kitchen to fix another cup of tea. She loved Alex's place. Its spacious, cool interior, filled with the clutter of a career traveler, could not have been more different from the stuffy confines of her student dorm.

The evening call to prayer droned over the sound of a Natalie Merchant album playing quietly over her iPod headphones. Balcony doors thrown wide and mug in hand, she stepped out into the hot evening air, humming along with the tune.

The view was dominated by the new Anglican cathedral compound across the street. Its predecessor had been located on the banks of the Nile, bulldozed to make way for the 6 October Bridge. The new building was now twenty years old but modern compared to its surroundings. Built to resemble a Bedouin tent, it looked more like a wine carafe, neck stretching up to eye level on the fifth floor.

The Sudanese refugees in the cathedral compound were settling down to their evening meal around green plastic tables. They would soon make the trek back across town to the vast necropolis known as the Northern Cemetery or, more popularly, the City of the Dead, where many of them slept. What had once been a place for the Mamluk sultans to bury their kin outside Cairo's walls, had, over the centuries, been subsumed within the city itself. Ancient tombs and grand mausoleums now served as homes to the city's homeless.

Sadie sipped her tea as social workers dished out steaming bowls of couscous and vegetable broth. Most of the throng were Christian and had fled strife in their homeland far to the south. A white-uniformed policeman, black beret pushed to the back of his head, lounged on a chair outside the gate, arm resting on the muzzle of a pump-action shotgun. Another knelt on a mat nearby, immersed in his daily prayers.

Sadie wriggled deeper into the padding of the low armchair and put her feet up on the small coffee table. Bliss. She was tired after her late night with the boys. Her tolerance for alcohol wasn't what it used to be, or maybe it was just the heat. Anyway, she'd stayed the night, skipped class, and hadn't left the apartment all day. But she felt better for having written to her parents, who hadn't heard from their globe-trotting daughter in more than a month.

She had not told them about Alex yet, waiting, she supposed, to see how things panned out. Maybe she would let her budding romance slip in her next email. But there was no point getting them unnecessarily excited. All her mother and father seemed to want was for her to settle down, find a nice man, and produce grandchildren. Her mom cried when she told her she was going to study Arabic in Cairo. "Darling, it's no place for a young woman," she'd said. Her father was more stoic but equally disappointed in his own quiet way.

Everything with Alex had happened so quickly. But she felt sure what she found with him was something special, the kind of connection she'd never experienced before. It seemed hard to believe they'd only met six months ago. She remembered the first time she noticed him looking at her in the university library. Slightly older than the other students. Good-looking, sure. But in a rugged, unselfconscious way. She smiled to herself. He'd thought his interest subtle, unnoticed.

Natalie Merchant's *Ophelia* continued to play softly in her ears. Sadie closed her eyes and drifted off. She didn't hear the sound of the front door opening and then closing again with a muffled click.

20

Traffic was backed up almost to the off-ramp onto Saray El Gezira. Smoke billowed in thick, black clouds from somewhere near the Marriott. Alex fished out his wallet and paid the driver before exiting the cab and setting out on foot, passing the rows of restaurant boats and feluccas moored at the Nile's edge.

Crowds of evening strollers stood in clusters staring at the smoke, chatting excitedly. Others sat on the stone fence separating the footpath from the rubbish-strewn concrete slope of the riverbank, munching peanuts or sipping Coke. Street hawkers, ice chests perched precariously on the backs of ancient bicycles, dripped their way through the throng.

The fire appeared to be in the hotel gardens. Distant sirens drifted through the stifling air, mingling with the raised voices of angry drivers and the incessant honking of horns. He pulled out his phone, hit redial, and waited for Sadie to answer. Maybe she had a better view of the action from the balcony of his apartment. The phone rang until her voice message came on. "Hi. Don't leave a message, I don't check them. Call back. Bye." He smiled and hung up.

Good old Sadie. You're a lucky bastard, mate. Shame needled his conscience as he thought about his encounter with the woman at the library.

■ ■ ■

Nearer the wrought-iron fence and pink facade of the Marriott, it is obvious the source of the smoke lies not in the hotel gardens but just beyond. The smoke is so thick now it blocks out the sun.

An invisible hand grips Alex's heart and lungs. His breathing quickens.

No, surely not.

Cars are parked on both sides of Sharia Michel Lutfallah, preventing the yellow fire tenders from entering his street.

Jogging now, beads of sweat sting his eyes, breath ragged. Fifty meters on, a small utility command vehicle and a white ambulance with red crescent markings are wedged in.

Alex is sprinting, leaping over hoses snaking through the muddy street.

"*Waqf!*" Somebody yells stop in Arabic.

The sound seems muffled, miles away, drowned out by the blood rushing in his ears. Black smoke and orange flames pour from his fifth-floor apartment.

Nearing the front steps to the lobby, he is screaming Sadie's name.

Firm hands pull him back. Sour breath: tobacco and coffee. Scalding heat. He thrashes wildly, arms flailing.

A dozen men in navy boiler suits and rubber boots wrestle a tangle of hoses, training plumes of water upward.

Boom! A gas canister in the kitchen explodes, throwing out horizontal tongues of fire and showering the street with debris. The fridge door, pots, utensils, the microwave. A shard of wood whooshes past his head and embeds itself in a car door a few meters away with a loud crack.

Focus, dammit. This isn't happening. Can't be happening.

"Mister, who is Sadie?" He spins, shaking off the officers gripping his arms. A man in the uniform of a police captain addresses him.

"You are yelling Sadie. Is this someone in the building?" More urgent this time. Flecks of spittle pepper Alex's face.

Across the street, a team of firemen in breathing apparatus and helmets emerge from the lobby and make their way toward the tenders. The flames are subsiding. One of the men looks toward the police captain and shakes his head.

Alex's voice is barely a whisper. "I...I'm...It's my apartment. Is anyone inside?"

"And, you are?"

"Alex. Alex Fisher. My girlfriend. I think she is inside. Is Sadie inside?"

The policeman's demeanor softened.

"I'm sorry, sir. Come with me, please."

21

Cairo
Friday, 10 July 2009

Alex lit a Marlboro Light and took a deep drag. From his perch just below the 6 October Bridge, he stared out at the river. The nicotine went to work, helping to focus his scattered thoughts. Just after 1:00 a.m. and crowds of strollers still thronged the wide Nile-front boulevard. The river formed a swathe of darkness running through the heart of the ancient city, defined at its edges by glittering streetlights.

The boulevard, dotted with large planters of papyrus and date palms, ended at the bridge. On the other side of the road that crossed it, light shone from the windows of some of the island's grander old mansions, their gardens running down to the water's edge. They faced the brightly lit Egyptian Museum and, farther down river, the old diplomatic quarter of Garden City.

The concrete balustrade retained some of the day's warmth and Alex leaned back, lost in thought as he observed his fellow night owls. Cairo was a city that never shut down completely. Few women were out this late. But men strolled hand in hand or with arms linked, smoking and chatting, as was the Egyptian custom.

In the days following the fire, a dense fog seemed to envelope him. He couldn't escape it. He had answered questions from the police and fielded concerned phone calls from his family, friends, the office, and consular officials.

There were several requests for interviews from journalists, interested in the death of a British woman in Cairo. He declined them. He called Sadie's parents, whom he had never met. Her father was calm, almost cold, her mother hysterical, sobbing down the crackling line.

He was numb, unable to summon up the range of emotions he should be feeling. *Anything would be preferable to this sense of emptiness.*

Head Office wanted him back in London, fearing he might have been the intended target of foul play. He would not have been the first foreign journalist to find himself on the wrong side of big business interests, or the many factions battling within the pressure cooker of Egyptian society. When he refused to leave Cairo, there was an offer to pay for a hotel room, and an assurance that, of course, he could take as much time as he needed. Instead, he accepted an invitation from Bairstow to stay in his riverside apartment a few blocks away on the island.

Sadie's body was not recovered.

But police forensics officers were still combing the shell of his apartment. The inferno burned so fiercely that fire crews were initially unable to enter. The police had no idea what started the blaze. But they assured him it was a miracle the entire building had not gone up in flames.

Alex spent his days sitting in Aubrey's seventeenth-floor rooms staring at the city, his nights roaming the island's streets. Was it possible Sadie had not been home? *With no body, surely there is a chance she is alive.*

"Don't be stupid," he muttered, exhaling a stream of smoke.

His eyes stung from exhaustion, yet he couldn't sleep at night and found himself taking these nocturnal excursions. Sometimes, he even ventured across the bridge to the city proper. Tonight, he'd opted for the waterfront.

Three days since the fire and the small grain of hope that Sadie might walk through the door or call his cell phone was dissolving in a sea of melancholy. Covering plane crashes, natural disasters, and terrorist bombings, he'd made a career of intruding on other people's grief, but experienced little of his own. Both his parents were alive and well, and his grandparents died when he was young. Intermittently he dreaded and longed for the moment he knew must come eventually, when the numbness wore off. But for now he was able only to glimpse what that lay ahead, and it frightened him.

He flicked the remains of his cigarette away. Its glowing tip spiraled into the inky water. He pulled his knees up to his chin and lit another.

There would be no quick fix. No shortcut.

He met a Catholic priest once who recounted a saying learned during a half century of luckless Christian mission among North Africa's desert tribes. How did it go? He tried to remember.

There is no way out of the desert except through it.

It had been the first anniversary of the 2004 Boxing Day tsunami and he was on assignment, following up on the families of tourists killed when the waves swept Southern Thailand's resort beaches. He was struck by how raw their grief still seemed, undiminished twelve months on. A year earlier, he'd landed on a cracked runway in Aceh on the northern tip of Sumatra aboard an Australian military flight, one of several dozen journalists plucked from their regular assignments in the region to cover the devastation.

He met the priest after a week of picking through the flattened, body-strewn debris of Banda Aceh, the once-beautiful city known as the Verandah of Mecca, where Islam was first introduced to the Indonesian archipelago by Arab spice traders.

They met again a year later, on a Thai beach. A memorial service.

Knowledge of the process of grief can provide a generalized map of the terrain we have to cover, the priest told the somber gathering.

Each of us will take a different path, each will choose landmarks and travel at his own speed, navigate using the tools provided by his culture, experience, and faith.

He racked his brain for the priest's name but came up empty. Over the past few days, his memory deserted him. He forgot basic things but remembered details. Sitting under the bridge, he wondered what tools his culture provided, what faith? He couldn't think of anything.

Alex's parents were missionaries, with strong beliefs. But almost as soon as he was old enough to choose his own path, he wandered from theirs. The patterns of his youth—Sunday school, Bible class, grace before meals, church—wove themselves into the fabric of his subconscious, a world view he'd come to think of as part of a grand plan. When it all began to unravel in his early twenties, when change came, his world shattered.

At fifteen years old, he'd gone through a phase of persistent religious brooding. He'd started attending a youth group at the local church. The leader would have been in his late twenties. For the impressionable kids, he was an attractive personality, younger than a parent but older and more experienced than those he was charged with looking after. His name was Tom Gilmore, and he had a seductive message—the void Alex and the other teens felt inside had an explanation; it was from not having Jesus in their hearts. If they would only ask Jesus in, then the void would be filled.

Tom could quote the Bible at will and did so often. It impressed his young charges. It was important to learn the Scriptures, he'd said, because they were *the very words of God*.

Alex eventually came to accept Tom's message of salvation. He didn't feel anything in particular, but he felt happy to be part of something and that feeling, which he years later came to recognize as loneliness, seemed to have gone. Tom was thrilled, as were Alex's parents. Tom told him only those who were saved, or born again, as he now was, were real Christians. Alex, born for the first time just a decade and a half earlier, felt privileged.

While studying history and classics at university in New Zealand some years later, his bubble burst. He'd found it increasingly difficult to take at face value the ancient Bible stories inherited from his parents and from Tom. Eventually he gave up trying and drifted away from the Church. He was sick of being treated as a simpleton every Sunday, told the version of the Bible in the pew in front of him, replete with its flowery language, was literally the word of God. He felt cheated.

Nobody stood in the pulpit and told the congregation that none of the original copies of any of the books of the New Testament survived, nor any of the first copies, or the copies of those copies. At university, he learned the versions of the four Gospels he'd been taught to revere, Matthew, Mark, Luke, and John, were hand copied over a period of many hundreds of years, accumulating all the scribal errors, additions, and omissions inherent in that very human process.

Alex found it irritating: the lack of willingness to accept that the canonical Gospels were not seen as sacrosanct until many years after they were first written down and put into circulation in the early Church. For hundreds of years, they shared the metaphorical library shelf with literally dozens of similar accounts of the life of Jesus.

One of Alex's favorite courses at university was on the late Roman Empire, spanning the period of the early Church through to the rise of Constantine the Great as emperor. He was fascinated. After three centuries of brutal persecution, Christianity made an incredible breakthrough. It became the official religion of the state. The faithful, no longer fearing for their survival, turned on each other in an attempt to answer the dual questions of how to define themselves and what constituted true beliefs. The outcome of those internal struggles was the Bible as it existed today, a collection of books, four of them accounts of the life of Jesus, bound into a single volume. The battle was hard fought, the spoils immense. The victors got to determine orthodoxy, the shape of Christianity for posterity. The victors wrote its history, dictated its rules, compiling its texts into a sacred canon.

Texts that did not make the cut were destroyed or marginalized, their proponents hounded as heretics. Alex realized that if things turned out otherwise, if a different faction had won the day, not only would the Christian Church have altered course but so too would much of modern history. The victors had done a thorough job too. More than two millennia passed, yet modern scholars were only just beginning to recover the voices of the losers in that early struggle for the heart and soul of the Church.

Sitting below the bridge, lost in these thoughts, Alex was reminded of his recent meeting with Professor Herman and the clippings he'd read from reviews of Smith's book on the discovery of the Secret Gospel of Mark.

The bitter battles over orthodoxy, over truth, are obviously still alive and well.

He returned his attention to the late-night strollers.

Their number was dwindling, but a dozen or more clusters of men remained on the boulevard. In a puddle of light cast by a streetlamp, a vendor selling coffee and tea, made on a small charcoal brazier, sat atop the river wall. Nearby another man sold snacks from a cardboard box fastened to the carrier of his bicycle with a section of rubber inner tube.

His gaze drifted to the old homes facing Garden City. He stood and stretched, stifling a yawn. *One more cigarette and then back to Bairstow's, try to get some sleep.* His friend would probably still be up. Perhaps they would have a nightcap together before hitting the sack.

He lit up. The glowing dial on his watch showed 1:59 a.m.

Quite a few men lingered on the riverbank, even at this late hour. He was about to jump down from his perch under the bridge when he recognized a figure standing alone, just at the edge of the huddle surrounding the coffee seller. Despite the distance of about forty meters, and the darkness, he was in no doubt. She smoked a cigarette and the streetlight reflected off shoulder-length blond hair tied into a ponytail.

What was Noora doing here? Then he remembered.

I share a house with several other postgrads, not far from that bridge.

Cairo was not unsafe for foreigners, particularly on the island. But it was unwise for a Western woman to be out alone on the riverbank at this hour.

He clambered down onto the boulevard and made his way toward her, weaving between the groups of men, occasionally nodding in greeting. Given his mood over the past few days, he was surprised by the excitement he felt at the thought of talking to this woman.

About ten meters separated them when a figure emerged from the gloom and stood next to Noora.

He froze in his tracks.

The man turned toward her slightly and touched her arm. He was older but well put together, distinctly handsome features. They did not exchange words, but there was no mistaking the smile of recognition she gave in return.

Even in the dark, with nobody watching, his face reddened. *How stupid of me to think she's alone.*

The pair began walking directly toward him, forcing Alex to take a seat on an empty bench formed by the edge of a large planter of papyrus. Embarrassed, he sat there, trying to look casual, expecting any second to be discovered. But Noora and the man stopped on the other side of the papyrus.

They were speaking a foreign language that he did not understand but recognized instantly. Hebrew.

Eventually, Noora and the man moved closer and took a seat on the edge of the planter. Although obscured from view, their voices were clearly audible. They had switched to English.

"Do they know you are out here?" the man said, keeping his voice low.

"I waited until they were asleep."

"Good."

Alex stood carefully and slowly walked toward the bridge, keeping the planter between him and the couple. He didn't want to be listening in on a lovers' nighttime tryst. As soon as he could, he turned off the boulevard onto a side street, heading in the direction of Bairstow's apartment.

He tried not to think about Noora, or the sense of disappointment he felt so unexpectedly when the man appeared. But questions, like angry bees, swarmed in his brain.

His dark mood returned, and he suspected a sleepless night lay ahead. Yet, he'd made a decision. He knew what he had to do.

22

Alex woke exhausted, mouth like an ashtray, throat dry. A few moments, and then his brain registered that he was fully clothed and lying on top of the covers.

The events of the night before came back slowly. Still wired from the bizarre close encounter with Noora on the riverfront, he arrived at Bairstow's apartment to find his friend already sound asleep.

Unable to sleep himself, he raided the liquor cabinet.

He'd avoided alcohol over the past few days, fearing it would only take him lower than he already felt. Uncorking a bottle of Laphroaig, he poured two fingers of the pale yellow liquid into a tumbler and drained it before helping himself to a generous refill. The single malt burned a trail down his esophagus and into his stomach. It felt good. So good, in fact, he finished the bottle and fell asleep on the couch. At some point in the night, he must have made his way to bed.

Now, bright sunlight streamed through the bedroom window. He pulled himself upright. A sharp pain knifed through his temples to the back of his skull. Saliva flooded his mouth. *Oh God, I'm going to hurl.* He swallowed hard. Groaning loudly, he lay down again. He stared at the cracks in the ceiling and thought about the decision he'd made while staring at the Nile. He couldn't bring himself to return to work, yet he would not sit around moping, waiting. For what, he wasn't quite sure.

The sounds of river traffic drifted into the bedroom. He forced himself upright again and padded through to the bathroom. Four Tylenol, downed with a glass of water. He stripped off and stepped into the shower. The cold jet drummed against his scalp and shoulders and he stood for a full ten minutes until the painkillers kicked in.

By 8:00 a.m. he was in the kitchen making coffee.

Keys rattled and the door to the apartment opened and closed. A double thud as Bairstow kicked off his shoes and shuffled into the lounge.

"It's me."

"In here. Coffee?"

"It'd be rude not to. I picked up some croissants from the Marriott Bakery. Glad to see the wounded are walking."

Aubrey was, as usual, direct. Alex appreciated it. He was weary of how everyone had been treating him with kid gloves lately. They stepped out onto the balcony. Below were the waterfront properties of the Vatican mission and Indian embassy, rooftops a mass of antennae and satellite dishes. A string of barges filled with sand and cement chugged upstream, passing under the 6 October Bridge. The dull throb of their engines made the balcony doors vibrate.

Alex lit a cigarette and handed it to his friend. He fired up another for himself. They stood, elbows on the railing, sipping their steaming drinks. After several minutes he broke the silence.

"I've decided to write about my friend Smith, track down his manuscript, or at least try to."

A horn sounded out on the river, and a slender taxi boat pulled up at the crowded pier under the bridge.

"It means probably going to Israel and God knows where else. I was wondering if you would come with me, a sort of road trip. It'd be fun," he said, trying to make it sound like an attractive proposition.

Bairstow didn't respond immediately. He exhaled a cloud of smoke and took another sip of coffee.

"Sounds like fun."

"Really?"

"I've got some leave owing that the ambassador wants cleared before Christmas."

"That's a yes, then?"

He grinned. "Very definitely, old boy."

PART TWO

23

Cairo

Saturday, 11 July 2009

Africa's largest city sprawls like a bloated serpent along the fertile banks of the Nile for nearly fifty kilometers. Home to twenty-two million people, it is not a gentle place. Its intensity provokes strong reactions, repelling and seducing visitors in almost equal measure.

When he first arrived, Alex felt as though he was climbing into the heaving belly of a pregnant monster. From day one he loved it. It was noisy, crowded, polluted, dusty, and dry. The poverty was raw and unflinching, the opulence of the wealthy equally so. But it was also a place of wonder and intrigue. The architecture and myriad cultures reflected all those who'd been seduced, those who'd coveted and conquered her—the Arabs, Romans, Greeks, Turks, French, and British.

Coptic Cairo is the oldest part of the ancient metropolis, inhabited for more than two thousand years, older even than the Islamic quarter with its bristling skyline of ornate minarets. The word Copt is taken from the Arabic word *Gypt*, literally meaning Egyptian. After conquering Egypt in AD 641, the Arabs called the population of Egypt *Gypt*, from the Greek word *Egyptos*. As the center of the indigenous Coptic Christian community, the quarter is home to many of Egypt's oldest churches. Hidden away in its narrow alleyways is the Church of St. Sergius, built in the fourth century on the site where, legend has it, the Holy

Family—Joseph, Mary, and the infant Jesus—rested in their flight from Herod's persecution.

Heavily armed, black-clad paramilitary soldiers eyed Alex suspiciously as he entered the enclave. They manned every gate. It had not always been that way, but America's "War on Terror" changed things, sometimes overtly and at other times just subtly. With such a distinctive Christian enclave in a majority-Muslim nation, the Egyptian authorities lived in constant fear of sectarian violence.

He entered St. Sergius through the small doorway in the southwest corner and was immediately enveloped in its cool, dim interior, infused with the scent of incense and beeswax. He loved the ancient Egyptian-Byzantine basilica and visited it often in his early days in the city. Its use of Islamic motifs, the inlaid wooden stars of the iconostasis screen, presented a certain harmony. It soothed him. An intermingling of Islamic and Coptic styles stretched back centuries and was a hallmark of this part of Cairo.

Rows of burnished wooden pews gleamed dully against ornate, almost gaudy walls. Exposed roof beams led toward a raised transept. A couple of tourists examined a fresco, while another, seated in a pew near the front, appeared to be deep in prayer.

Two rows of pillars, one above the other, stretched out on either side toward the sanctuary. The marble columns, he knew from earlier discussions with his friend, Father Emil Boutros, whom he had come to visit, were pilfered from more ancient buildings and used without regard to their diameter or architectural form.

Steps led up to the sanctuary, its two side chapels obscured by wooden screens elaborately adorned with carvings in wood and ivory. He could barely discern the canopied high altar or the apse with worn steps on which the priests of ancient times used to sit. Somewhere below his feet, beneath the cool flagstones, was the flooded crypt where it was believed the infant Jesus had taken shelter.

The whole place was infused with a calm that was absent in the rushing city outside. It seeped into his body.

A voice boomed from the direction of the sanctuary, jolting him out of his reverie.

"Welcome, welcome! It has been too long, Alexander Fisher." Father Boutros, chest-length beard swaying from side to side, hurried down the center aisle.

"Thank you for making time to see me at such short notice, *Abuna.*" Alex used the Egyptian term for father.

"Don't be ridiculous! For you, nothing is too much." The priest enveloped Alex in a bear hug.

"The architecture never ceases to impress me," Alex said, breaking away reluctantly and indicating the room around them as they took a seat, side by side, in one of the pews.

"It is a living embodiment of a saying often heard in this part of the world: 'We are all People of the Book.' It actually comes directly from the Koran. The Arabic *Ahl al-kitab* is usually translated as 'people of the book' but it literally means 'people of an earlier revelation.'"

Alex had heard this said before, particularly in his early days in the city. Asking a stranger's religion was not uncommon here. Faith was not a private affair as it so often was in the West. If pressed, Alex usually categorized himself as an atheist or agnostic, someone who just wasn't sure. But as a Westerner he was invariably regarded by the locals he came into contact with as Christian. He quickly learned that to be an atheist in this part of the world was regarded as an absurdity. To have no god, no faith, was quite possibly the direst of all fates.

Father Boutros continued, "It is something few Christians in the West realize, but Jesus featured as the Prophet Isa in the Islamic Scriptures. Christians, Muslims, and Jews all worship one Abrahamic God and share some of the same ancient stories. The Old Testament, the Koran, the Talmud, in many respects are all the same story. The Prophet Muhammad did not, in fact, claim to be founding a new religion when he had his visions and began to preach; he was simply bringing the old faith in the One God to the Arabs. Non-Muslim peoples, according to the Koran, received Scriptures revealed to them by God before the time of Muhammad. The Koran is taken to represent the completion of those Scriptures."

The priest broke off and smiled. His eyes twinkled with mischief, and he lowered his voice to a whisper. "You know, Muhammad originally had his followers pray in the direction of Jerusalem, turning their backs on the pagan associations of the *Kabah* in Mecca."

He chuckled and then raised his voice again. "But enough of that. I'm sure you didn't come to hear a sermon!"

Alex had called Father Boutros the morning after his decision to follow Smith's trail, wherever it led, and he explained a little of his quest. The Harvard-educated Coptic priest possessed an encyclopedic knowledge of Church history, as well as extensive contacts in scholarly and religious circles. It often seemed to Alex that there were few of the Middle East's main players the sixty-one-year-old cleric had not met, or did not know personally. It was a resource he'd often tapped into as a journalist.

But he was a little nervous about calling the old priest. The Coptic Church was founded on the teachings of the Apostle Mark, who introduced Christianity to Egypt in the first century during the Roman emperor Nero's reign. Alex wondered how Father Boutros would view his quest to track down an alternative, and possibly blasphemous, version of the venerated saint's sacred writings. Christianity spread rapidly throughout Egypt within fifty years of Mark's arrival in Alexandria in about AD 68. A fragment of the Gospel of John, written using the Coptic language, was found in Upper Egypt and dated to the early second century. The Coptic Church was now more than nineteen centuries old. Copts liked to point out that their Church was the subject of prophecy in the Old Testament. The Prophet Isaiah foretold that "in that day there will be an altar to the Lord in the midst of the land of Egypt."

Alex was encouraged to see the priest appeared not to have taken any offense and decided to get straight to the point.

"Is it really possible that Smith discovered a secret Gospel nobody else ever heard of? I have to say it sounds a little farfetched."

Father Boutros was thoughtful.

"I've given some consideration to your quest. The authenticity of your friend's discovery is something beyond my area of competence, but I took the liberty of contacting a friend of mine, an American priest and scholar who is currently the librarian and conservator at the Greek Orthodox hermitage of St. Catherine's. Father Julian has agreed to meet you."

Alex knew of the monastery, a formidable walled redoubt built at the base of Mount Sinai, a two-thousand-meter rocky outcrop held to be the place where Moses received the Ten Commandments as he led the Israelites on their flight from Egypt.

"Thank you, Emil."

"It is nothing." The priest waved a bony hand in the air, as if shooing away a pesky insect.

"But, I have to say, there is nothing in itself extraordinary about the discovery in modern times of ancient Christian documents. Few people know this, but the four Gospels of the New Testament were written anonymously and only later came to be called by the names of their reputed authors. I often hear people these days bemoaning what they see as the decline of Christianity into liberalism, by which they mean beliefs they see as unorthodox, not matching their own. Yet, if anything, the faith is becoming narrower. The diversity of early Christianity is staggering when compared with today.

"What is more, the early Church knew far more Gospels than those that eventually came to be included in the New Testament. Sadly, most have not survived the centuries. But they have turned up in this part of the world with incredible regularity, particularly in the period following World War II. The Dead Sea Scrolls themselves were found around that time, as was the so-called Gospel of Thomas."

In his heavily accented English, Father Boutros recounted the discovery in Upper Egypt of a stash of manuscripts in 1945. In the village of Nag Hammadi, not far from Luxor and the Valley of the Kings, thirteen ancient codices were unearthed, containing over fifty crumbling texts once thought to have been destroyed during the early Church's struggle to define orthodoxy.

The priest was a good storyteller and had Alex's full attention.

"A group of peasants were digging for nitrate-rich fertilizer at the base of a Jabal al-Tarif, near the banks of the Nile, when one of them struck a hard object with his mattock."

Father Boutros spoke of places in a matter-of-fact manner, as if everyone knew of them. He would refer to rock formations as if they were well-known street corners in Paris or New York.

"After more digging, it turned out to be a human skeleton. Next to it was a jar, sealed with bitumen, which the peasants were initially afraid of opening. They are a superstitious lot, feared they might release a genie!" Boutros chuckled.

"They debated awhile, but greed got the better of them. After all, the jar could just as easily contain gold, couldn't it? The manuscripts inside were hand-written on papyrus in ancient Coptic, but scholars agree they were originally composed in Greek, the language of the New Testament.

"Among the books in the jar, none has sparked more controversy than the so-called Gospel of Thomas, a collection of sayings of Jesus, some of which may well be authentic and many of which were previously unknown. Come, I will show you."

They made their way to the back of the basilica where a small door was set into the stone wall.

Surely he doesn't have the manuscripts here.

Passing through, they entered a small, brightly lit vestry. There were chairs and a small table covered in a patterned cloth. A selection of richly embroidered priestly vestments hung in an open-fronted wardrobe. The desktop computer looked out of place in such ancient surroundings.

"My office," explained his friend. "Can I offer you tea, or perhaps some cof-fee? Coca-Cola? You look tired, Alexander. I will ask one of the boys to go out and fetch us some food, yes?"

"Just water would be fine, thank you." Alex had always felt relaxed around this friendly man of God. He battled a sudden urge to pour out the anxieties of the past few days. Father Boutros poured him some water from a pitcher on the table.

"The Nag Hammadi Library, as its collection of works is now known, has, since its miraculous discovery just after the war, been published in its entirety. It is freely available on the Internet."

The priest switched the machine on and the hard drive whirred into life.

"Let me read you some passages, and you'll see how they differ from the modern Gospels. The differences are in many ways quite subtle, but the Gospel of Thomas when it was discovered provoked strong reactions, not least from the Vatican, which expended considerable energy trying to suppress it and question-ing its authenticity."

Father Boutros began to read, translating as he went.

"The disciples said to Jesus, 'We know that you are going to leave us. Who will be our leader?' Jesus said to them, 'No matter where you are, you are to go to James the Just, for whose sake heaven and earth came into being.'"

It was immediately obvious what the Church would have objected to. Peter, according to Jesus in the canonical Gospels, was the rock on which the Church was built. The two hundred and sixty-five men who've served as the head of the Catholic Church over the centuries all trace their lineage back to Peter, the first Pope whose authority was ordained by God. That line of papal succession, Alex knew, was based on Matthew 16:18. "The Lord says to Peter: 'I say to you,' he says, 'that you are Peter, and upon this rock I will build my Church, and the gates of hell will not overcome it.'" But here was a very different version of events, a suppressed version that had Jesus anointing a different disciple: his brother, James, as his earthly successor.

The significance was stunning. Nothing less than the unquestioned authority of the Vatican was at stake.

Father Boutros selected another passage and was again reading and translating from the screen.

"Jesus said, 'If your leaders say to you, "Look, the Father's kingdom is in the sky," then the birds of the sky will precede you. If they say to you, "It is in the sea," then the fish will precede you. Rather, the Father's kingdom is within you and it is outside you.'

"I can see from the look on your face that the second saying here is more confusing to you," said Father Boutros. "It is indeed a little more cryptic, but think carefully and you can see what the Church might object to. Holding out the promise of a reward, paradise in the next life, is a very powerful thing. In Catholicism, it is only priests who can grant absolution and entry into the Kingdom of God. That kingdom is a reward for a life of hard work.

"The idea that Jesus anointed someone other than Peter to lead the Church and that the Kingdom of God was not something to strive for, but already here, was anathema to the Holy Roman Church.

"See, here is another verse that is more explicit."

The priest was reading again.

"His disciples said to him, 'When will the kingdom come?' Jesus said, 'It will not come by watching for it. It will not be said, "Look, here!" or "Look, there!" Rather, the Father's kingdom is spread out upon the earth, and people don't see it.'"

24

The motorcycle repair shop on the narrow side street off Sharia Al-Azhar had no name and was virtually indistinguishable from thousands of other small businesses in Islamic Cairo. Wedged between two ugly brown-brick buildings, it was impossible to say exactly where one structure finished and another began. The street number, large Arabic numerals daubed in black paint, had mostly peeled off the entryway, sealed with a green steel roller door. The door was open.

Hatim wiped his hands on his grubby galabaya and squatted on the footpath out front. He greeted a steady stream of neighborhood folk as they brought in punctured tires, headlights in need of new bulbs, and brakes requiring repair. Short and fat, with a bushy black beard and thick hair crowned in a white skullcap, the young man exuded a cheerful piety and greeted each customer by name. He made it his business to recognize people.

He'd run the shop for nearly three months and shared the squalid three-room flat at the rear with two men of a similar age, Abdul-Aziz and Dhul Fiqar, devout Muslims for whom he felt great affection. They called each other brother, although they were not related and did not even look alike. While Hatim was short and round, the other two were harder, sullen men with dark skin and darker eyes.

Their arrival in the inner-city community drew little attention. It was the way they preferred it. The trio slept in the same room on foam-rubber mattresses yellowed with age, shared simple meals cooked over a gas hob, and worked on motorcycles in the shop. The little money they earned more than covered their daily needs, with some to spare for charity.

As often as they could, they attended the local mosque. But if business was unusually brisk, they would roll out their *sajjadah*, or woven prayer mats, on the pavement outside, which they kept freshly swept and watered to tame the dust that plagued the city at this time of year.

Today was busy, but for the sake of routine, so as not to attract attention, Abdul-Aziz and Dhul Fiqar had gone to the mosque, anyway. To all who asked, they would say their beloved brother was busy at the shop, which indeed he was.

Hatim had made a point of bathing his feet, forearms, and face at the spigot on the street in an unhurried fashion, before kneeling to pray. Yet he found it difficult to concentrate. His mind was on the guest who arrived the night before, bundled out of a nondescript Suzuki van.

The brothers were given only a few hours warning of the operation, but they were ready. The spare room was blacked out and soundproofed with blankets and rugs. They stockpiled food in small quantities over the weeks, so the local shopkeepers would not notice the presence of a guest.

Despite having so little privacy, the three men did not in fact know each other's true names. Neither did they want to. They'd met in a camp in the Libyan desert a year ago, where they were given their monikers, good Muslim names that indicated functions. They were names all three felt proud of, even though they knew that kind of pride was a sin and could be dangerous. Hatim's name meant Judge. Abdul-Aziz was Arabic for servant of Allah. Dhul Fiqar was the name of the Prophet Muhammad's sword. They were names matching the gravitas of their mission. Hatim felt they also imparted a certain fearsome quality.

The trio received their instructions by cell phone phone using a card bought for the purpose and which they immediately destroyed. The guest was to be accorded every courtesy and treated with as much dignity as the situation allowed, in accordance with the dictates of their Muslim faith.

Yet, when all was said and done, Hatim had to admit he was surprised, and more than a little uncomfortable, when the visitor's hood was finally removed and he saw it was a woman kneeling on the carpet before them.

25

The battered Fiat taxi rattled to a halt a few blocks short of Al-Azhar mosque in El Hussein Square. One of Cairo's oldest houses of worship, it once doubled as a university, renowned in Europe and throughout the Arab world for its scholarship. Standing on the footpath, Alex took a moment to admire the structure, named after Fatima al-Zahra, daughter of the Prophet Muhammad. Five minarets stretched toward the sky, each with balconies and intricately carved columns. There were six entrances. The main one now before him was built in the eighteenth century and known as Bab El Muzayini, the barber's gate. Students had once been shaved there. The mosque was a potpourri of architectural styles, built piecemeal over its thousand-year history. But the overall effect was quite beautiful.

It was just after midday. Hordes of faithful Muslim men spilled out onto the wide thoroughfare. They blocked traffic, chatting in small clusters before drifting back to their various jobs in the city's main market area, Khan el-Khalili, a district immensely popular with foreign tourists, its narrow alleys and colorful shops perfectly fitting their preconceived notions of the Orient.

Alex chose the hottest part of the day in hope of avoiding the crowds of visitors, which as evening approached would arrive by the busload from their luxury hotels closer to the Nile. He picked a side street devoted almost entirely to stationery shops and plunged into the bazaar, heading roughly northwest in the direction of the tailors' and tent makers' *souk*. A donkey-drawn cart, stacked high with colored bolts of cloth, jostled for right of way with a smoke-belching Vespa scooter, shrill horn blaring. Shop owners barked short phrases in English and beckoned for him to examine their wares.

"Hello, Mister."

"Cheap price."

"Everything free for you today. Come take a look."

He passed through the metalworkers' quarter, where most of the shops were devoted to mending and dismantling vehicles. The constant racket of metal striking metal made it by far the noisiest part of the souk. A prayer mat was rolled out on the oil-stained footpath in front of him and Alex was forced to step onto the road to avoid it, almost tripping over a dripping spigot. A short, plump young man with a bushy beard and white skullcap looked up from his position squatting outside a motorcycle repair shop. A brief look of surprise crossed his dark features. Few foreigners ventured into this part of the bazaar.

A rhythmic thunk, thunk, thunk drifted out of the workshop.

"Mut'asif." Alex apologized in Arabic.

The suspicious look faded and the man smiled.

"Ahlan wa sahlan." Hello, welcome.

"Ahlan bik," Alex responded, with a slight nod. He turned into another street, this one crammed with stalls selling clothes, an incongruous mix of full-length black gowns and racy undergarments, cotton shirts, T-shirts, jeans, and jackets.

Unlike the most popular shops with tourists in the brass workers' and coppersmiths' quarter closer to the market's medieval gates, this was where locals came to shop.

Alex needed clothes. Other than the grab bag with a change of shirt and pants he kept at the office for emergencies, he'd lost everything in the fire. He spent about half an hour buying shirts, several pairs of cotton pants, and a selection of T-shirts, socks, and underwear at the stalls. When he was finished, he found a café, where he drank an ice-cold Coke and ate a plate of fresh dates.

He tried not to think about the events of the last few days and to focus on the journey ahead. He'd arranged with Emad for a vehicle to make the trip to St. Catherine's monastery the next morning.

But something about being in Khan al-Khalili reminded him of Sadie. She loved spending hours burrowing into the alleyways of the spice quarter, haggling for textiles and other trinkets with which she decorated her room at the language institute and presented regularly as gifts to friends. It required physical effort for Alex not to think about her.

He summoned the waiter and ordered a glass of water to wash down the Coke. He drank quickly, before paying and threading his way back through the thronging bazaar to Sharia al-Azhar. The square around the mosque was deserted, peaceful, the faithful having returned to their businesses.

He hailed a taxi. The ride back to Bairstow's apartment took an hour.

26

Cyrus Gelb was frustrated. He carefully smoothed out the letter on the desk and proceeded to read it for the umpteenth time. There had to be a message, a clue in it somewhere, but if there was he couldn't see it. He'd held such high hopes that they were nearing the end of their quest, even told the Heart Master as much. With the benefit of hindsight, a very unwise move. He'd raised the boss's expectations, making the ensuing rage that much more frightening.

He stared at the page.

I have been doing some very interesting research in Egypt and Israel for the past three months...

Leaning back in the chair, he ran a hand through his pale-blond hair.

He stood and walked to the window of the luxury room on the eighth floor of the Marriott. Below, he could make out a cluster of naked children splashing in the water at the edge of the Nile. Three boys, a slightly older girl, perhaps six or seven at the most. The boys were trying to hold each other under the muddy surface. The girl squealed and clapped with delight. Their firm little bodies glistened in the sunlight.

Cyrus allowed himself a moment to watch. They reminded him of seal pups. Even in the morally relaxed environment of the Communion, his interest in young children was frowned on, regarded as unhealthy, perhaps even dangerous. But, as the Heart Master's private secretary, he was beyond reproach. It would be a brave person who challenged him.

He turned and strode back to the desk.

Under strict instructions, Cyrus's team had kept a round-the-clock watch on the professor for weeks. Using a rental car, they set up surveillance on the quay outside his rundown hotel in Haifa, watching as the old man wrote at the desk by the window.

He returned to reading the letter.

Do you remember the story I told you in Phnom Penh about my discovery of Mark's Secret Gospel and the pious outrage it stirred up among my academic colleagues and the lay community? Of course, you will not have forgotten! As I'm sure a fellow with such a finely tuned nose for a story quickly surmised, there is more to it. I rather think it is something you will find interesting in your line of work.

...some very strange things have been happening. I sometimes feel that I am being watched, but perhaps that is just the foolishness of an old man.

They were not completely misguided in deciding to steal the letter. There were direct references to the Secret Gospel in the handwritten missive, and it was obvious Smith was planning to share something important with the journalist.

But he needed more.

It was also clear their surveillance had not gone unnoticed. He would have a word with the team about that kind of carelessness.

The letter gave no clue as to where the manuscript was hidden. He would have to come up with another plan, and a way of explaining this mess to the Master. He thought about his boss. The Heart Master had never for a second doubted the authenticity of the professor's find from the moment it was announced, avidly devouring his books and essays on the topic. It explained the visions and voices he, as guru, had so often heard. It fit perfectly, too, with the beliefs on which he had founded the Community in southern California during the sexual and political revolution that marked the 1960s.

Of course the Heart Master had not always been called the Heart Master. The guru changed his name by deed poll from the far more mundane Franklin Albert Jones to Da Free John and adopted the illustrious titles Heart Master, Transmitter, and Baptizer. When the professor's books on the Secret Gospel of Mark went out of print, the guru had even obtained the rights, reprinting them under the banner of his own publishing house. He'd written to the professor, invited him to join the Communion. The invitation was declined. Gaining possession of the original manuscript would be a real coup. It had become an obsession.

The Master's voice echoed in Cyrus's head. *What the professor stumbled upon in the tower at Mar Saba is an ancient confirmation that Jesus, too, was a Spirit-Baptizer. He inducted his devotees into the Kingdom of Heaven through an authentic spiritual and yogic process, by night and in sacred privacy.*

Because of the obvious parallels between Smith's interpretation of the Secret Gospel and the beliefs of the Free Daist Communion, the guru had chosen to sanction and spread his theories. It was a close fit. The Heart Master saw himself as a natural successor of the Christian philosopher Carpocrates, whose breakaway sect was mentioned in the ancient fragments found at Mar Saba. Like Carpocrates, he required his devotees to explore a broad range of sexual and emotional possibilities.

Cyrus grew up in the Communion. He knew no other life.

When his parents died in the car crash, which left him with terrible facial scarring, the Heart Master took a personal, and more than spiritual, interest in the youngster. Under the guidance of his teachings, Cyrus explored many states, from celibacy through promiscuity, heterosexuality, homosexuality, monogamy, and polygamy. The Master had once even instructed another devotee to watch while Cyrus borrowed his wife, an exercise the man was told would help free him from the sin of egotistical jealousy.

Cyrus returned to the window of his hotel suite, but the kids had gone, replaced by an old woman washing aluminum cooking pots. His team had kept up its surveillance of Alex Fisher after the incident in the library, in which the young female devotee played her part so brilliantly, allowing Cyrus himself to snatch the letter.

His spies tailed the journalist to the basilica in the Coptic quarter. Posing as tourists, they overheard most of the conversation with the priest, until the pair moved into the vestry at the back of the old church. It was frustrating not to know what was discussed there, but his agents heard enough to gather that Alex Fisher's next destination would be the library at St. Catherine's monastery.

They would follow him there. It shouldn't prove too difficult. Cyrus felt sure he had the perfect agent to carry out the task.

27

Her eyes were wide open, but she was blind. Breath rushed in her ears. She was hyperventilating. Then rough hands smelling of grease and soap removed the hood. It was still dark, but not completely so.

"If you continue to make noise, I will be forced to gag you." Feet stomped out and the door thudded closed. A narrow band of light remained visible at its base, casting a welcome glow across the floor.

Sadie lay on her side in a pile of stale blankets, hands bound in front with a plastic tie. Her feet were shackled with a chain and padlock to a ring in the floor.

She must have been dreaming again, crying out in her sleep. How long had she been here? Two days, perhaps three, maybe a week? It was hard to tell. Her days were punctuated by the removal and replacing of the hood, meals brought in at intervals and irregular visits to a tiny, foul-smelling toilet.

There were three of them, although they had at first been careful not to show their faces. The same one always brought the food. He had a hard voice, and while the other two treated her with a degree of deference, respect even, this one had roving hands that became bolder as the days went by.

Night was the worst, without the strip of light that somehow gave perspective to her surroundings. The sounds of the household, muffled conversations, the clanking metal on metal in what she guessed must be a workshop, became less and less and eventually ceased. Then she was suspended in silent blackness, alone. Deprived of sensory input, her mind played tricks on her, and her body felt like it was floating. She lay there, her consciousness expanded, ears sensitive to the slightest sound. With each passing hour that consciousness grew, a spider's web, delicate tendrils spreading under the door and throughout the house, returning to her the slightest tremor or footfall, the breathing of her sleeping captors.

Sadie pretended she spoke no Arabic, all the while straining to catch snatches of conversation, anything to get a sense of where she was being held and by whom. They were careful not to talk in her presence. She had only vague memories of the kidnapping: Fire, a loud explosion as she was forced onto the floor of a van. Screeching tires. A journey that could have been one hour or three, she did not know.

She did her best not to think about Alex. Did he know she was alive? Was anyone looking for her? Her parents would be frantic. Not for the first time since her ordeal began, she fought back tears, swallowing hard and biting her lip until she felt the metallic taste of blood on her tongue.

Perhaps an hour passed. She was just beginning the descent into troubled sleep, when keys rattled in the door and the bolt was forced back. A harsh voice commanded her in broken English to face the wall.

She rolled over.

Footsteps and the clank of a tin plate on the cement floor near where she lay. The door closed again. Silence.

She lay still, ears straining, body rigid. Her skin crawled. She could still hear the man's ragged breathing. Then he spoke.

"You must be terrified, sister. There is nothing to fear if you cooperate. I have brought you food."

The tone was caustic, condescending. Sadie recognized the voice as belonging to the man called Dhul Fiqar. From her Arabic Studies, she knew it was the name of the Prophet's sword.

"The brothers have gone out for supplies. They will be a while."

A hand touched her leg.

Tears pricked Sadie's eyes and she swallowed hard, body trembling. The hand moved up to her waist and under her shirt. Then he was touching her breasts, pulling at her bra, squeezing painfully.

She fought to keep her voice steady.

"You should be ashamed of yourself. Is this how Muslim men behave?" she said through gritted teeth. "You are a disgrace to your religion."

"What do you know of Islam, whore!" The blow landed on her right temple. Light flashed behind her eyes. Searing pain knifed through her jaw and her head spun as she slipped into unconsciousness.

28

The Heart Master had been furious, but he was determined that the mission to find the precious manuscript should continue. He'd assured his private secretary that cost was no obstacle, none at all. He must employ all means at his disposal to ensure success.

The house on the banks of the Nile that Cyrus Gelb rented as headquarters for the duration of the operation was a beautiful old wooden structure. It sat protected from prying eyes behind a three-meter wall topped with barbed wire and broken glass. Set in a manicured garden on Gezira Island, it faced the broad sweep of the river across from the well-ordered diplomatic quarter known as Garden City.

Despite there being no shortage of space in the mansion, he kept the hotel room at the Marriott as his private lodgings. It helped set him apart from the others, reinforcing his authority. Solitude also enabled him to focus on what lay ahead. Tonight, he would deliver to the team their instructions for the next phase of the operation.

Discretion was central to the choice of accommodation. Since a high-profile series of court cases in 1986, the leadership of the Free Daist Communion to which they all belonged claimed to have abandoned sexual experimentation as a spiritual practice. Of course that was a carefully cultivated deception. The use of spiritual theater, in which devotees were encouraged to release sexual and emotional problems and seek union with God, remained an integral part of the Master's teachings.

The public exposure from the court case was traumatic. It nearly saw the Master thrown into jail. A twenty-nine-year-old former member claimed she was traumatized by a spiritual theater session at the group's hot springs resort, near Middletown in Lake County. As a child, she was sexually abused by a neighbor. To help her through her resulting fears and anxiety, the Master instructed her to have oral sex with three group members. He then indulged himself, in front of a selection of the community's elders. Over the years since the court case, disgruntled former members would occasionally go public with fresh claims of abuse. Those claims were difficult to prove and routinely denied.

It was early evening by the time Cyrus showered, shaved, and splashed on some expensive cologne. Although the Master always assured him that physical beauty was unimportant, he felt compelled to make an effort. He saw the way the younger devotees looked at him, barely able to hide their shock, revulsion even, at his facial scarring. He knew the taught ridges and valleys of puckered, reddened skin made him ugly. But they also inspired fear and gave him power. He liked that.

When he arrived at the Nile-side mansion from his hotel that evening, he was ushered in by one of the young male devotees wearing an ankle-length, hooded robe of white linen. They had followed his directions perfectly. The team needed to be in the right mind-set to receive their instructions. Ritual was the key.

Rows of flickering candles lit the hallway. Soothing music drifted from somewhere deep inside the residence. He could not identify what it was, but he made out the plucked notes of a sitar and some kind of flute. Appropriately Eastern, perhaps Indian. The Heart Master would approve. Anticipation of what was to come gave him a surge of pleasure.

He followed the devotee into a large living room. It, too, was illuminated by dozens of guttering candles, the air rich with their scent. The French doors to the garden were thrown open, allowing the warm night air to carry in the perfume of jasmine flowers and distant sounds of river traffic.

His pulse quickened. Five devotees stood in a wide circle. They, too, wore loose robes. Adding to the effect of anonymity and androgyny, faces were covered with white, expressionless masks. The devotee who'd shown him in slipped on his mask and joined the group. Against the far wall, a low table held ritual offerings of flowers and a picture of the Heart Master.

Soft chanting filled the room.

Cyrus got comfortable in a large armchair and inclined his head slightly. "Let the ceremony begin."

The only female in the circle stepped forward as the chanting droned on. The swell of breasts under loose cloth was all that betrayed her sex. The woman was their newest recruit, the one he intended to use for the next phase of the assignment. His excitement was building. A tingling sensation rippled beneath his skin.

The group's chanting suddenly ceased, replaced by the woman's lone voice.

The hood and robe slipped from her shoulders and fell soundlessly to the ground as her body undulated to the music. Candlelight flickered off honeyed skin. Although her face was masked, she seemed a little nervous. That was understandable. The four male devotees moved closer. Shedding their robes, they sank to their knees, arms outstretched, pawing at the woman's naked flesh, raking her flanks. Hands pulled her to the floor as the first of the masked devotees mounted her. Cyrus allowed all five men their turn before he satisfied himself, first in front of them and again in private in an adjoining room. Within an hour of arriving, he was back at his hotel.

On the second floor of the Nile-front mansion, the woman sat alone on the edge of her bed. She'd spent half an hour in the shower, swallowing down the bile and allowing the water to wash away the tears streaming down her face. The tears were unexpected. She'd thought herself ready for this assignment. Her training at the academy had been grueling, but nothing could prepare her for the ordeal she'd just endured.

Soon the team would leave for the monastery, but for now she needed to calm herself. She went over her instructions. The phone Cyrus gave her lay on the pillow. She picked it up and slipped it into the pocket of her shorts. Her hands trembled as she pulled on a pair of thick white socks and laced up her leather hiking boots. Then she lay on the bed and waited.

Cyrus's instructions were to make contact as soon after arrival as possible, to update him on the journalist's movements. Getting a line out might require her to climb at least part way up Mt. Sinai. But posing as a tourist meant she needed to act like one, and the best way to do that was to do what tourists did, which was climb to the bloody thing to watch the sunrise.

29

Cairo
Sunday, 12 July 2009

Emad was late, and they didn't set out for St. Catherine's until after 8:00 a.m. The smoke-belching Peugeot spent at least an hour snarled in Cairo's notorious morning traffic as the temperature climbed steadily and the sun burned through the thick layer of air pollution hanging over the city. Neither Alex nor Bairstow was in an expansive mood, and they sat in silence as the city thinned around them. Dusty apartment buildings in dormitory suburbs gave way to the rubble of the desert's fringe.

They headed north toward the Suez Canal. The Red Sea coast, with its myriad beach resorts and sleepy fishing villages, lay somewhere far off to their right through the heat haze rising off the sand. Alex sat up front, lost in thought, while his friend spread himself across the backseat, using their packs as armrests.

He knew Sadie wasn't coming back, but leaving Cairo felt like a betrayal. Shouldn't he still be searching, waiting? Holding on to the vain hope she might walk through the door, explaining breezily she'd just popped out to buy supplies for dinner and asking what on earth happened to his wrecked apartment? Such thoughts were illogical, ridiculous. He pushed them aside, thinking instead about his meeting with Father Boutros. He was beginning to discern the vague outlines of what he was dealing with. Under any other circumstances he would be thoroughly enjoying himself. After all, it was a good yarn; the discovery of a previously unknown Gospel, a secret text, suppressed by Church authorities, picturing Jesus initiating his disciples with a hallucinatory, nocturnal and quite possibly homosexual rite. It was scandalous. It seemed more like the stuff of fiction, a thriller you might pick up at an airport bookstore before a long flight.

The desert outside the speeding Peugeot was baking. Emad passed around a pack of Cleopatra cigarettes, and they wound down their windows before lighting up. Pop music blared from the taxi's ancient cassette deck. Alex recognized the tune as one from Mohamed Mounir. The Nubian-Egyptian singer and actor from Aswan made regular appearances on the local news. He cut a handsome figure with his shock of curly black hair and was considered the darling of the North African nation's youth. His infectious pop-oriented tunes had their roots in traditional Egyptian and African styles, and the lyrics usually carried social and political messages. The album playing was one of his more controversial offerings, *Earth...Peace*.

The song "Give Me Strength, O Messenger of God" came on as the Peugeot chugged onto the massive white suspension bridge spanning the Suez Canal. The historic waterway spread out below them. A convoy of hulking oil tankers and an American frigate made their way toward the Mediterranean.

Displaying a surprisingly rich voice, Emad sang along with Mounir, slapping out the beat on the steering wheel with the palm of his right hand. Alex tried to make out the lyrics. His Arabic was still rudimentary. Something about all killing being abhorred by God. He'd read about this particular single.

"Have you heard this one before?" he said, breaking the silence.

"Huh. What's that, old man?" Bairstow's eyes were closed, head back.

"This song. It has an interesting history."

Bairstow yawned and stretched, flicking the butt of his Cleopatra out onto the rushing tarmac. Alex took a final drag of his and did the same.

"It sounds familiar, but buggered if I can make out a word of it."

"It was written soon after 9/11. You know, a lot of ordinary Muslims were shocked such a thing could be done in the name of Islam."

"Remember how CNN and BBC showed people dancing in the streets in some parts of the Middle East?" asked Bairstow. "I'm told that was some stunningly selective reporting. Did a lot to fuel the fires of Western outrage, and what followed...Afghanistan, Iraq."

Alex agreed. "Yeah, those images certainly did nothing to ease tensions. I was based in Cambodia at the time, but friends here tell me they really upset some people.

"Anyway, the singer of this track, guy called Mounir, was driven to learn more about his faith by the whole thing. He performed the *hajj* for the first time, returning to Egypt from Mecca critical both of his fellow Muslims, who he said didn't bother to seek a true understanding of the faith, and of the West whom he felt misunderstood it, sometimes deliberately.

"So he released this album, which surprised a lot of people because it seemed very religious for such a secular artist. But for others it wasn't religious enough. The video for this song was banned by most Arab satellite television channels. A number of *Imams* spoke out against it, claiming the religious terminology he used was inappropriate. Mounir's response was that they could go take a hike, the fight against rigid thought was what makes us human was how he put it."

Bairstow grunted and closed his eyes again, listening to the tune. Several seconds passed.

"It's not really my bag to be honest. Tell you what, though, I could eat something."

"It's only 10:00 a.m., Aubrey," Alex said, rolling his eyes.

"Well, I've packed us some lunch. We can stop at a rest area by the water at some point."

They descended the large span to the other side of the canal, stopping briefly at a police checkpoint to show their passports and have their names and nationalities recorded in a logbook. Before long, the taxi was speeding south along a coastal plain with the deep blue of the Red Sea sparkling enticingly to their right, providing a striking contrast to the sandy landforms and the darker black-and-tan hills and mountains of the interior. Alex recalled that some of the beaches were still strewn with mines and explosives left over from World War II and subsequent wars between Israel and its Arab neighbors. Some time ago, one long-dormant piece of ordnance claimed the lives of six expatriate children from the British International School in Cairo. Those beaches that were cleared now hosted local resorts and condominium developments in varying states of repair.

Alex marveled at the resilience of the locals as he stared out the open window at the passing landscape. Located between the Gulfs of Suez and Aqaba at the northern end of the Red Sea, the plateau known as the Sinai Desert covered sixty-one thousand square kilometers of harsh, arid terrain. Its highest peaks soared more than two thousand meters above the surrounding plains and rocky valleys.

Despite the hostility of the terrain, people had lived here since prehistoric times. The region was famous as the route the Israelites took on their exodus from Egypt. For centuries, the desert's northern coast bordering the Mediterranean was the main trade route between Egypt and Palestine. From the second century until the rise of Islam in the seventh century, it was part of the Roman Empire and then its successor, the Byzantine Empire.

After years of rule by Islamic dynasties, it became part of the Ottoman Empire and was turned over to Egypt at the end of World War I. As a result of its strategic location at the crossroads of the Middle East, it was the scene of heavy fighting between the Allies and Axis powers during World War II. Then came the 1956 Suez Crisis, followed by a series of wars between the fledgling state of Israel and its Arab neighbors. Beneath the exterior beauty, the region was soaked in blood.

It was in the third century that hermits found seclusion in the craggy peaks of the St. Catherine region. There they developed the idea of Mt. Sinai, or *Gebel Mousa*, the mountain of Moses in Arabic, being the place where Moses found the burning bush and received the Ten Commandments. After visiting the region in around AD 330, Empress Helena, the mother of Constantine the Great, ordered a chapel be built at the site. She dedicated it to the Virgin Mary.

Nearly two hundred years later, following reports of massacres among the monks, Emperor Justinian ordered the construction of the fortifications that now surrounded the monastery. Its survival was greatly aided by the construction of a mosque within its walls in the year 1106. With the raise of Islam in Egypt in the mid-seventh century, it had become an isolated enclave of Christianity on the peninsula.

Tradition had it that a delegation of monks visited the Prophet Muhammad asking for protection. That protection was granted in a document still preserved within the hermitage's ancient library, the same library where Alex hoped to learn more about Smith's discovery of the Secret Gospel from a librarian named Father Julian.

They pulled over for lunch by the roadside on a narrow strip of rocky beach. Alex wasn't hungry and stripped down to his boxer shorts and went for a swim. The water was cool and helped to clear his head. He lay on his back and stared up at the perfectly clear sky. The thin white contrail of a jet made slow progress across the dome of blue, heading toward Europe. He wondered absent-mindedly if any of the passengers was looking down at this moment and what they would see from such a height.

Emad eventually wheeled the taxi inland, away from the glittering sea. They were climbing now. The road narrowed, winding between walls formed by high rocky outcrops. Canyons periodically opened out onto small, secluded plains studded with twisted trees. They sped past the occasional Bedouin herder with his ragged collection of goats and camels grazing on thorns and patches of brown scrub. Every now and then, fortified stone houses came into view, perched high up on the rock wall of a wadi, a rift formed by an ancient watercourse, but it was obvious few people lived in this hostile terrain.

The sun was setting as they finally approached St. Catherine's.

The monastery was perched on the slope of a steep valley half buried in shadow. The pillared spire of a church and delicate white dome of the monks' living quarters peeked above high stone fortifications as the taxi pulled to a halt on a dusty patch of ground near the main gate.

■ ■ ■

Three rooms were reserved for them in the guesthouse outside the walls of the hermitage. It was built in the same style and of the same stone as the monastery proper on a series of natural terraces, nestled in a grove of date palms and olive trees. Lush vegetable gardens, tended during the daylight hours by the two dozen resident monks, infused the burning desert air with the unfamiliar smell of wet earth.

The bulk of the rooms at the hostel were situated around a courtyard. At one end, a set of stone stairs led down to a narrow terrace lined on one side by more cell-like rooms, each with a single arched window. The terrace had a low wall. On the other side was a drop of about two hundred feet to a narrow track on the valley floor. Opposite and separated from the guesthouse by a rift in the rock, a sheer granite wall soared upward nearly a thousand meters.

After settling into rooms next door to each other on the lower terrace, Alex and Bairstow took a wooden table outside the kitchen. The bottle of Laphroaig materialized from their luggage, and they sat smoking cigarettes while the manager went in search of the cook. With the sun gone, the temperature dropped dramatically, forcing them into long-sleeved shirts. An hour or two earlier, their perch would have afforded a sweeping view of the plain below, on which some historians believed the fleeing Hebrews camped as Moses climbed the mountain toward his rendezvous with God. Now, all that was visible was blackness pierced by the flickering amber of Bedouin campfires far below. Their meeting with Father Julian was not until the morning, and the gates of the monastery were firmly sealed against outsiders for the night.

There was no evidence of other guests, although the hostel manager, a tall, spare figure in a threadbare but neatly ironed galabaya, said a number of the rooms were occupied.

30

St. Catherine's Monastery, Sinai Peninsula
Monday, 13 July 2009

Alex woke with a start. The glowing hands on his wristwatch showed 12:17 a.m. Asleep for less than an hour, he was wide-awake. Pale moonlight filtered through the open window. He'd been dreaming, but something caused him to wake. Had there been a sound at the door? He could feel a slight headache behind his eyes from the whiskey and realized he was still wearing his clothes.

This is becoming a habit.

He lay still, ears alert. The complete silence of the desert at night was almost deafening, but he fancied he heard a faint scuffing, possibly footfalls.

He pulled back the blanket and padded over to the window, pushing it closed before unlatching the door and stepping out onto the deserted terrace. The air was cold. It held almost no moisture and, aided by clear, cloudless skies, retained little heat after the sun set. Moonlight cast the world in black and white, dipping the date palms and olive trees in silver. He collected his boots from the stoop and tucked them under his arm, pausing outside Bairstow's door. Faint snoring.

The residual warmth from the flagstones was pleasant under his feet as he took the stairs to the upper terrace, where he paused to slip his boots on. The air was completely still. A few campfires still burned in the valley below. He walked to the low wall at the end of the terrace and peered into the darkness. The surrounding peaks were etched against a slightly lighter sky.

Again that noise, more distinct this time. Footsteps.

Alex crouched down, scanning the terrace. By the kitchen area, the chairs were turned upside down and placed on the tables, legs like anti-aircraft batteries pointing skyward. The dining room and small coffee shop were shuttered.

There it was. Movement by the stairs leading to the car park and monastery gate. A figure just visible, moonlight glinting off pale hair. After the events of the past week, his nerves were ragged.

You're getting jumpy, mate. This is a guesthouse. Why shouldn't others be up and about? Yet he felt a compulsion to follow.

The person moved and disappeared. All was still again.

He moved as silently as he could around the perimeter of the terrace, sticking to the darker moon shadows cast by the low buildings. At the edge of the coffee shop, he peered carefully around the corner at the stairs. They were empty. Taking them three at a time he reached the top and paused. Nothing moved. Left was the path to the monastery gate. Gravel crunched underfoot. He considered removing his shoes again, but pressed on toward the dark walls of the hermitage.

31

Sadie came to with a jolt. Her head throbbed, but her body was numb, as if still asleep.

Metallic jangling, a key turned in the lock, and the steel door swung open. For the first time since she'd arrived, the main light in the room flicked on. The world flared a brilliant white. Her head felt like it was going to explode.

Hands pulled her into a sitting position, back against a black blanket hung on the concrete wall. The numbness was gone now, and her body screamed with pain, as if red-hot coals were forced into her joints.

A few seconds and her vision cleared.

The man called Hatim was holding a long, curved knife in his right hand. Light from the fluorescent bulb glinted off its wicked blade.

This is the end. This is where I die.

Her breath came in ragged gasps. The Arab tightened his hold on the knife and stretched toward her. Sadie's whole body tensed and she closed her eyes.

Surely this could not be the end. She always felt she would die before growing old. But it would be a car accident or falling off her vintage Enfield Bullet, the motorbike she had stored in her parent's garage back in England, not in a filthy cell at the hands of a knife-wielding Egyptian psychopath.

"Try to relax, sister. This will not hurt."

She felt a tugging at her wrists and her hands came free as Hatim hacked through the plastic ties.

Relief flooded her body. She opened her eyes and saw someone had placed a plastic tub of water before her on the floor. A towel lay next to it.

"Please, clean yourself." The voice this time was that of Abdul-Aziz.

Both men turned and left the room, closing the door but leaving it unlocked. Sadie wondered where Dhul Fiqar was. She looked down at herself. Her feet were still shackled to the iron peg. The buttons on her skirt were undone, several torn off. Handprints in dried blood smeared the waistband. She felt her chest tighten. Tears pricked the back of her eyes.

What did that bastard do to me?

Sadie lifted her skirt and examined herself. There was a dull ache at the base of her stomach, discernable despite the pain in the rest of her body. Dark blood smeared the inside of her thighs. Between her legs was wet with the stuff, but her underwear remained in place.

In her dazed state, it took her a moment to comprehend what happened. For the second time in as many minutes she felt wave of relief and uttered a silent prayer of thanks to a God she was not sure existed.

The evil bastard must have been furious to find she was menstruating. She imagined the wave of anger and revulsion surge through him. A smile, the first since her captivity, spread across her face. For Muslim men, menstruating women were considered unclean and untouchable.

She quickly washed her hands, arms and face in the tub. The water was cool against her skin.

A few minutes passed and the men returned.

This time her attacker was with them, carrying a tripod and video camera. He did not look at her directly and kept his distance. To Sadie's horror, two of the men had automatic rifles slung over their shoulders. They set up their equipment near the door, camera pointed to where she was chained to the floor. Hatim hung a black-and-white banner on the wall behind her. As he stepped past, she recoiled at the sight of the pistol stuffed into the waistband of his pants.

"We are going to make a little video for your boyfriend," Dhul Fiquar sneered.

"You will read the message we have prepared for him."

32

St. Catherine's Monastery
Monday, 13 July 2009

Moonbeams painted the roofs of the monastery's taller buildings in soft silvery light. Slender cypress trees stood sentinel at the southwest corner of the wall, casting shadows across the car park, long black stains like seeping water. The tiny, steel-studded wooden door set into the base of the western wall of the hermitage was firmly sealed for the night.

Alex marveled at the sheer walls, rising fifty or sixty feet into the gloom. He could just make out a small room perched on wooden beams at the top. From reading about St. Catherine's, he knew it was where monks in less secure times had entered with the use of baskets and thick ropes. His boots made little sound as he skirted the car park, picking out a path toward the stairs at the northwest corner. Descending them, he was soon walking along the base of the northern wall. Still no sign of the person he'd seen on the steps of the hostel. He began to relax a little.

Perhaps he'd been imagining things.

Clambering over a rough stone wall, he entered a large, dusty courtyard strewn with boulders. A slight breeze plucked at his shirt, raising goose bumps on his arms and causing him to shiver.

Halfway across the open expanse one of the boulders moved.

Alex froze in his tracks.

A deep roar pierced the silence. He dived, wincing as sharp stones pierced the skin on his elbows and forearms. He cast around wildly for the source of the noise.

One of the huge boulders a few feet away appeared to sway, first forward and then back as it rose from the ground. Another inhuman moan rent the air as a second boulder began to rise. A third and a fourth followed.

He almost laughed out loud with relief as the camels straightened their legs and continued to grumble at the indignity of being awakened in the middle of the night.

Soft laughter drifted from the edge of the compound.

A group of Bedouin men huddled against the wall, wrapped in thick blankets against the night chill. *Bedu*, the Arabic word from which their name was derived, simply meant "inhabitant of the desert" and referred generally to the nomadic peoples of Arabia, the Negev, and the Sinai. Their lives were harsh and their hospitality legendary. In the vast solitude of the desert, encountering another person was often still celebrated as a noteworthy event. For most people, the word Bedouin conjured up images of sand dunes, billowing robes, and the graceful loping stride of camels. But in truth it was a dying lifestyle. Modern society made the traditional ways less attractive, particularly to the young. Many Bedouin tribes began to settle in urban areas for at least part of every year. Governments, too, made efforts to regulate their nomadic lifestyle, often seen as representing a military threat to urban rulers.

"Did Abdu frighten you, friend?" One of the men rose from his haunches, gesturing to his camel.

"Yes, he did. I thought I was alone out here."

"You are never alone in the desert. Do you want to go up the mountain? I will take you for sixty pounds."

Alex shook his head and checked his watch. It was 1:30 a.m.

"No thanks, I'm just walking," he said, realizing after the words were already out how ridiculous they must sound. But the Bedouin man simply nodded, as if it was the most natural thing in the world to be wandering around the desert in the dark.

"You are a little early, but not the first. Most tourists don't start for several hours. The sunrise from the summit of *Gebel Mousa* is a beautiful sight," the man said, using the Arabic name for the mountain.

"You are American?"

"My father is English. My mother is from New Zealand."

"Ah, a Kiwi. Gidday, mate."

"Yes." Alex smiled.

Treated with suspicion by the Egyptian authorities and marginalized by big operators from Cairo, these tribesmen eked out a meager living from the tourist trade.

They could probably greet me in two dozen languages. Another thought struck him too. They would have seen anyone else passing by.

"Have you seen any other foreigners come this way? Just now, I mean."

"Yes, we thought she must be your friend." The men giggled.

Alex was startled. *She.* So he hadn't been imagining things.

"When? Which way did she go?"

"Not long ago, my friend. Ismail has taken her up the mountain on his camel. She wanted to see the sunrise. What is your name?"

"I'm Alex."

"Alex. Fifty pounds and Abdu will carry you up the mountain."

"Forty."

"Forty-five. Best price. There will be no profit. Do you want my wife and children to go hungry?"

"Ok, forty-five. Fifty, if you can catch up with Ismail and the woman."

33

Several hours before dawn a camel and rider loomed ahead in the darkness. He could just make out the swaying beast was led by a lone figure walking a short distance ahead.

Emerging from the trail onto a ridge, Alex shivered, wishing he'd thought to slip on a sweatshirt before leaving his room. His mouth was dry and tasted of stale alcohol and cigarettes. Far below, a light on the fortified walls of St. Catherine's pierced the darkness. It burned in the same spot for centuries, lighting the way for weary travelers, an oil cauldron replaced by an electric bulb in the early 1960s.

I must be losing my mind, chasing a stranger through the Egyptian desert in the middle of the night. There was no reason to suspect she was doing anything other than getting a head start on the other tourists and pilgrims staying at the guesthouse, a nighttime ascent of the mountain to catch the sunrise. Perhaps he should have told Aubrey or Emad where he was going before setting off on this wild goose chase.

As he swayed through the darkness, he reviewed the questions he wanted to ask the monastery librarian, Father Julian. Who was the scribe that wrote the letter in the back of the seventeenth-century edition of Saint Ignatius's work, and when was it written? Did the scribe have a fragmentary copy of Clement's letter at his disposal? If so, was the letter actually written by Clement or could it have been forged? If Smith was the scribe, the perpetrator of an elaborate hoax, why would he do it? It made no sense that he would risk a distinguished academic career on a prank. Finally, and perhaps most important, would anyone decades later really care enough to kill him?

It was easy to see why the Church might, over the years, have found the appearance of new versions of ancient Scriptures disturbing and even have sought to suppress them. An account of the life of Jesus that portrayed him as something of a magician, a libertine, and a homosexual was explosive stuff. It challenged the strict, controlling sexual mores of the Church, portraying Jesus engaged in sexual activity with his young devotees. Rigid rules on sexuality were, he knew, a powerful tool used to great effect over the last two thousand years to control not only the clergy but also millions of ordinary followers around the world. Alex chuckled mirthlessly under his breath. Power via guilt; it was crude but effective. In many Christian denominations, sexual activity outside marriage, outside the purpose of procreation, was deemed a sin. Although his own parents had a somewhat less judgmental approach, Alex had Roman Catholic friends who were taught that masturbation was the greatest sin. Such teaching had left generations of young boys either pent up or requiring absolution, terrified and ashamed to find they'd already committed the greatest sin upon their own bodies by the tender age of thirteen.

The implications were staggering. If authentic, Smith's find would raise significant questions about the study of early Christianity and force a reassessment of the historical Jesus. It would, in fact, require theologians to rethink much of their interpretation of the New Testament.

The stakes in the battle for the heart and soul of Christianity are extraordinary.

If some other form of the faith had won the struggles for dominance, the familiar doctrines now adhered to by hundreds of millions around the world might have been different. Bloody wars were fought over what now seemed to be minor points of doctrine. Those wars determined the history of civilization, particularly in the West.

My friend Morton Smith had a message for me. He sent me a letter and he wanted to meet. He wanted to add something to the story he told me in Cambodia of the discovery of the Secret Gospel of Mark.

The world was silent, except for the faint scuff of camels' feet on rock. Ahead, the mountain reared up, a deep inky mass in the predawn darkness. The sky cleared, illuminated by a quarter moon and dusted with millions of bright stars.

The gap was now about ten meters and slowly closing. Alex could see that the figure on the camel ahead wore shorts and a dark sweater, hair pale at shoulder length. A twinge of recognition rippled through him Within a few minutes, his mount had almost drawn level, and the two Bedouin guides greeted each other.

The figure turned.

"Alex! What are you doing up here?"

The surprise seemed genuine.

"Hello, Noora."

His introspective mood evaporated. He had enjoyed their conversation at the university library the week before. But since spotting her out late at night on the banks of the Nile, he'd barely given this woman another thought.

All of a sudden, his fears about noises outside his room, footsteps in the night, the subsequent pursuit of a shadowy figure up the mountain, seemed foolish.

"I'm up here on research, meeting the monastery librarian later this morning. Thought I'd best make an effort to see the sunrise from the top while I'm here."

Noora pulled back her hair, fastening it in a ponytail with an elastic band. The camels were now side by side and Alex and Noora's knees were almost touching. The guides continued chatting.

"What about you? Fancy bumping into each other like this, so soon. What brings you to St. Catherine's?"

"Oh, I'm being a tourist, I'm afraid." Noora grinned, that same beautiful flash of teeth he'd found so appealing at their first encounter.

"Getting an early start on the climb?"

"The guidebook says sunrise from the peak is spectacular." She tapped the small bag slung over her shoulder, indicating the book within.

One of the Bedouin guides made a clicking sound, and Noora's camel moved forward. Alex's beast followed and they resumed their ascent. He wrapped his right leg around the pommel of the saddle, tucking his foot into the crook of his left knee as he had seen locals do. Within half an hour, they reached a small plateau where several other beasts were tethered. A handful of local men sat around a small campfire sipping tea and eating *halawa*. The sweet smell of the crumbly sesame paste hung in the air alongside the odor of fresh dung and straw.

Dawn was just over an hour away.

His guide tugged the rope and his camel swayed forward sharply and then back, first kneeling and then lying down for him to dismount. Noora's did the same and they both stretched their stiff limbs.

"Ouch. I'm not sure I could do that for much longer. The book said it is about thirty minutes to the top. We can take the steps cut into the rock."

He noted the assumption implicit in her words. They were now traveling partners. He did not correct her. "It seems amazing that these desert tribesmen can ride their camels for days without dismounting."

After paying the guides, they began up the steps, Alex in front. The air was fresh and a soft breeze began to blow. All around, the jagged, blackened shapes of the mountains were superimposed on the slightly lighter hue of the night sky, like a child's cardboard cutout.

As they climbed, he found himself telling Noora about the events of the past week. He hadn't spoken much about his feelings to Bairstow, and somehow it felt easier to talk to a stranger. The memory of Sadie was fresh, and a sudden physical pain shot through his chest. It was better than the numbness he'd experienced earlier.

For the first time since her death, tears pricked the back of his eyes. He blinked rapidly.

"I don't know how you can go on here, in Egypt I mean. You must be devastated," Noora said.

"I'm not sure either. I guess I feel like I've been swept out to sea. I'm floating on an unknown ocean. If I stop swimming I might sink."

"You will make it, Alex. It is amazing our capacity to cope with sadness. I lost my father a few years ago. We were extremely close."

"I'm sorry to hear that."

Noora brushed his arm. A hand pressed into his, squeezing, fingers briefly intertwining before letting go. "Let's talk about something else, shall we? Tell me about your research. What story are you writing?"

They scrambled over a large rock. The small Greek Orthodox chapel at the top of the mountain was visible in the predawn gloom thirty meters distant. He thought about Smith and his quest. He was about to begin telling Noora the whole story, but something he couldn't quite put his finger on stopped him.

"Maybe later. Let's just enjoy the sunrise."

A small stone kiosk was built into a cave at the base of a massive boulder below the Chapel of the Holy Trinity. A boy offered to rent them a soft felt blanket. Alex dug in his pocket and pulled out some loose notes. The sky lightened almost imperceptibly. Dawn was less than half an hour away.

They climbed the final few steps, and Noora took Alex's hand again. He did not object. The contact, the warmth of another human being, felt good.

A handful of tourists milled around the chapel, and they made their way to the other end of the plateau, over a jagged outcrop of red granite. They were now standing in a tiny bowl of rock. Nobody else was near. A faint orange glow appeared over the mountains to the east. The breeze was stronger here and tugged at the collar and sleeves of his shirt. He fought a sudden urge to hold Noora, who was standing slightly in front of him, gazing out over the desert, still invisible nearly two thousand meters below.

In the darkness, Noora's long, tanned legs were a mahogany color. She wore brown leather hiking boots and ankle socks. Her fine navy merino jumper hugged her slender shoulders and narrower waist, accentuating boyish hips.

Noora caught his gaze and held it. He quickly turned away, reddening. A sudden image of Sadie flashed through his mind, and he was filled momentarily with guilt, as if he had already betrayed her memory.

Noora turned fully to him. Her eyes searched for his. This time Alex held them. She reached out and stroked his cheek, sending a tingling sensation pulsing through his jaw. Desire washed over him as Noora stepped forward and kissed him on the mouth. Her lips parted slightly, the hot wetness of her tongue on his.

Sadie's image did not return. Hands loosened his belt, releasing the buttons on his pants, sliding them over his hips. Cool air touched his skin, arousing him. Noora turned to face the abyss, back pressed against his chest as he pushed his hands up under her jumper and cupped her breasts. She wriggled her own shorts to her knees, pressing her buttocks hard against him and he pushed himself inside her.

Afterward, they huddled under the felt blanket in the cleft in the rock. Exhausted, he fell asleep almost immediately. When he woke, he was alone.

His watch showed less than twenty minutes had passed. Dawn was breaking over the mountains, bathing the valley far below in deep purple and orange.

34

St. Catherine's Monastery
Monday, 13 July 2009

"Let me say for a start that we know with absolute certainty that Mark's Gospel circulated in different versions in the early Church. This is beyond dispute by any reasonable scholar."

Father Julian had the look of a man who rarely saw sunlight. He was tall and gaunt with a beard that grew down to the knotted rope cinching the waist of his black woolen habit. Whiskers were streaked with a shade of gray that matched the pallid skin of his bony face. He appeared in his midfifties, yet the sparkling green eyes behind thick bifocals hinted at a much younger age.

The monk spoke with a twang that betrayed his American roots. He greeted them warmly, eager for news of his old friend Emil Boutros. Alex liked him instantly.

The monastery library was cool and dimly lit. The smell of dust and brittle parchment filled their nostrils as he and Bairstow took the seats offered them at a scarred wooden reading table. A single room enlarged by the removal of several interior walls, the library took up two floors along the eastern wall of St. Catherine's. The upper and lower levels were separated by an ornate wrought-iron railing. Tall glass-fronted shelves held thousands of volumes; four thousand five hundred, if Alex remembered correctly, mostly in Greek. But Arabic, Coptic, and Syriac were also among the many languages represented. He could see many were bound in rich flaking leather, intricately illuminated with delicate miniatures in gold leaf that glowed warmly in the light shed by two rows of bulbs high above.

Despite the enthusiastic welcome, Alex was on edge.

The events of the early morning troubled him. *Only hours ago I made love to a stranger in one of Christendom's most holy places. Now I'm here in a monastery where the oldest complete copy of the New Testament was discovered. My life is being turned upside down. I'm losing control.*

After waking on the summit of Mt. Sinai, Alex found Noora standing on a boulder next to the old chapel, staring at the dawn. Like several other tourists, she was taking advantage of the clear airspace to use her phone. She ended the call and smiled at him as he approached. They descended the mountain via a valley with three thousand steps carved into the rock face. It took three hours, and with trembling legs they returned to their separate rooms at the hostel. Alex showered and fell into a deep sleep. Bairstow woke him an hour and a half later for breakfast in the coffee shop; freshly baked bread and jam washed down with instant coffee sweetened by condensed milk. There was no sign of Noora.

Alex hauled himself back to the present. He forced himself to concentrate.

Father Julian continued.

"After all, even the four Gospels of the New Testament, known as the synoptic Gospels because they always appear together, say that Jesus did many things and performed many miracles that are not recorded in their pages."

He quoted from memory, "'Now there are also many other things that Jesus did. Were every one of them to be written, I suppose that the world itself could not contain the books that would be written. John 21:25.'"

"There are numerous manuscripts of the books of the New Testament, and none of them are identical. In fact, there are more than five thousand partial or full versions in Greek, and you may be shocked to learn there are more differences than anyone has been able to count. Estimates go up to three hundred thousand. Nobody knows for sure."

The two visitors looked incredulous. Father Julian chuckled.

"Rest assured, gentlemen, most of these differences are minor, scribal errors of transcription, little changes in wording. But some are significant, the result of intentional omissions or additions that betray the biases and beliefs of the copyists.

"For example, when Jesus is approached by a leper wanting to be healed in Mark 1:41, rather than feeling compassion, as the familiar story goes, the oldest Greek versions of the text show he became angry. You have to admit, this paints a rather different picture of the Messiah.

"I'll mention one other case that helps illustrate the point. It is perhaps the most striking example of the differences between various Gospel texts. It involves the last twelve verses of Mark, in which Jesus, after the resurrection, appears to his disciples. It is one of the best-known sections of the Gospel tale and often cited by the more fundamentalist, mission-oriented sections of the Church. Indeed, it is a favorite of many sects and cults."

"I know the section you mean," said Bairstow, glancing at Alex and noting, with apparent satisfaction, his look of surprise. "Jesus tells his disciples to go out and preach the Gospel to all nations and says those who believe in him will manifest signs such as speaking in strange tongues, handling snakes, and drinking poison without any ill effects."

Bairstow caught himself, "Sorry, Father. It's just that the chaplain at my old boarding school was really into this stuff. We were herded into chapel every morning and forced to hear his tales of the mission field in Southeast Asia. We all thought he was a complete nutter. Rumor was he had been ordered back to England from Sumatra by the Archbishop of Canterbury after an incident with an Indonesian choirboy." Bairstow reddened. "Bugger, sorry, carry on."

Alex glared at his friend.

Father Julian cleared his throat, "The oldest and best manuscripts of Mark end at chapter sixteen, verse eight. Those last twelve verses are not there. The women gathered at Jesus's tomb are told he has been raised and are instructed to inform Peter. They flee in fear and say nothing to anyone. For a lot of scholars, this ending is even more astounding than the one that came to be included in the canon of scripture. There was no account of Jesus appearing to anyone after he is raised from the dead."

Alex said, "So, there really is nothing at all implausible about several versions of the Gospel of Mark circulating in a large city like Alexandria in the first century?"

"Precisely."

Alex continued, "Before we go on, can I ask you about something that has been troubling me since my meeting with Professor Tarb Herman of the American University?"

"Certainly."

"He told me the so-called Secret Gospel of Mark could be older than the four accounts found in the New Testament. But how can that be if Clement says it was an expansion of Mark's original work?"

"Clement was writing a century after the fact and may have got the story wrong. It's as simple as that," said Father Julian.

"It is believed by many scholars that the Gospel of Mark as we have it today is a contraction of a longer text. That could mean the secret version is Mark's original. Think carefully about that narrative glitch in the story about Jesus and the disciples arriving in Jericho. In one sentence they arrive at the city, and in the next, they leave. Why would the writer bother to mention their visit if he did not plan to say what happened there? The Secret Gospel would solve that problem. It fills that gap. It seems most likely that the Mark of the New Testament is a contraction of an earlier, longer account. At some point somebody decided to cut parts out. Clement quite simply had the order confused."

Bairstow butted in again.

"Father, all this uncertainty about the actual text of the Bible, doesn't it make you question your faith? I know it is a bit off topic, but, I mean, isn't scripture meant to be the word of God? Yet if it is so full of errors, we have no idea what was originally written."

The monk smiled.

"I have no problem believing the Scriptures are inspired by God, or that many inspired writings exist outside the twenty-seven books of the New Testament and thirty-nine in the old. But it is important for any serious Christian intent on studying the Bible to understand how it has been passed down through the centuries. With the advent of the printing press, the number of errors entering the text of has fallen significantly. These days the scribe has been cut out of the equation. But his role was a very human one. God created humans with an incredible capacity for intellectual thought, and it's a shame when people fail to use that capacity to foster their own faith and better understand their creator."

Father Julian looked up at a narrow window set high in the library wall. Bright sunlight painted the rock face of the mountain.

"Please, join us for a simple lunch in the refectory. We can continue our discussion this afternoon."

35

"For God's sake, rape is rape, Eli! Let's get her out of there." Zvi Zamir was yelling, forcing the spy chief to hold the phone from his ear.

A brief silence, filled by the static whine of the secure line as the signal bounced off Amos-2, the IDF's dedicated military communications satellite high above the Earth.

Eli Zeira moved uncomfortably in his folding chair. He was not bothered by his colleague's tone. He would deal with that particular issue later. But the situation with the air conditioning, or lack of it, was getting on his nerves. He mopped his face with a damp handkerchief. Anyway, it was too late to pull the plug, even if they wanted to. Nothing could be undone, and there was nothing to be gained from losing focus now. He had always been good at compartmentalizing. Partitioning was the term used by the Institute's psychologists, trained at spotting and encouraging such things. Most people could do it, but he was especially good. He could create separate worlds within his own universe, a handy attribute in a job where he was required daily to send young Israeli men and women into harm's way. He could separate out the various aspects of his life so they did not taint each other, and he could do it as neatly and efficiently as a skilled surgeon using a scalpel to excise a deadly cancer. Some would call it a survival technique, others an extremely useful tool.

Once, during a particularly bitter argument, Zeira's wife pointed out that psychopaths and serial killers had the same ability. At the time her observation had stung, but over the years he came to see the truth in her words.

In the universe in which he operated, there was no black and white, just millions of shades of gray. He was reminded of something Stella Rimington, the first female head of Britain's MI5, once said to him. Something along the lines of the espionage world attracting some of the oddest characters ever to get involved in serious matters. He was one such character.

"Calm down, Zvi. You know as well as I do how—" He paused, searching for the right word. "—how *distasteful* some of these Christian sects can be."

But they can also be extremely useful. Most reserve a special place in their worldview for Israel, God's chosen people. Unfortunately many were terrorists, just like the Muslim extremists he spent his career combating. Their motivation was rooted in an idiosyncratic interpretation of the Bible and tenets of their faith. From their viewpoint, scripture provided ample justification for violence. Such groups existed all around the world, from God's Army in Burma, to the Christian militias in Uganda, and the states of the old Soviet Union. In India's Nagaland, Christian militants routinely engaged in gunpoint conversions and even ethnic cleansing in a bid to carve out a separate Christian state. And although in the United States Christian terrorists had fallen off the radar of law enforcement authorities in the wake of 9/11, there was a time when three of the FBI's top ten most-wanted criminals were antiabortion activists.

Islam is often characterized as being a religion of violence, but is Christianity any better? Or for that matter Judaism? He should know. He'd made a career of sowing terror among Israel's enemies.

The man on the other end of the secure line was still whining. Zeira was getting annoyed.

"We don't train our people for that, for rape. Think about it. Imagine if she was your daughter, goddammit! She *is* someone's daughter."

Finally, Zeira snapped. "She is not my daughter and neither is she yours."

He was tempted to continue chastising the man but held his tongue. The chief of psychological warfare was too emotionally involved. But Zeira had no doubt that their conversation just ten days ago would still be fresh in his mind. *The cost of backing out now is too high for him.*

For now, there were more pressing issues. Things were not going entirely to plan. The bomb threat delaying the ferry worked beautifully. But they came close to losing control of the operation after that. How could his agents have missed that damn letter? By the time they'd discovered it had been sent to the journalist, it was too late. A schoolboy error that, quite frankly, left them in a pile of donkey shit.

"I hope you're not going soft, Zvi. That would be a mistake. Perhaps it was unwise for you to go to Cairo, to handle your agent directly, in the field."

Silence again.

A fly had somehow made its way into the stifling subterranean operations room. Zeira shooed it away from his face. Then he tapped a cigarette loose from the pack on the table and lit it with his free hand. It took several attempts for the lighter to catch. He stared at the pack, absent-mindedly reading the surgeon general's health warning. He was having second thoughts about this new brand. They didn't have the same kick as the Arab varieties he was used to. A man with mouth cancer—blackened lips, missing teeth, hollow cheeks—stared back from the carton. Not among the most disturbing images he'd faced, but unpleasant nonetheless. A few years back, on the advice of his doctor, he tried to change to lights. They tasted terrible then and they tasted terrible now. This would no doubt be another failed attempt.

The fly buzzed Zeira's face and landed on the table. It rubbed its hind legs together.

Amazing creatures; so quick, so skilled in flight that even our best engineers and scientists can't replicate their abilities. He crushed the insect with the edge of the cigarette carton.

On the other end of the line, he could almost hear Zamir marshalling his emotions, pulling himself together.

Zeira softened his voice. Partition, compartmentalize. "Let's go through it again, see where we stand, shall we?"

"All right, okay."

36

St. Catherine's Monastery
Monday, 13 July 2009

During his nineteen years in the desert, Father Julian never wore a watch. His days began two hours before dawn with the ringing of a wooden bell, calling the monks to prayer. They ended long after sunset, when his eyes were too tired to focus. The spaces between were calibrated by meals and the angle of the sun on the rocky desert landscape.

At St. Catherine's, time in the way most people understood it meant little. Alex struggled not to smile when, over lunch, the monk described his last visit to Cairo three years earlier, referring to the trip as recent.

After eating, Father Julian insisted on explaining in painstaking detail a project he was engaged in, cataloguing and photographing the monastery's vast archive to make it more accessible to scholars around the world. The library at St. Catherine's received thousands of emails each year, requests from researchers seeking access to its priceless collection of documents. The monk proudly showed them a room off the main library with several computer terminals and a complicated-looking digital camera mounted on a purpose-built metal frame. Requested documents were photographed and compressed into computer files before being emailed out. The room was the only one in the monastery with air conditioning, a necessity to prevent the sensitive computer equipment from overheating.

"Eventually, we hope to have this whole library stored safely in a digital archive. As you can see it's an extremely slow process, but you have to start somewhere," Father Julian said.

"At the rate we are going, I estimate it will take another fifty to seventy years."

■ ■ ■

It was after 1:30 p.m. by the time they were once again seated around the reading table. Father Julian explained that two key questions needed answering in regard to the discovery of the Secret Gospel of Mark.

"Were the quotations of the secret account attributed to Mark actually written by the author of the canonical Gospel of Mark? And was the letter the professor photographed an authentic letter of Clement, or was it forged?

"Plainly, since Clement's letter was discovered in the back of a 1646 edition of the letters of another early church father, St. Ignatius, it cannot have been written into that book before the book was made. It is, therefore, at best a seventeenth-century copy.

"Given that the handwriting is not Clement's, the only way to know if the words were indeed originally written by Clement is through a careful analysis of style. It is a question of vocabulary, modes of expression, and theology. The majority of scholars Smith showed the photographs to during his research, more than eight world-renowned experts of the day, agreed that the letter was indeed authentic.

"A slightly smaller majority agreed that the segments of quoted texts from the Secret Gospel were indeed written by the same author as the Gospel of Mark. While not in the style of Clement, they were very much in the style of Mark as found in the New Testament. Even today, nearly fifty years after Smith's find, these remain the majority opinions, although there has never been complete consensus.

"As I explained earlier, there are a number of features of the canonical Gospel that can be explained if the secret version were indeed the original. Students of the canonical version of Mark have long been puzzled by a passage near the end of the Gospel, where Jesus is arrested by soldiers in the garden at Gethsemane.

His disciples flee the scene, but there is someone else there, 'a young man' who is 'clothed in a linen cloth.' When the Romans try to grab him he runs away, naked, leaving the cloth in their hands. Mark 14:51–52. Who was this strange figure who had never been mentioned before?"

Alex saw the link immediately: the boy Jesus resurrected and introduced to the mysteries of the Kingdom of God.

Father Julian continued. "I'm sorry to say that I will not be able to give you a definitive answer as to whether the letter attributed to Clement is genuine or not. But it is worth bearing in mind that among the earliest doubters was the first person Smith showed the photographs to, one of his old teachers at Harvard, a man by the name of Arthur Darby Nock. Nock was one of the few people in the field of biblical scholarship who could genuinely claim intellectual superiority over Smith in his chosen field. He maintained until he died some years ago that it was a 'mystification for the sake of mystification,' in other words a forgery by someone who simply wanted to see if they could get away with it. But he did not point the finger at Smith. He believed the forger was likely to have been someone in the seventeenth century. It has to be said, though, others have thought otherwise."

Father Julian removed his glasses and proceeded to clean them on a section of his cassock. As he did so, another monk entered the room carrying a tray of glass coffee cups, which he placed on the table before leaving.

Father Julian replaced the glasses on his nose. "Ah, excellent. Please, help yourselves."

The sweet black liquid was spiced with cardamom in the Arabic style and Alex sipped his appreciatively, remembering with a shudder the instant brew at breakfast in the guesthouse.

"Now where were we? There are a number of factors to consider here. First, a point you may find quite surprising. Since Smith photographed the Clementine manuscript, no other scholar has been able to subject it to a careful examination.

"Of course, there is no doubt the book existed, or that a letter was written into the back of it in a seventeenth-century Greek style of handwriting. But without a proper chemical analysis of the ink, it is impossible to determine if the scribe was writing in 1758 or 1958."

The monk stood and walked over to a glass cabinet. Putting on a pair of white cotton gloves, he removed a fragile-looking codex and brought it over to the table. He flicked on a desk lamp and adjusted it to a low angle. The brittle sheets of parchment were covered in neat Greek script.

"Look closely at the script and you can see there are no hesitations in the author's hand. That tells you he was not copying an earlier document or pausing repeatedly to imitate a style of handwriting. Such details can be lost in a photo.

"Early Christian texts were copied by hand, and the copyists naturally made mistakes. Those mistakes were repeated and added to by later scribes. If Smith's letter is authentic, it was written in the early third century and copied over another thirteen centuries. Yet the manuscript he discovered strangely has few of the major copying mistakes you would expect to find. In that respect at least, it appears that the author was not copying a text but composing one."

Alex was incredulous. "Why, if this manuscript caused such a stir, did nobody go and look for the document? Many forgeries have been uncovered through a close analysis."

Father Julian said, "It is much to the professor's credit that he left the volume where it belonged, where it survived intact for hundreds of years due to the hot, dry desert climate. It simply was not his to take. And you forget, Alex, that Mar Saba was, back then, quite remote. It sits in a region that has not always been accessible due to political turmoil. Besides, not anyone can just waltz in there. You have to be invited by the Greek Orthodox Patriarchate of Jerusalem.

"Let me show you something. Many ancient monasteries, including this one, have had to learn the hard way in their efforts to distinguish scholars from treasure hunters."

Father Julian led them across the floor of the library to the far wall, where a typed document hung in a black frame.

"This is a receipt given to one of my predecessors for the Codex Sinaiticus, the oldest known text of the entire Bible in one volume. See, it was signed in 1859 by the German scholar Constantin von Tischendorf. During a visit here, Tischendorf borrowed the codex on behalf of the czar of Russia so a copy could be made and studied. It was never returned.

"As you can see from the receipt, he promised the safe return of the codex to the St. Catherine's library. More than 150 years later, we are still waiting. For many decades, this priceless treasure was preserved in the Russian National Library. In 1933, Josef Stalin sold it to the British Library for £100,000, a fraction of its real worth."

37

They finally exited the tiny door in the western wall of the monastery after 5:00 p.m. Father Julian had given Alex a phone number to contact him if there were any further questions.

His head buzzed with the possibilities. He needed a cigarette and a chance to quietly sift through his own thoughts. In some respects, the visit did little to clarify the situation, leaving him yet again with more questions than answers.

"I'll see you back at the guesthouse. I'm going to take a walk."

"I'll be on the terrace by the coffee shop, having a sundowner. The single malt beckons." Bairstow waved a beefy paw and lumbered off in the direction of the stairs to the hostel.

Alex watched him go before heading along the base of the wall, taking the same route as in the early hours of the morning. He could appreciate what Father Julian said about the difficulty scholars would have experienced gaining access to Clement's letter at Mar Saba. But why had Smith himself not gone back to take a look? He was an expert in manuscripts and would have known what to look for. He knew he had not properly examined the pages themselves under a magnifying glass or a microscope but only photographed them. Why spend the next twelve years of his life painstakingly verifying the text without taking the most important step?

He passed through the courtyard where the camels had been sleeping. He pulled out his pack of cigarettes and shook one loose. He fired it up and drew in the smoke and then exhaled it in a long, breath. The sun was low over the mountains and the nicotine went to work on his frayed nerves.

A modern forgery of an ancient letter that contained an even more ancient fragment of a Gospel that tricked world-leading experts in the field of Clementine and biblical scholarship would be an amazing feat. But it would not be impossible for a person with the requisite set of skills.

Alex sat on a low stone wall and stared up at the mountains for a good five minutes, moving only to draw in fresh hits of nicotine.

Have I missed something? There was something about his conversation with Father Julian that was niggling, floating just below the surface of his conscious mind. He tried to think harder. Something to do with the mention of Smith's old professor, Arthur Darby Nock. He never mentioned him in our conversations in Cambodia. *I've heard that name, or seen it, somewhere before.*

Then it clicked. Alex dropped the cigarette in the dirt and ground it out with the toe of his boot.

Bairstow was nowhere to be seen as he quickly made his way back to his room. The two books he checked out of the library at the American University, the volumes written by Smith about his discovery, were in his bag. One was a thick volume for scholars and the other the thinner version for the general public, which read like a detective novel. Pulling out the thick, learned volume first, Alex turned to the dedication in the front.

There it was, that name: Arthur Darby Nock.

He was floored. Smith had dedicated the book to one of the earliest doubters of his find, the brilliant scholar who concluded Clement's letter was a "mystification for the sake of mystification."

He opened the second book. The dedication struck him like a lightning bolt. It read simply "To the one who knows."

Alex closed the volumes and returned them to his pack.

Who is the "one who knows"? Could it be Nock?

He pulled his cell phone from his pocket and punched in a number. It rang for a long time before finally being picked up.

"Father Julian speaking." The line was terrible and Alex recalled that cell phones only had patchy reception here.

"Father, it's Alex. Sorry to disturb you again so soon."

"Not at all, it is always refreshing to meet a fellow seeker. I very much enjoyed our meeting today."

He explained his discovery about the dedications. He had to repeat himself several times to make himself understood.

"I hadn't noticed, to be honest," said the monk. "But it certainly fits with another curious fact that I neglected to mention earlier. If the letter is original, it is ironic to say the least that it appears in the back of the book that it does: Isaac Voss's 1646 edition of the letters of St. Ignatius."

"How so?" Alex's voice had a new urgency in it.

"Voss's is the first edition of the works of Ignatius to remove several letters that had come to be recognized as forgeries. He also excised additions to the text that are generally believed to have been inserted by theologically motivated scribes. There is another interesting bit of symmetry, too. Clement talked about two versions of the Gospel circulating in Alexandria, as you know, one for the spiritually advanced and one for ordinary believers. Smith produced two accounts of his find, one for scholars and one for laymen. It is a neat piece of mirror imaging, perhaps too neat. Are these coincidences, or the craftily placed fingerprints of a forger?"

Alex was about to hang up when he remembered the original reason for his call.

"How does one verify Clementine vocabulary?"

Father Julian said, "The work of past scholars has over the years made it easier, one in particular.

"Just before World War II, a German academic, a fellow by the name of Otto Stahlin, published a four-part criticism of Clement's work. The final volume, titled *Clemens Alexandrinus*, was published in 1936 and contained an extensive index and complete vocabulary list, with notes on how frequently each word was used in Clement's writings. Smith said he was able to use Stahlin to determine whether his discovery followed Clement's writing style."

"Thanks, Father. You've been most helpful," Alex said, but he realized the connection had already been lost.

He stepped out onto the terrace. The sun was very low. He closed the door to his room and went in search of Bairstow. His friend was on the upper level, slouched in a plastic chair, sipping a glass of whiskey. Alex flopped down next to him at the table and poured himself a healthy measure of single malt as he recounted his telephone conversation with the monk.

"Are you thinking what I'm thinking?" asked Bairstow. "I mean, let's assume, for the sake of argument, that it was forged. It almost certainly would have had to have been produced after Stahlin's 1936 edition of Clement's writings was published, right?"

Alex's pulse quickened. Smith made his discovery in 1958. "Exactly, and it would have to have been forged by someone who went to Mar Saba and had access to the library. The monks, after all, had had the rare Isaac Voss edition for centuries. What's more, if its placement in that particular book was not merely coincidence but a carefully placed set of fingerprints, then it would have to have been put there by someone who knew the book was in the library, someone who had been there before, someone like Smith, who was stranded in Palestine during World War II."

Bairstow cut in. "But why would he do that? I find it hard to believe a leading academic like Professor Smith would pull such a stunt."

Alex thought for a moment. The Smith he knew certainly had a healthy disdain for his fellow academics. The man also had a wicked sense of humor, and he could imagine him taking great pleasure in pulling the wool over the eyes of his contemporaries. Could he have found the Isaac Voss edition during his first visit and then used the intervening years thinking it over and working out the wording of a letter that was so like Clement that it fooled even those who had spent their lives studying him? Could he have produced quotations from Mark that were enough like the original to fool yet more experts?

"Few others in the twentieth century had the skill to pull it off, but I'm not convinced. If he did it, there must have been another reason."

"Like what?" said Bairstow.

"I don't know. But I have the feeling there are still pieces of the puzzle we haven't found."

"You know, I can't help but feel as if Smith wanted to get caught. Not immediately, but eventually."

"Me, too."

38

The Bedouin campfires were again visible on the plain below. Alex was beyond tired.

"I need a shower and I'm going to try and check my email before dinner. See you in half an hour."

Bairstow put his feet up on the plastic chair his friend had just vacated. He reached for the bottle of Laphroaig, sloshing a healthy measure into his glass.

"You know where to find me."

Alex made his way to the stone flight of steps leading to the lower terrace. His legs ached from the early morning ascent of the mountain and his long day sitting in the library. He briefly wondered where Noora was as he started down the stairs. There had been no sign of her since they parted that morning. She must have taken one of the popular guided tours of the monastery and its grounds.

A sound on the terrace below caught his attention. A stifled cough and then a soft click. Alex reached the bottom and turned the corner, still thinking about the girl.

The Arab spotted him first.

He'd just pulled the door to Alex's room closed and was wiping the handle with a handkerchief, replacing it in the pocket of his galabaya, when Alex looked up.

Their eyes locked.

He thought he detected a brief flash of panic replaced quickly by a steely determination on the unshaven face. Despite the warmth of the evening, a chill ran down his spine. Beads of sweat broke out on his forehead with the sudden realization that the stairs he had just descended were the man's only exit route.

The intruder charged.

For a heavyset man, he moved with startling grace and speed. In a flash, the gap closed. Alex was too slow, and the shoulder blow to his sternum left him sprawled on the flagstones gasping for breath. Pain shot through his chest as he tried to rise.

The Arab hoisted his robe, taking the stairs four at a time.

Working on pure adrenaline, Alex scrambled to his feet and ran after the man, catching a glimpse of the startled look on Bairstow's face, mouth half open as if searching for words, as he sprinted past the coffee shop on the upper courtyard. At the top of the second flight of steps, the Arab briefly lost his footing on the gravel before recovering and darting right, disappearing into the monastery gardens.

Alex slowed to a jog and looked around for his assailant. The air was warm and still, and he strained for the patter of running feet.

To the left, he could just make out the fortified enclosure of the hermitage with its massive rectangular-hewn blocks of hard granite rising above the olive trees. Ahead, a small stone church that he recognized from the guidebook as the Chapel of St. Tryphon, the early Christian martyr considered by many farmers to be the protector of fields. To its left and attached to the main church stood a smaller structure, its steel door slightly ajar.

Steep stairs cut from the hard rock of the mountain descended into darkness. There was nowhere else the man could have gone.

I shouldn't be doing this, but to hell with it. He pushed the heavy door open wider and stepped inside, ears straining for any noise. Nothing was audible over the ragged sound of his own breath.

The air was stale, and there was a taint to it that he could not quite place. Electric cables snaked along the ceiling of the passage between a series of caged bulbs, and he felt around on the wall for a switch.

He sensed a presence at the door behind him. Before he could react, a hard object connected with the back of his head. He was unconscious before he hit the ground.

39

Solid rock, cold against his palms. He blinked hard, still nothing. The thick, velvety darkness was complete. Alex gingerly inspected the back of his head. Pain shot through his skull and his fingers came away sticky.

"Shit." His panicked voice doubled back, echoing in the subterranean space.

Hands shaking, he hauled himself to his feet and rummaged in his pocket for a cigarette lighter. The tiny flame sparked to life. Inky shadows flickered on the rough-hewn walls. The light was just enough to make out his immediate surroundings.

He gasped in horror. The lighter clattered to the floor, and he dropped to his knees, scrambling in the dust to find it.

The flint sparked a second time.

I've been buried alive.

It was some sort of chamber. All around were bones. Stacks of bones lined the walls, neatly separated into body parts; tibia, femurs, ribs, scapula. Against one wall a pile of yellowed skulls, eyes and mouths gaping, touched the ceiling. A niche held a full skeleton, dressed in the black vestments of a monk. A black cap emblazoned with a white cross sat atop the grinning skull in a perverse parody of the living.

His heart hammered in his chest. Since childhood he was prone to claustrophobia. He recalled one particular game of hide-and-seek with his older brother, Simon. He must have only been about six years old. Simon was nine and something of a bully when it came to his younger sibling. He peeked as Alex crawled into the linen cupboard and promptly drew the bolt, firmly securing the door. He'd remained there for several hours while their mother was out running errands. Angry yelps soon turned to floods of tears. Ever since, he'd hated confined spaces. The fear manifested itself in ways that were often inconvenient and sometimes embarrassing as a foreign correspondent. It was a large part of his pathological hatred of flying and, on a recent excursion to Luxor, he'd drawn the line at clambering down the narrow sandstone passageways of a newly discovered tomb in the Valley of the Kings.

This was fast turning into his worst nightmare.

Forcing himself to remain calm, he began a more thorough inspection of his surroundings. The chamber was long, with a low vaulted ceiling that disappeared into the gloom. The walls were hewn from the rock, and he searched for the stairs he must have come down. They were nowhere to be seen. He pulled his phone out and flipped it open. The screen lit up, a green puddle of light in the darkness. No signal.

"Fuck, fuck, fuck."

There are hundreds of bodies here, hundreds of skulls. This must be what hell is like.

Covering natural disasters and human conflict, Alex had seen plenty of dead bodies before, many in far worse condition than the dry brittle remains now stacked around him. But down here, in the dark, he was powerless to look away, to escape them.

With the lighter in one outstretched hand and phone in the other, he began making his way toward the far end of the chamber. The stairs must be in that direction. Something crunched under foot. Looking down he recoiled, realizing he'd stepped on the leg of a skeleton.

A loud screech came from his left, in the darkness up ahead. He stifled a yelp and spun to face the noise.

"Hello!" The terror in his voice distorted as it bounced off the walls. "Who's there?"

Silence.

Ten seconds passed and he slumped to the floor, careful not to touch any more of the ancient bones.

There it was again, metal hinges and then shuffling footsteps.

Alex crawled carefully behind a chest-high pile of femurs and extinguished the lighter. Footsteps echoed through the underground space and then silence again. If this was his attacker, he needed a weapon. He felt around for something heavy. Reluctantly he closed his fist around a femur. Old and brittle, but it would have to do. One end of the bone was jagged. If it came down to hand-to-hand combat he'd use it to stab his opponent.

A shaft of light pierced the darkness and bobbed over the rocky floor from the back of the cavern. The footsteps came closer.

A bulky figure loomed behind the beam. The Arab must have dragged him unconscious across the floor before returning to the stairs to make sure nobody had spotted them. With the coast clear he was now returning.

He held the bone in front of him like a swordsman preparing to strike.

■ ■ ■

"Anyone down here? The light at the top of the stairs doesn't work."

Relief washed over him. He'd know that voice anywhere.

"Aubrey, thank God. You've no idea how glad I am to see you."

He rose from behind the bones and stepped into the beam of his friend's flashlight.

"Ah, there you are. My God, man, you look terrible! Is that blood on your shirt? Who was that you were chasing?"

"I have no idea. But I caught him sneaking out of my room. What the hell is this place?"

Bairstow played the flashlight over the walls. "By the looks of things, it's the charnel house. The rocky ground in these parts doesn't permit many permanent graves, so for centuries the monks have first buried their dead in the cemetery on the far side of the orchard and later exhumed their bones and placed them here. Some of these skeletons will be more than fifteen hundred years old. All in the guidebook, old boy."

Alex shuddered.

Bairstow continued, "Look over here. Christ, they even have the remains of the archbishops in special niches. I suppose it serves a sort of spiritual purpose. It certainly makes you meditate on life and death."

Alex cut in. "Let's get out of here. This is all too bizarre."

"What the devil was that Arab up to, anyway? We'd better take a look at that head of yours and then see if anything is missing from your room."

Alex thought back to his brief encounter with the intruder. "I didn't see him carrying anything when I surprised him at the door."

"Well he must have been up to something."

They picked their way across the chamber to the stairs. At the top, it was wonderful to be in fresh air. The night had cooled and the sky was salted with stars. Bright moonlight enabled them to make their way out of the orchard to the hostel without the aid of the flashlight.

40

Alex opened the door to his room and flicked on the light. He realized as he did so that he must have left the place unlocked as he and Aubrey sat talking on the upper terrace. He stepped cautiously into the room, Aubrey close behind.

All the rooms at the monastery guesthouse were small and decorated in an identical fashion; two single beds separated at their head by a simple cabinet. A thin, reddish camel-hair mat covered the strip of floor between the narrow cots. To the left of the door, a writing desk doubled as a dresser. Next to it, on the other side of a wardrobe, a door opened into a tiled bathroom.

His backpack lay undisturbed where he'd left it on the spare bed closest to the window. The bed he'd slept in was still unmade, as he left it just after midnight. As far as he could tell, everything was as it should be.

Then he saw it.

Atop his pillow someone had placed a manila envelope, the kind lined with bubble wrap. Alex picked it up carefully. He'd stopped breathing. It wasn't sealed and he tipped out the contents. A single DVD fell onto the bedspread.

Bairstow looked over at his friend, cleared his throat, and then sighed, as if he were about to speak but changed his mind. Alex hadn't moved. His eyes were riveted to the disc.

A knock on the door startled them both.

"Pardon the intrusion, Mr. Alex, but is there a problem?" It was the guesthouse manager, his gaunt frame filling the door. He must have seen Alex sprinting after the intruder. The fellow was nervous, hands fidgeting with a string of prayer beads. Then, catching the sight of blood on Alex's collar, his face paled.

"Perhaps we shall call the police, sir? There is a doctor in the village nearby, but a few minutes by car."

Alex hesitated and then shook his head.

"I fell on the stairs. Nothing has been taken, so no harm done. I must have startled the man before he had a chance to go through my bags."

The caretaker looked doubtful but very much relieved as he prepared to leave. Like most Egyptians, he had a healthy aversion to the country's security services.

"As you wish, sir. If there is anything I can do, please let me know."

The manager departed, and Alex and Bairstow looked at each other. Neither man knew how to express the kaleidoscope of emotions and thoughts running through his head. Both were shaken.

"What the bloody hell is going on?" was all Bairstow could muster.

"Is it a message? It looks like a message."

"Perhaps we *should* be going to the police. There is something seriously fucking weird happening."

41

A graphic in black and white appears on the laptop screen; a circle containing a sword and an automatic pistol crossed with an open Koran in the middle. It is flanked by text in Arabic.

After a few seconds, another graphic, with more text in Arabic, replaces it. In the lower-right-hand corner is a picture from a Muslim funeral; two men carrying a dead body on a stretcher.

The two graphic images together last about nine seconds.

Cut to a medium shot with no camera movement. Sadie is facing the lens, eyes lowered, hair tied back under a blue headscarf. Other than the scarf, she is still wearing the same clothing as the last time Alex saw her. The barrel of a machine gun is visible in the upper-right-corner of the picture. On the left side, part of a figure dressed in olive- green battle fatigues and in the upper-left-hand corner more text in Arabic, in bold red letters.

Sadie is in the center of the picture and looks directly into the camera as she recites the message written by her captors.

"I am Sadie Cooper, a citizen of the United Kingdom…and I think this is possibly my last chance to speak to you."

Alex is confused. None of this makes any sense at all. *Sadie alive?* Elation battles with rising panic. He cannot trust his eyes. Bile rises in his throat. He has to remind his lungs to draw in oxygen as a burst of bitter saliva floods his mouth, forcing him to swallow. His face, drained of blood, has gone white.

Bairstow takes his friend's arm and guides him backward to the edge of the bed, forcing him to sit.

Both men are trembling. Their eyes never leave the screen.

Sadie continues to speak. "I don't want to die, I don't deserve it and neither do those women and children held in the Israeli prisons, people living in Palestine, suffering under the yoke of Zionist oppression. Please help me."

Alex can tell she is reading from a script. The delivery is wooden, the words belong to someone else.

"I need you to help me. Please do what is asked of you. You are the only person on God's earth that I can speak to. I now realize how much the faithful have suffered with the approval of the Crusader powers. The warming of relations between the Catholic Church and the Jewish-Zionist oppressors is a plot to destroy the people of the one true religion. It is not the fault of the Palestinian people that Hitler hated the Jews. All massacres of the innocent are to be denounced, but a certain massacre should not be used for political gain and blackmail."

Abruptly, the image cuts away to a short, fat man. He is standing in front of the camera wearing a black balaclava and white headband emblazoned with red Arabic writing. He has a pistol in one hand and is reading from a piece of paper.

"The Islamic Army has passed a death sentence on Sadie Cooper."

Alex emits a low moan. "This cannot be happening. It must be some kind of joke."

The sound quality on the DVD is poor and there are muffled metallic, clanking noises in the background. The camera pans jerkily to the left. A man, visible from the chest down, stands directly behind Sadie, who is still kneeling. Tears stream down her cheeks. The man has her hair and scarf balled in his fist. A long, wickedly curved *jambiya* is held at her throat.

Sitting on the hostel bed, Alex's whole body convulses violently. Tears sting his eyes. His throat feels like something is wedged in it. He cannot swallow and it's difficult to speak.

"Aubrey, I can't watch this."

Shooting to his feet, he sprints to the tiny bathroom. His stomach contracts, and he bends over the sink and vomits. The night is cool, but his forehead and cheeks are flushed, shiny with sweat. Breathing in short gasps, he tries to calm himself. Blood hammers in his ears and his vision is blurred.

"Turn that fucking thing off."

Bairstow remains riveted to the screen, unmoving. "We have to watch this, Alex. Keep it together, man."

As a journalist, Alex has covered hostage situations before. While he knows most end in release, he also knows some do not.

I don't need to watch her die. He storms over to the laptop on the desk and makes to switch it off.

The camera swings back to the man in the balaclava.

"Only you can save her, Alex," says the man, eyes boring into the lens.

He freezes, as if electrified, shocked by the direct mention of his own name. But what he hears next stuns and confuses him further.

"We know Professor Morton Smith has contacted you. That book is the rightful inheritance of the Islamic Army. You have until the end of the week to return it, or the sentence of the court will be executed. Do not go to the police. If the authorities are brought into this in any way, Sadie Cooper will die."

The camera pans to the right, showing a closeup shot of a man in military-style fatigues with his face masked by a scarf. He is carrying an automatic weapon pointed to his right. The camera pans left, showing a similarly uniformed, masked, and armed person. It pans to the middle, showing the two gun barrels pointing at Sadie, tilts down showing her hands cuffed, and tilts upward again, briefly showing her tear-streaked face looking straight into the camera before the scene ends.

The circular logo from the beginning of the video reappears. The image lasts three or four seconds and the screen goes blank.

PART THREE

42

"*Eight people were killed by a direct rocket strike on the train depot at Shemen Beach at rush hour this morning. Paramedics from Magen David Adom treated dozens of wounded and evacuated them to hospitals in Haifa. The IDF has begun an investigation of the incident.*

"*Army sources said Hezbollah guerrillas in southern Lebanon have used an enhanced type of rocket against the city. They said it has a forty-kilometer range, and can carry a larger amount of explosives than the older-type Katyushas.*

"*Northern Front Commander Udi Adam said that following the heavy rocket attacks on Haifa, the IDF is responding with attacks on areas from which terrorists are firing the rockets…*"

Avigail Stern sighed and twisted the dial on her small radio sitting atop the concrete wall. Even in the darkness of late evening, with the temperature edging down, the air so close to the seafront was saturated, heavy.

"War, always war," she muttered, returning her attention to the garden.

Five sirens in less than half an hour that morning had drowned out the distinctive scream of the Russian-built rockets as they passed overhead. The World War II-design Katyushas were usually launched from a series of tubes mounted on the deck of a heavy truck that fired volleys of the inaccurate yet nonetheless deadly missiles. The weapon of choice for Islamic militants in southern Lebanon.

Easy mobility made detection and destruction tough work. Now feared by Israeli civilians, the irony was not lost on Avigail that the same rockets once rained down on German troops on the Russian front. Those troops quickly learned to dread their peculiar whine.

She was unable to finish her cup of coffee at breakfast, forced to take shelter in the basement with the neighbors. The rocket attacks and inevitable retaliation by the IDF were unrelenting. It was a self-perpetuating and brutally destructive cycle of violence. Haifa, Israel's third-largest city, perched between the Mediterranean and the picturesque slopes of Mount Carmel, was increasingly in the firing line.

Avigail uttered a silent prayer for the boys and girls of Magen David Adom, Israel's national disaster, ambulance, and blood bank service. They would have been busy today. The name meant "Red Shield of David" but was usually translated as "Red Star of David," after the symbol emblazoned on the side of its emergency vehicles. Many years ago, Avigail's adopted daughter, Rachel, had joined up straight from medical school. It changed her from a laughing, bubbly twenty-four-year-old to, well…Avigail didn't want to think about it.

She flicked through two other news bulletins carrying accounts of the morning's mayhem before finding what she was looking for on a music station. She paused to listen.

"Temperatures will drop by three degrees Celsius overnight. As the weekend approaches, the thermometer will begin to rise. The long-range forecast calls for slightly warmer-than-usual-temperatures later in the week. By Thursday, the mercury will pass thirty-five degrees Celsius. No precipitation is expected until next month."

She sighed again. Not good news for the flowers. She turned off the radio and went back to gardening. Wincing as she knelt, she ignored the ache in her legs from the old wounds where the bones had set badly. She was close to eighty years old, and not a day had gone by in well over half a century that she had not felt that pain.

Of all the flowers in her garden, the *Anemone coronaria* were her favorite. She was determined they would survive the summer. Their large, poppy-like blossoms in scarlet, crimson, blue, purple, and white were a common sight throughout Israel. Her bony fingers worked the fresh manure into the soil around the base of the flowers. June to August, and sometimes September, were considered summer in Israel. Temperatures in Haifa would routinely reach the midthirties. Tomorrow was shaping up to be no different.

Sweat ran down her face, and she wiped her forehead with a soil-stained sleeve. The action caused the white fabric to ride up, revealing the blurred blue lines of a tattoo on the outer side of her left forearm. She paused to contemplate the series of numbers and letters.

In a strange way, this mark etched into her leathery skin was a good-luck charm. Only those selected for work were issued serial numbers. Those sent directly to the gas chambers were not registered and received no mark.

43

St. Catherine's Monastery
Monday, 13 July 2009

Alex's mind was a cauldron of emotions. He sat terrified on his bed at the hostel outside the walls of the hermitage.

For a while relief had washed over him. One thought had run through his mind over and over. *The woman I believed was dead is alive.* Tears rolled down his cheeks. It had taken a full hour to calm down and stop his entire body from convulsing.

Now the dominant emotion was fear, fringed with panic.

Alex wiped his nose with his sleeve and forced himself to concentrate. The reality of the situation was sinking in. A frightening series of incidents concerning his own security as he researched the story of his friend's life and untimely death had become a whole lot more serious.

Until now, it hadn't occurred to Alex that Sadie's fate might be connected to that of the professor, or to his own.

Something pricked his memory, something about the DVD he and Bairstow had just watched. He thought hard for a moment, playing the scenes over in his head.

The graphic in black and white; a circle containing a sword and an automatic pistol crossed with an open Koran...Sadie facing the lens, eyes lowered... the barrel of a machine gun...a figure dressed in battle fatigues...Sadie looking directly into the camera...the wickedly curved sword...a clanking noise in the background.

Nothing of any significance came to him.

Turning to Aubrey, he said, "There is something here I can't quite put my finger on. We'd better watch the DVD again, see if there are any clues to who this group is."

His friend shrugged. "The Islamic Army. I've heard that name before. It's come up in a number of the classified briefings I've been to at the Security Ministry on the Muslim Brotherhood..."

Bairstow stopped midsentence. Alex had noticed he was always careful not to talk about the specific nature of his work at the British embassy, but he had long suspected his responsibilities extended to liaising with other foreign missions on intelligence and counterterrorism issues.

His temper flared.

"For fuck's sake, Aubrey. "Classified my ass! Don't clam up on me now."

Bairstow appeared hurt.

As quickly as the anger had come it was gone. There was grief in Alex's voice.

"Mate, fuck your job, this has gone beyond a story. The last thing on my mind is writing. This is serious shit, really serious. Sadie's life may depend on it. Anything you know that can help make sense of what has happened, help locate her, is important."

■ ■ ■

Neither man could stomach the thought of dinner that evening. They chain-smoked, filling the room with a gauze-like haze that eventually forced them to open the door and window. After a heated discussion, they concluded that going to the Egyptian authorities was not an option. Alex was adamant. The message was clear; they were being watched by some sort of extremist group and Sadie would die if they did so. The group called itself the Islamic Army, and for some reason neither he nor Bairstow could fathom, they wanted to get their hands on Morton Smith's manuscript.

Worse still, they believed Alex had it, or knew where it was, and they had given him just four days to hand it over. Alex had no idea how to make contact, to let them know they were mistaken. He had absolutely no clue where the book was. Bairstow lit a fresh Marlboro Light, using the glowing butt of his last cigarette. He walked over to the door and peered into the darkness, as if he expected someone to be lurking there. The effect would have been comical under any other circumstances. Except for a sicklylooking gray cat stalking insects in the shadows, the terrace was empty. The sound of laughter drifted down from the restaurant.

"Look, Alex, I'll tell you what I can. I'm relatively junior, so it's not like I'm privy to everything. This group, the Islamic Army, has cropped up, but only in passing. How much do you know about the Muslim Brotherhood?"

"Only that it is illegal but tolerated. It's Egypt's most popular and powerful nongovernmental organization, has its own website, and is heavily involved in charity work. Its power and influence is growing."

Bairstow ground out the remainder of his cigarette. He took a deep breath, exhaling loudly. "It has an interesting history. Let's start from the beginning."

He got comfortable on Alex's bed, locking his fingers at the back of his neck, elbows pointing to the ceiling. Alex took a seat on the other cot, under the window. He poured himself a slug of whiskey to calm his nerves and lit a cigarette.

The Society of Muslim Brothers was founded in 1928 by a young schoolteacher named Hasan al-Banna. As a Sunni Islamic revivalist movement, its establishment followed the collapse of the Ottoman Empire after World War I and the subsequent end of the caliphate system of government that had united the Muslims for many hundreds of years. Al-Banna, who was just twenty-two years old, believed Islam was not only a religion but a fully comprehensive way of life, based on the tenets of Wahhabism, a strict and repressive form of the religion better known these days as Islamism and espoused by the Saudis, as well as unsavory characters such as Osama bin Laden.

Alex recalled their discussion of Wahhabism in his apartment with Sadie, the night before the fire. He motioned for Bairstow to go on. Aubrey pulled himself upright and reached for Alex's cigarettes on the low nightstand between the beds. He extracted one from the pack and placed it between his lips. Alex leaned over and lit it for him, impatient for his friend to continue.

Al-Banna had supplemented the traditional Islamic education for the Brotherhood's male students with training in jihad, holy war. It was not a fact many people knew, said Bairstow, but while studying at university, Osama bin Laden was influenced by the religious and political ideas of several professors with strong ties to the Brotherhood. He exhaled a perfect ring of blue-gray smoke. It drifted to the ceiling and broke apart before he picked up the thread of his story again.

The Brotherhood grew as a populist movement over the next two decades, encompassing not only religion and education, but also politics, through the establishment of the Party of the Muslim Brotherhood, the *Hizb Al-Ikhwan Al-Muslimoon*. It blamed the Western-leaning Egyptian government for doing nothing against Zionists flooding into the land on the eastern seaboard of the Mediterranean in the wake of the war and Hitler's Holocaust in Europe. Naturally, the Brotherhood joined the Palestinian side in the war against Israel. It also started organizing and executing attacks inside Egypt, which led to an official ban on membership. It is believed a member of the Brotherhood assassinated the prime minister, Mahmud Fahmi Nokrashi, in 1948. Al-Banna himself was gunned down by Egypt's security services in Cairo a year later.

About that time, due to its growing popularity, the Egyptian government legalized the Brotherhood again, but only as a religious organization. It was, however, again banned in 1954 because it insisted that Egypt be governed under shari'a, or Islamic law. That year, Abdul Munim Abdul Rauf, a Brotherhood activist, was accused of trying to assassinate President Gamal Abdel Nasser and was executed, along with five others. Four thousand members were rounded up and jailed, and thousands of others fled to Syria, Saudi Arabia, Jordan, and Lebanon.

A decade later, Nasser granted amnesty to the imprisoned Brothers, evidently hoping their release would weaken interest in Egypt's recently formed Arab Socialist Union party. Three more assassination attempts occurred in quick succession. The most senior-known members of the Brotherhood were executed in 1966. Hundreds of others were imprisoned. Nasser's successor, Anwar al-Sadat, promised the Brotherhood that Islamic law would be implemented and released all of the prisoners. But the Brotherhood soon lost its faith in Sadat, accusing him of the ultimate betrayal when he signed a peace agreement with Israel in 1979. Sadat was assassinated in September 1981. The blame fell on the Brotherhood.

Despite being officially outlawed, the Muslim Brotherhood had over the years captured seventeen seats in the Egyptian Parliament through members standing as independents. They also held important offices in banks, local government, and professional organizations throughout the country. Today, explained Bairstow, an extremely complex financial network connected the operations of over seventy branches worldwide.

Bairstow said, "During their seventy-plus years of existence, there have been cycles of growth, followed by factional splits forming violent jihad-oriented groups, such as al-Jihad and al-Gama'at al-Islamiyya here in Egypt, Hamas in Palestine and mujahideen groups in Afghanistan. In Egypt, the Brotherhood is a far-reaching operation. Its members see themselves as unjustly oppressed. The current president routinely has them arrested."

"So the Islamic Army is one of those offshoots?" Alex asked.

"You've got it. Their motto is taken directly from that of the Brotherhood: 'Allah is our objective. The Prophet is our leader. Koran is our law. Jihad is our way. Dying in the way of Allah is our highest hope.' They have been blamed for a slew of beheadings in recent times and are known to have links to al-Qaeda in Iraq. Needless to say, they are a tough bunch, and they mean business. It would be hard to overstate the danger Sadie is in."

Alex digested this last piece of information, and he felt his stomach tighten. He lay back and stared at the ceiling.

It was just after 3:00 a.m.

44

Tuesday, 14 July 2009

Alex was fully awake. Despite the physical exhaustion, his conscious mind refused to be decoupled from the racing train of recent events. Bright moonlight filtered through the curtains, projecting slow-moving shadows across the bedspread and walls. The effect was like being underwater, and he had to remind himself he was surrounded by thousands of kilometers of barren sand and rock.

An owl hooted somewhere in the monastery gardens, and a dog barked out a staccato response. Otherwise, the desert was silent.

Every time he closed his eyes, Sadie's face was there, pleading. Pale, tear-streaked cheeks and dark hair framed by the blue headscarf. He replayed the footage in his head; the wicked-looking muzzles of AK-47 rifles, the short, fat man in the balaclava pronouncing the verdict of "the court," the automatic pistol crossed with a sword, the open Koran.

The jambiya.

We know Professor Morton Smith has contacted you. That book is the rightful inheritance of the Islamic Army. You have until the end of the week to return it or the sentence of the court will be executed...

It was now the early hours of Tuesday.

I have just four days. The worry gnawed at him. It was Tuesday a week ago that Sadie disappeared in the fire, ten days since he identified his friend's body at the morgue in Alexandria, just eight since he received the intriguing letter, now stolen, saying there was more to the story of the Secret Gospel of Mark.

So much had happened in such a short time.

It was hard to comprehend that just the previous Monday he was having dinner at his apartment with Sadie and Aubrey. They discussed 9/11, America's War on Terror and religious fanaticism, the so-called Clash of Civilizations. Theory, an intellectual debate, had somehow become all too real, a living nightmare.

Alex still could not pinpoint what was playing on his mind earlier in the evening, pricking his memory as he watched the DVD. Perhaps it was something in the background, a noise. He knew he had to watch the footage again in its entirety, looking beyond the painful image of Sadie. The thought sent a fresh wave of nausea and panic crashing over him.

There was also something interesting about the language that stuck in his mind. He rubbed his face hard and tried to focus.

That was it. It was the use of the word *inheritance*. Why would the speaker use that word? Why would a group of Muslim fanatics committed to jihad feel that the writings of an early church father were part of their inheritance? It made no sense.

Sadie's words, obviously written for her by her captors, played in his head on a continuous loop.

I don't want to die, I don't deserve it…You are the only person on God's earth that I can speak to…

What was she feeling now? How were they treating her? He was helpless, impotent.

Alex, don't wallow in it, you've got to focus.

The warming of relations between the Catholic Church and the Jewish-Zionist oppressors is a plot to destroy the people of the one true religion. It is not the fault of the Palestinian people that Hitler hated the Jews. All massacres of the innocent are to be denounced, but a certain massacre should not be used for political gain and blackmail.

The reference to Hitler was intriguing but not particularly mystifying. Arab leaders and media had long been fond of comparing Israel to the Nazi regime while playing down the extent of the Holocaust. *A certain massacre* was an obvious reference to the extermination of the Jews during World War II. As a journalist living in the Middle East, Alex had gotten used to the constant comparisons drawn between the fate of the Jews in German hands and the treatment of the Palestinians by the state of Israel. He had long ago ceased to be surprised by them.

Like many of his fellow Western journalists, he knew the comparisons were simplistic and a gross exaggeration, but he found himself sympathetic to the plight of the Palestinian people. Dispossessed of their ancestral lands, their general powerlessness and discontent were easily exploited by those who saw violence as the only solution.

But the mention on the DVD of the *warming of relations* between Israel and the Vatican struck Alex as significant. He had read something recently on the subject. He swung his feet out of bed and sat for a moment. His body was weak and unsteady, as if recovering from a bout of illness. He reached for his cigarettes on the nightstand and lit one, breathed in the smoke.

Slowly it came to him. *It was an article. I was sitting in the café near my apartment, reading* Al-Ahram, *something about the Vatican and Israel ending a dispute.*

He moved over to the desk and switched on his laptop, finishing the cigarette as the hard drive whirred into life. It took some time to get a connection using his cell phone.

It did not take long to find the article from the Associated Press.

> *Vatican, Israel end spat over terrorism*
> *Tel Aviv (AP)*
>
> The Vatican and Israel have agreed to end a public feud over terrorism, with Israeli Prime Minister Ariel Sharon calling Pope Benedict XVI "a true friend of Israel."
>
> The dispute erupted when the Pope failed to include Israel on a list of countries that had been victims of terrorism. The Vatican rejected Israeli complaints and suggested that Israel routinely breaks international law when it cracks down on Palestinian militants.
>
> The public spat had threatened to damage improving relations between Israel and the Vatican.
>
> Israel's ambassador to the Holy See, Oded Ben Hur, delivered a letter to Vatican Secretary of State Cardinal Angelo Sodano that said Israel was ready to move on to a more constructive dialogue.

"We definitely see this thing behind us and are looking forward to improving our relationship," Ben Hur said.

The letter from Sharon called Benedict "a true friend of Israel, genuinely committed to advancing tolerance, understanding and reconciliation."

Ben Hur said Sodano was pleased with the letter and indicated that the Holy See was ready to resume normal relations. Sodano said the omission of Israel was unintentional and the result of hasty preparation of remarks.

As a kid, Alex was fascinated by World War II and took several papers on the subject at university. But his memory was hazy. Improving relations between the Vatican and Israel was mentioned in the DVD message. It seemed to be a theme worth exploring.

He saved the story to the desktop and logged on to *The Guardian* website. A few clicks later he was in the archives section and punched several key words into the search engine.

About a dozen stories came up, and he scanned their headlines before selecting one. It was from Reuters, several years earlier.

Publication: Reuters   Date: 24 Mar 2000 Page: 5
Headline: Pope tells of grief over Holocaust
Subjects: CLERGY; ROMAN CATHOLICISM
(ISRAEL; POLITICAL IDEOLOGIES; WORLD WAR TWO)
Section: NEWS Sub Section: INTERNATIONAL
JERUSALEM

POPE John Paul expressed heartfelt grief for centuries of Christian persecution of Jews yesterday, but stopped short of the apology Israelis had sought for the silence of the Catholic Church during the Holocaust.

"I assure the Jewish people that the Catholic Church...is deeply saddened by the hatred, acts of persecution and displays of anti-Semitism directed against the Jews by Christians at any time and in any place," the Pope said during an emotional visit to Israel's Yad Vashem Holocaust memorial.

He expressed intense grief for the horrors of the Nazi extermination of European Jewry, saying the memory "lives on, and burns itself on to our souls."

Saying he had come to pay homage to the millions of victims, the Pope said: "There are no words strong enough to deplore the terrible tragedy of the Shoah"—the Hebrew word for Holocaust. Many of those present wept openly.

The Pope did not apologise for the actions of the Roman Catholic Church or its wartime leader, Pope Pius XII, who is said by many in Israel to have looked the other way.

The Pope said: "Men, women, children cry out to us from the depths of the horror that they knew. How can we fail to heed their cry? No one can forget or ignore what happened. No one can diminish its scale."

Alex was intrigued. It was obvious there was a battle going on between Israel and the Palestinians for the affections of the Catholic Church and its millions of members around the globe. What's more, it had been going on for some time. Alex closed the story and exited *The Guardian* site.

Using Google, he entered a final search, this time for more recent stories. He quickly found what he was looking for, a short piece from Agence France-Presse two weeks ago.

Pope to make first visit to Holy Land
Vatican City (AFP)

POPE BENEDICT XVI will make his first visit to Israel next month.

Vatican officials said the visit to Jerusalem, which will also take in the Palestinian territories, would take place in September, although the exact dates had yet to be determined.

Israelis are likely to examine every word the Pope utters for hints of an apology as he honours the memory of six million Jewish dead, in a hall built in Jerusalem on the cremated ashes of Holocaust victims.

The Pope's visit to the memorial will give him an opportunity to high-light closer ties between the Vatican and Israel, a day after a visit laden with religious and political symbolism to Palestinian-ruled Bethlehem in the West Bank.

Benedict's predecessor, Pope John Paul, traveled to Israel and the West Bank in March 2000.

Visiting Jesus's birthplace and a nearby refugee camp, the Pope delighted Palestinians and their leader, Yasser Arafat, with a passionate recognition of their "natural right to a homeland."

Israeli officials played down the significance of the papal statement, saying it reflected long-standing Vatican policy.

Alex saved the stories and shut the computer down. A new picture was emerging slowly in the developing fluid of his mind. But it was indistinct. He had to get a clearer idea of what he was dealing with. So much of what happened in the past week and a half still made no sense.

He was burned out and knew he needed sleep. He lay back on the bed and closed his eyes. The sky outside the window was beginning to brighten, and he hauled the pillow over his head. Sleep seemed to swallow him whole. Like an exhausted swimmer caught in a strong current, he slipped beneath its dark surface.

It was 4:59 a.m.

■ ■ ■

Someone was thumping on the door.

Alex opened his eyes and raised himself slowly from the bed. His wristwatch showed it was 7:01 a.m. Just two hours had passed. Sunlight filtered through the curtains. The bed sheets were twisted around his legs, soaked with perspiration.

He'd been dreaming, a nightmare of which he could no longer remember precise details. The rhythmic banging penetrated his sleep and mingled with the sounds in his subconscious.

"Alex, you awake, old chap?"

"Hang on, Aubrey." He rubbed his face and yawned.

Kicking the sheet away, he swung his feet out of bed, suddenly wide-awake, mind alert, despite having hardly slept. Briefly it was as if the events of the night before hadn't happened. But in the few seconds he sat there, it all came flooding back. He tasted the bile in his throat. Fear gripped his intestines.

Yet something in his dream stirred a memory. He tried to take hold of it, coax it from the depths of his unconscious mind, but it remained flickering just below the surface, slippery as an eel.

45

The portions were not large to start with and became progressively smaller. At first, Sadie was grateful. In the half-light of her prison, she found cockroaches crawling around the bland vegetable gruel dumped at irregular intervals in her bowl. Tiny insects inhabited the folds of coarse *baladi* bread she used to scoop the slop into her mouth.

Water arrived only at mealtimes, after the clanking sounds of what she felt sure was a metal workshop somewhere nearby ceased. Even then, the liquid usually filled less than half the plastic beaker now lying on its side next to her mound of blankets. More than once, Sadie reached for the water greedily with bound and shaking hands, only to spill it. The room was hot, and her mouth was perpetually dry and sticky. Her parched throat ached when she swallowed. On her visits to the stinking toilet down the hall, her urine was dark yellow, viscous. She was beyond thirsty and her stomach hurt.

Much of the time she was blindfolded, but when she was not she saw dull flashes of light in front of her eyes and small animals and insects on the periphery of her vision. Becoming hypervigilant, she heard strange sounds and voices whispering death threats. She wondered if they were real or imagined.

Since making the video, hopelessness had become the soul mate of terror. Hearing loud noises, she was convinced that her captors were coming to kill her. It was at such moments that her whole life ran like a rapid slide show before her eyes.

Long hours were spent thinking about Alex. His voice was often in her head. He told her again about a course he attended as part of the preparation for his Middle East assignment. Tailored to journalists, it was called Hostile Environments Training and involved a week on a farm just outside London in the capable hands of a team of former British Green Berets. Such courses were common for media organizations, and the number of private security firms running them had multiplied as a result of the War on Terror.

On day three of his course, Alex and his fellow journalists were driven to a field where they were to be shown methods of collecting and purifying drinking water. Their Land Rover bounced along a rutted lane until it was prevented from going any farther by an older model Mini Cooper parked diagonally across their path, apparently broken down. A man, head under the hood, appeared to be examining the engine.

As soon as their vehicle pulled to a stop, shooting erupted.

Firing blanks, former elite soldiers dressed as balaclava-clad hostage takers bundled the journalists out of their vehicle and forced them to the ground, removing belts, tying their arms and legs, and blindfolding them. They were subjected to verbal and mild physical abuse in a process designed to mimic that which hostage takers would use to terrify and break them. All the evidence said that people who were prepared suffered the least physical and emotional harm when held captive. The more they knew about what to expect and the techniques to cope with abduction, the better their chances of survival.

But Sadie had no training for the situation in which she now found herself.

She reminded herself repeatedly that her captors were also under huge strain. Hostage taking was not for the fainthearted. *They will fear attack from me or my rescuers. They must maintain constant vigilance. They will be tired, irritable, and perhaps even afraid of me.*

There had been an initial lack of confidence. They appeared unsure of what to do, how to treat her. But that uncertainty soon evaporated. As the days passed, her captors become cruel, even careless. Sadie tried early on to establish a friendly rapport, focusing on the man called Hatim. Careful to disguise the fact that she spoke some Arabic, she tried to strike up conversations, and to identify common, benign human experiences that would enhance the likelihood of her being seen as a human being. At first, her efforts were greeted with stony silence. Eventually, Hatim lashed out with a punch that left her nose bleeding and her right eye blackened and partially closed.

46

The sprawling British embassy at No. 7 Ahmed Ragheb Street was a stone's throw from the American University's innercity campus. It reminded Bairstow of the White House without a dome. Up until the fall of the empire, the ornately columned, two-story edifice symbolized British power in the Middle East. It was the palace from which London ran Egypt's affairs in typical imperial fashion.

For Britain, the ignominy of losing superpower status was brought home in the mid-1950s, when Ambassador Sir Ralph Stephenson saw a large chunk of his precious embassy grounds emancipated by President Gamal Abdel Nasser in the first flushes of nationalist fervor. In one fell swoop, the swimming pool, Nile-side dock, and about five thousand square meters of impeccably manicured lawn disappeared. In their place, newly liberated Cairo built a riverside corniche.

Just two years later, the empire struck back. Britain and France, in alliance with Israel, occupied the zone surrounding the Suez Canal. British diplomats were given twenty-four hours to leave the country, and the Union Jack stopped fluttering over Garden City. By the time it was discreetly rehoisted a few years later, the mystique of the sprawling complex built by the first Earl of Cromer had faded. The earl himself was never popular with the Egyptians. His memorial tablet occupied a prominent spot in the city's old Anglican cathedral. It was now hidden away in the basement of the new one, opposite Alex's old apartment block, the current bishop having decided it would not take its place alongside plaques commemorating regiments who fought in both world wars.

Except for faint echoes of its earlier glory, brought on by the infrequent visits of minor royals, the historic British residence—thought to be the most picturesque outside India—was now used mostly to promote trade deals and cultural exchanges. State dinner parties, thronged by courtly ladies and gentlemen in white ties had long ago been replaced by charity bazaars, cake stalls, and workmanlike diplomatic functions.

Bairstow entered the compound through the wrought-iron gates, adorned on each side with the crest of Queen Victoria. A pair of marble lions guarded the entrance, acquired by Lord Kitchener, Britain's proconsul in Egypt until 1914. Instead of heading to the main residence, he took a path through the gardens to one of several dowdy, modern office blocks.

■ ■ ■

He'd left Alex in the bar at Shepherd's, three blocks north along the Corniche el-Nile. The new hotel remained a Cairo institution, but it was nothing like the old one it replaced. That one was built in 1841 and served during both world wars as a social hub where diplomats, spies, and socialites from dozens of nations mingled. During World War II, the city's streets were filled with soldiers, British civilians, Americans, White Russians, and stateless Jews. There were a half-million Allied troops in the country and over one hundred thousand refugees.

The modern cube-shaped hotel, perched on arched columns beside the Nile, did not look like much from the outside. But the interior retained some of the old character, with its dark wood, plush Turkish rugs, and antique furniture. Guidebooks called it "atmosphere." To Alex, it mostly looked crass. The bar served excellent coffee, and Bairstow chose it because of its proximity to the embassy.

They left St. Catherine's monastery midmorning and, aside from Emad's usual haste and general disregard for the rules of the road, the drive through the Sinai Desert and along the Red Sea coast was uneventful. Not far from the monastery, before joining the main coastal highway, they passed a Bedouin butchering a camel. The brake lights on the truck in front glowed red, and they were forced to slow to a crawl.

The huge animal was already dead, lying on its back. Long legs pointed skyward like broken straws. The butcher went about his work efficiently with an old saber. It reminded Alex uncomfortably of the hostage video. The tribesman was naked from the waist up, brown skin bathed in sweat and blood. Flies swarmed as he swung the jambiya.

Alex witnessed similar scenes in Southeast Asia, the slaughter of water buffalo at certain festivals. But the sight of the dead camel and the man with the sword left him sullen, and most of the rest of the trip was spent in silence. In the desert, every kilometer looked the same, as if they had not moved. Yet they passed places with exotic names like Abu Rudeis, Hammam Fura'un, and Ras Sudr. The uniform landscape did nothing to alleviate the hopelessness that hung in the air. Neither Alex nor Bairstow could think of a way forward.

Before leaving the hostel, they had forced themselves to watch the hostage video again, looking for clues. Nothing. Yet this time the bile did not rise in Alex's throat. The fear and panic were replaced by a smoldering anger, mingled with frustration. They seemed to be at an impasse, a dead end. They did not have what Sadie's captors demanded of them and had no idea of how to get it. They knew who her captors were but not why they wanted the book. Most important, they had no way of making contact.

On several occasions, Alex scanned the road ahead and behind their speeding Peugeot, searching for familiar vehicles. If they were being watched, those tracking their movements were good and to all intents and purposes invisible. Not prone to carsickness, he spent the journey reading Smith's account of the discovery of the Secret Gospel at Mar Saba, borrowed from the library at the American University the day his bag was stolen. He was struck by the sheer weight of scholarship, the detail and the number of learned scholars Smith consulted. Once again, he was assailed by doubts. Perhaps it was a genuine find. After all was said and done, the dedication at the beginning, to "the one who knows," could easily be a reference to God, couldn't it? Or perhaps the dedication was to the Gnostic tradition more generally, the tradition of secret knowledge.

When Alex pulled the book from his pack, it fell open to the picture section in the middle of the volume, the ones Smith took during his stay at the ancient hermitage in 1958. The first showed the bearded Archimandrite Kyriakos on horseback. The Greek Orthodox priest, who acted as Smith's guide to Mar Saba, wore steel-rimmed glasses and a black cap as he stared into the camera lens with obvious intelligence from atop his mount. In the background of the overexposed black-and-white image, a stone gateway was just visible.

He turned the page to two photographs facing one another. The first image showed Mar Saba, built into a steep rock wall, taken from the opposite side of the canyon. The caption said the monastery was one of the two great hermitages of the Greek Orthodox Church, the other being St. Catherine's. The facing image was of the hermitage from within. Soaring above its stone walls, domes, and sloped roofs was the square library tower, a single window in its eastern wall. Despite the image being black and white, he could almost feel the hot desert sun beating down on walls the color of parchment. A photo of the interior showed the library shelves as Smith had found them. Untidy stacks of leather-bound books and piles of loose manuscripts lined the walls and lay scattered on the floor. A wooden chair sat in front of the shelves, its straw seat collapsed inward. In his mind's eye, Smith sat on its torn surface as he worked to catalogue the priceless collection.

The final photograph was of the first page of the manuscript of Clement's missive, scrawled in the back of the early edition of the letters of Saint Ignatius of Antioch. Tight, spidery handwriting, which the experts had all agreed looked very much like a seventeenth- or eighteenth-century hand, covered every inch of the page.

"It just seems so incredible that this could have been a hoax," Alex said, breaking the silence. "It's too elaborate, isn't it? I mean, it was the twentieth century for Christ's sake. Surely, it would be impossible to pull off a stunt like that."

Bairstow stared blankly out the window. They were approaching the outskirts of Cairo, and the taxi sped through another kilometer or two of desert before he replied.

"Do you remember the Hitler Diaries?"

Alex did. They were discussed extensively in several of his history classes at university. In April 1983, the popular West German magazine *Stern* made an announcement that shocked the world and, like Smith's discovery some three decades earlier, it caused an unholy uproar.

Stern claimed to have discovered Adolf Hitler's personal journal, sixty-two handwritten volumes, the contents of which challenged accepted historical views about Germany's most notorious exchancellor and one of history's most famous characters. As the story went, the diaries were discovered in East Germany in the possession of peasant farmers, apparently rescued from a downed Nazi plane in April 1945. The story seemed to be corroborated by historical facts. The memoirs of Hitler's personal pilot mentioned the crash of a plane carrying the Fuhrer's papers toward the end of the war.

Stern hired several world-renowned experts to test the authenticity of the diary. Others also engaged scholars in the field. Among them was British Historian Hugh Trevor Roper, employed by *The Times* of London, which had paid a huge amount of money to *Stern* for serial publication rights. Trevor Roper said he believed the diaries were original.

Stern employed handwriting experts. Among them were the famous Swiss academic Dr. Max Frei-Sulzer, and an American, Ordway Hilton. They were each provided several photocopied pages and asked to compare them with other samples of Hitler's handwriting from the federal archives. Based on the samples provided, the men determined the handwriting was a match.

It was not until days before publication of the diaries was to begin in *The Times* that Trevor Roper began to get nervous and recommended further forensic testing. Those tests determined the diaries were, in fact, elaborate forgeries. Eventually, the world learned the identity of the mastermind behind the hoax, a Polish petty criminal, art forger and Hitler enthusiast named Konrad Kujau.

"Some people will go to extraordinary lengths to perpetrate fraud. If a man like Kujau could whip up sixty-two volumes and fool the experts, imagine what someone of the intellect of your friend Professor Smith could get away with," said Bairstow.

Alex had to concede the point.

Again silence descended on the occupants of the taxi. They were in the city now, and progress slowed to a crawl. This time it was Bairstow who eventually broke the silence as they approached the banks of the Nile.

"You know, we never did manage to find any relatives."

"What?" Alex had lapsed into a stupor, eyes glazed over, exhausted from lack of sleep.

"For Smith, I mean. We couldn't locate any next of kin. His body has, of course, been flown back to the UK. But there was no family that we know of."

Bairstow drawled on, but Alex tuned out. He imagined a coffin being lowered into the ground in a cemetery somewhere in England. Sodden earth, grass wet with rain. No mourners, a simple service. It was depressing. Just as he was about to close his eyes again, something Bairstow said caught his attention.

"Sorry. What were you saying?"

"His stuff, it's still at the embassy, in the storeroom of the consular office. We had nowhere to send it."

"Maybe we should take a look at it."

"Whatever for?"

"Got any better ideas?"

It took another half hour to reach Bairstow's apartment on Gezira Island. Emad waited while they ran their bags upstairs, and then he drove them back across Tahrir Bridge to Shepherd's on the east bank of the river.

Alex was on his third coffee by the time Bairstow returned, carrying the vinyl suitcase.

47

The medal was heavy and beautifully crafted, attached by a gold clasp to a wide, bloodred ribbon bordered with thin black-and-white stripes. The Nazis didn't do things by halves.

The decoration itself was simple and designed to be worn at the throat. It consisted of a white-enameled Maltese cross with gold borders. Four German eagles, also in gold, perched between the arms, each clutching a swastika in its talons, angular black crosses superimposed on a circular white background. Alex turned it over, half expecting to find a name engraved on the back in gothic script, like a school prize. Nothing identified its owner, just a date, 1942. He laid the medal on the dining room table and picked up the black velvet slip. It, too, was devoid of inscriptions.

The rest of the contents of Smith's suitcase spread over the tabletop. Bairstow sat in an armchair sorting through a pile of papers on his lap. A cigarette rested on the lip of an ashtray at his elbow. He had put the soundtrack to *The English Patient* on the stereo. It was one of Alex's favorite films, perfectly capturing the romance of North Africa during the turbulent 1930s and '40s. Ella Fitzgerald's smoky voice crooned in the background.

The balcony doors were thrown wide. There was no breeze, but the sun had disappeared below the horizon, and the air was pleasantly cool. The lights of Garden City and a row of houseboats on the far bank reflected off the black waters of the Nile. Alex removed his laptop from its satchel and set it on the table. The apartment had wireless Internet and as soon as he booted up, he was online.

He called up Google and punched in "Nazi medals." A long list of pages appeared on the screen, and he scrolled down through the headings.

Gordons Medals Ltd.
Specializing in Militaria of all nations, incl, UK & Germany.

Nazi Long Service Medals; Nazi rings
In all cases service time before the **Nazi** Party came to power counted for long service **medals** so WW1 service was counted and if Active Service was DOUBLE…

PzG—Nazi Iron Cross Knights Cross German Medals!
HISTORY BOOKS • ADOLF HITLER MILITARIA • **NAZI** FLAGS POSTERS & PICS • UNIFORMS • WAR MOVIES • PINS • BADGES **MEDALS** • **NAZI** MUSIC • WW2 PROPAGANDA • DAGGERS…

The History Bunker MEDALS—Reproduction WW2 Medals (Nazi medals…
Online Shop | **MEDALS**—Reproduction WW2 **Medals** (**Nazi medals** Third Reich awards)…WW2 German **Nazi** Party District Commerative badge **medal…**

Orders, decorations, and medals of Nazi Germany—Wikipedia, the…
Orders, decorations and **medals** earned by Germans before the **Nazi** assumption of power…

Within fifteen minutes he found what he was looking for on Wikipedia.

"Aubrey, take a look at this."

Bairstow peered up from reading a pile of receipts. Cigarette clamped between his lips, he carefully placed them on the coffee table before hoisting himself out of the low armchair and making his way over to where Alex was staring at the computer.

A full-color picture filled the screen. It was captioned "Service Order of the German Eagle."

Alex held up the professor's medal next to it.

"It's a match, don't you think?"

"Mmmm, appears to be. What on earth was Smith doing with this thing, anyway?"

Alex ignored the question and scanned through the online encyclopedia entry. The Order of the German Eagle was instituted in May 1937 by Adolf Hitler for service to the Thousand-Year Reich and was awarded with swords to military personnel and without swords to civilians.

He examined the medal in his palm. No swords.

He read on. It was not known exactly how many were given out before 1945, and the whereabouts of most of them were now not known. Since the end of the war, few of the recipients were eager to advertise their stellar service to the Reich and, in any case, by the late 1950s it was illegal in Germany and most of Europe to wear the swastika, or any other Nazi symbols for that matter.

"Wow, look at this."

Alex read from the screen, "The Order of the German Eagle was a diplomatic and honorary award also given to non-Germans who were considered deserving. The known recipients have included some of the great names of modern industry and achievement."

There was a list. It included Thomas J. Watson, president of IBM, awarded the medal in 1938. Henry Ford, founder of the Ford Motor Company, was awarded one on his seventy-fifth birthday, also in 1938. James Mooney, General Motors' chief executive for overseas operations, had one, too.

"Look," Bairstow was pointing at the screen. "Charles Lindbergh, the first man to fly solo, nonstop across the Atlantic was awarded one on 19 October 1938. Hang on, how's that service to the German Reich?"

Alex knew the answer.

"People conveniently forget that in the years prior to World War II, Lindbergh was a noted isolationist, and a leader in the right-wing America First Committee whose goal was to keep the United States out of the looming war with Germany. Even after Hitler rolled into Czechoslovakia and annexed Austria, he continued to be an apologist for the Nazis."

"Damn. So what was your friend Smith doing with one of these bloody medals?"

Alex shrugged. "I guess people collect all sorts of things, but it is strange that he never spoke about collecting in all the years I'd known him. What else have we got? You find anything in that stack of papers?"

"A couple of things that might be of interest," Bairstow said, making his way back to the coffee table and jabbing at the receipts.

"I've been sorting through these. Several of them are for bank transfers. It seems the professor was regularly sending money to someone by the name of Avigail Stern. Not large sums, just a few hundred dollars here and there, wired at odd intervals to an account at a bank in Haifa, Israel."

"Haifa, that's where Smith boarded the ferry, right?"

"Yup."

There is something else. That's it. The letter Morton Smith sent me was postmarked Haifa. It was on hotel stationery. He tried hard to recall the name of the hotel, but it wouldn't come to him.

"Is there an address or phone number for this Stern woman anywhere among his stuff?"

"Nope, I've had a thorough look."

"Hmmm. You said there were a couple of interesting things."

"There is also a letter here from a guy by the name of Gunther Hesse. It appears he lives in Cairo, and they were planning to meet."

Bairstow pulled it from a pile on the table and handed it to Alex. The letter was handwritten in English on unlined typing paper.

It was just seven lines long.

Dear Herr Professor,

I am intrigued by your most interesting research project. The things you are interested in occurred many years ago, but I have found that age has only sharpened my memory of those turbulent times. Please feel free to call by at your convenience.

Yours sincerely,

Gunther Hesse

Alex laid the letter on the table.

"No phone number or address? Is there an envelope? Please tell me there is an envelope." His despondent mood lifted and, although the worry still gnawed away at his guts, at last they had something to go on, a direction.

Bairstow was standing, rummaging through the pile of papers.

"Got it," he bellowed, holding a small white envelope triumphantly above his head and performing an ungainly jig.

Alex snatched it. He winced as the sudden movement sent pain shooting through the back of his head, where he was struck the night before during his pursuit of the Arab. The envelope was addressed, in a neat hand matching that of the letter, to Professor R. Smith, c/o Port Inn Guesthouse, 34 Jaffa Road, 33261 Haifa, Israel.

He flipped the envelope over. Bairstow craned over Alex's shoulder.

But it was blank, no return address.

"Damn! I really thought our luck was changing for a minute."

"How about this, though? It looks like a couple of phone numbers." Bairstow tapped the back of another envelope mixed in with the receipts. A string of numerals was scribbled in Smith's own hand: +29132174, +2532360.

Alex pulled out his cell phone and punched in the first series and waited before pressing the end call button. He paused before trying the second. Then he tried again, on a hunch putting the calling codes for the United Kingdom and Cambodia before the numbers. Disappointment was written all over his face as he slumped into a chair beside the table.

"Neither seems to work." He sighed.

"At least we have an address for the hotel in Haifa," said Bairstow.

48

Alex pulled a thick book from the ornate wooden stand next to the couch and flicked through its pages. People were often impressed by the ability of journalists to track people down; hardened criminals, grieving relatives, fugitives, and lottery winners. Few stopped to consider just how the Fourth Estate actually achieved this, and even fewer realized that nearly every manhunt began, and often ended, with the obvious: the telephone directory.

In recent years, another even more powerful tool had been added to the arsenal of newsrooms around the world: the Internet. Alex had already exhausted that option, punching in the name Gunther Hesse into to every search engine he could think of.

He was surprised to find how many small cities and towns around the world bore the name Cairo and had online phone listings. It seemed that in the United States alone there was one in every state from Alabama to Wyoming. But the only Cairo that appeared not to have an online phone book was the real one, in Egypt.

Alex found H in the fat volume and flicked his way through Hamid, Hassan, Hamza…It didn't take long for him to find there were three Hesses listed in the city, and only one G. Hesse, in Heliopolis, a district straddling the main road to the international airport, northeast of the downtown area.

Heliopolis, literally Sun City in ancient Greek, had once been an enclave for wealthy expatriates and aristocratic Egyptians, built as a small town in its own right at the turn of the twentieth century by Belgian industrialist Édouard Louis Joseph, popularly known as Baron Empain. After Nasser's revolution, the enclave was commandeered by Cairo's educated middle classes and now hosted the presidential palace as well as Egypt's army and air force headquarters.

As the city expanded, the distance between Heliopolis and Cairo vanished, and it was now well inside the city limits. The lush gardens that once defined the district were now mostly paved over with multilane highways and dun-colored apartment blocks.

■ ■ ■

The taxi dropped them at the Palmyra, opposite the leafy grounds of the Uruba Presidential Palace. It was just after 8:30 p.m. Away from the cooling river breeze, the air was thick, suffused with fumes from the traffic on Sharia Al-Ahram. As the crow flies, the distance from Bairstow's apartment was only about four kilometers, but it had taken all of an hour. As far as either man could tell, they had not been followed.

With the clock ticking on Sadie's life, there was no debating their course of action. The sense of urgency was palpable. Waiting until morning hadn't been an option. Tomorrow would be Wednesday, leaving precious little time to find the manuscript, or Sadie, whichever they could manage first. Alex did not hold out high hopes of achieving either objective, but the forward momentum helped subdue the fear that lay coiled and heavy in the pit of his stomach.

The Palmyra Café was almost as old as Heliopolis itself. Like the bar at Shepherd's, it was a popular drinking spot for Allied troops during both world wars. Nowadays, along with the Amphitrion nearby, the Palmyra was one of the few places in the city outside the main five-star hotels where foreigners could drink alcohol without enduring the disapproving glares of more pious passersby.

A waiter showed them to a table near the front. Alex rated the place as one of Cairo's best eateries. A beautifully preserved time warp with marbled floors and silk-upholstered chairs was how he'd once described it in a travel piece. Vintage black-and- white photos hung from the walls.

They were starving. He ordered a plate of *kofta* with a generous baladi salad. Bairstow had the grilled pigeon, a local delicacy. The sight of the tiny bird made

Alex feel queasy as his friend picked through the mound of bones and greasy flesh. They discussed their plan as they ate. Although there was a phone number in the book, Alex decided it was best to turn up in person. The address for Hesse was listed as 23 Sharia Cleopatra, a stone's throw from the Baron's Palace, a gaudy structure built by Empain entirely out of concrete that resembled hewn stone. Its spires and pointed domes resembled a Hindu Walt Disney fantasy, although it had actually been modelled on the thousand-year-old Angkor Wat temple complex nestled in Cambodia's northern jungles.

■ ■ ■

Hesse's street was quiet.

It was 9:30 p.m. by the time Alex knocked on the door. Not wanting to frighten the old man, he'd decided it was better to split up and for Bairstow to wait this one out at the restaurant. The house was nestled in a small garden, one of the district's better-preserved relics of the early 1900s Heliopolis style, a distinctive mix of the Moorish, Arabic and European architecture.

The door was answered immediately, by a man somewhere in his eighties. Tall and gaunt, with a mane of silvery hair flowing back from his forehead, nearly touching his collar, no signs of thinning. A long, straight nose sat astride a handsome, almost equine face. Alex's first impression was that if he'd been asked to imagine a Prussian cavalry officer, this is what he would have conjured up.

"Mr. Gunther Hesse?"

If the man was surprised by the arrival of a visitor at such a late hour, he did not show it. "May I help you, young man?"

"My name is Alex Fisher. I'm a friend of Professor Morton Smith."

The reaction was as he'd hoped. Recognition flickered across Hesse's craggy, sun-lined features, and he stared past Alex as if expecting to see Smith standing behind him. Then he bowed graciously, opening the door wider to admit his guest.

"And where is the good professor?"

They stood in a short hallway, the walls dark red, covered with old prints, scenes from Asia. White lilies stood in a vase on an antique wooden sideboard, giving the room the vague air of a funeral parlor.

Alex cleared his throat "I'm afraid I bring bad news. The professor died just over a week ago. A heart attack."

"Dear God!" Hesse took a step backward. He looked genuinely shocked. "You'd better come in." He led Alex through a large, sparsely furnished living room and into his study. Walls lined with glass cabinets, every inch crammed with what appeared to be militaria and war memorabilia. Black-and-white photographs adorned those surfaces not covered with display shelves. Alex spotted an image of a much younger Hesse in the dress uniform of a German army officer. He was not expert enough to identify the rank.

Alex's host noticed his surprise.

"It was many years ago," he said, his tone matter of fact, neither apologetic nor defiant. "You must tell me what brings you here, Mr. Fisher."

"Alex."

"Ah, yes, Alex." He chuckled. "Forgive me. The younger generation is so familiar."

"Mr. Hesse, did you know Professor Smith well?"

Alex had not meant it to sound like an interrogation, but Hesse's face hardened momentarily and he detected a glint of suspicion in the German's pale-blue eyes.

"We have never met actually, just corresponded about the research he is conducting. Which takes me back to my earlier question, what brings you to my door? Surely you did not come here at such an hour to inform me of the professor's untimely passing."

"No, indeed not," Alex said. "I'll try to explain as best I can."

Alex described as succinctly as he could the circumstances of Smith's demise, focusing on his own visit to identify the body at the morgue in Alexandria, and the letter he received two days later. Leaving out Sadie's kidnapping, he explained finding Hesse's note among the professor's belongings.

Hesse said, "So, it seems Professor Smith had traveled to Egypt to meet with both of us."

"Yes, it does. What I need to know from you, if you would be so kind, is if he told you anything about what he was up to, his research?"

"And you are a journalist, writing a story about this?"

"The professor's letter to me made it plain he wanted me to write about his work. Now the shock of his passing has begun to wear off, as a friend, I feel some obligation, a duty to at least try and tell his story."

Hesse inclined his head, an almost indiscernible movement of his great, silvery mane. Alex could tell he was a man for whom loyalty and duty were important concepts. He stole another glance at the photo of Hesse in the officer's uniform. They were still standing, and finally the German gestured toward an overstuffed leather armchair.

"Please, have a seat." He lowered himself into a couch opposite. It creaked loudly as he settled in. "What do you know about the Abwehr, the German High Command's intelligence agency during World War II?"

"Only a little, I'm afraid. As I recall, it was abolished by Himmler in early 1944, about a year before the end of hostilities."

"Ah, a student of history!" Hesse said with obvious pleasure. "The Abwehr and its operations were integrated into the SS intelligence service to destroy what had become a hotbed for dissent against Hitler. The service was discovered to have been at the center of the failed plot to assassinate him. In the wake of that, its director, Admiral Canaris, was hanged."

Alex nodded, encouraging Hesse to keep talking. But he wondered where the old man's story was going.

In 1939, Hesse explained, with war in Europe coming, he was a captain in the regular German army. From there he was drafted into the Abwehr. At that time, the British Army was in Egypt to protect the Suez Canal, a vital link between Europe and possessions in the Far East. The rationale was that if Britain controlled the Suez, then Germany and the other Axis powers could not use it. Also, if the Allies could build up bases in North Africa, there was potential to launch an attack on what Prime Minister Winston Churchill called the "soft underbelly of Europe."

By 1941, the Italian Army was all but beaten, and Hitler was forced to send German troops to North Africa under Field Marshal Erwin Rommel to try and clear out the Allies. Hesse went in with those forces and was posted to Abwehr headquarters in Tunis, where he helped run German agents across the Libyan desert into British-occupied Egypt.

By August of 1942, the British were in full retreat, suffering defeat after defeat at the hands of Rommel and his desert-hardened Afrika Korps. But August saw the arrival of General Bernard Law Montgomery as head of the British Eighth Army, a man who was to prove Rommel's equal. In September 1942 he defeated Rommel at Alam el Halfa. The two armies clashed again at El Alamein in October. Eleven days later, the Eighth Army smashed through the German lines and Rommel escaped to Tunisia.

The Germans and their Italian allies now controlled only a narrow strip along the Mediterranean coast between Tunisia and Egypt. On November 8, 1942, Operation Torch was launched with American and British forces under command of General Dwight Eisenhower. The invasion of North Africa was made up of three separate task forces. The first, mostly of British troops, took Algeria with little difficulty. The second and the third ran into tough resistance, but by mid-November the Allies had taken Oran and Morocco.

By the beginning of 1943, the Eighth Army took Tripoli. Rommel made his last stand at the Mareth Line. Montgomery attacked from the front and on both flanks. Against bitter resistance, the British pushed through the final two hundred miles and took Tunis on May 7. Six days later, the Axis powers surrendered in Tunisia.

As Hesse spoke, Alex's mind wandered. While all this was going on, Smith had been stranded in Palestine. This was the period when he'd first visited Mar Saba in the Judean desert, and done his doctorate in Jerusalem.

Hesse said, "The British captured a quarter of a million soldiers. I was among them, a young captain." Alex's focus returned to the man before him.

Uninjured but thoroughly sick of fighting, Hesse spent the rest of the war as a British prisoner at a camp for officers at Grizedale Hall in Lancashire, grateful not to have shared the fate of his comrades defeated on the Russian front. The British and Americans at least abided by the Geneva Conventions. His stay at Grizedale Hall, once a stately country home, had not been unpleasant. The camp famously prompted one British politician of the day to grumble that it would have been cheaper and more punitive to hold German prisoners at the Ritz in London.

After the war, Hesse was released and shipped to Germany. A native of Dresden, he returned to find his family long dead and the city crippled by Allied bombing. He eventually made his way back to North Africa during the 1950s and had lived in Cairo ever since.

Alex was enthralled by the tale but must have begun to look impatient because Hesse at that moment seemed to snap out of his reverie. The leather couch complained as he shifted his weight.

Alex prompted, "So the professor was interested in your war service in the Middle East?"

"Indeed. But more specifically, it was the days just ahead of the fall of Tunis that appeared to be of interest to him. He said he found my name in the records of Grizedale Hall, or Camp 1, as it was known at the time, in the course of his research."

Alex frowned. The Morton Smith he knew was a biblical scholar, a world expert on ancient history and theology, not World War II. What on earth had his friend been up to?

"What exactly was it about that time that interested him?"

"He was going to explain more to me on arrival. I was expecting him any day. In fact, I thought it might be him when you knocked. We had spoken on the telephone several times, but most of our correspondence was by letter. The professor was very old-fashioned in that way. No emails.

"As you may have guessed, I run an antiques and war memorabilia business," he said, gesturing to the walls of his study. "Most of my transactions are done online. I have a website, Gunther Collectibles and Militaria. I chose not to use the name Hesse for my business. Too much like that of a certain Nazi," he chuckled mirthlessly.

"But I digress. In the last few days of the war in North Africa, Abwehr headquarters in Tunis was a hive of activity. The same can be said of the German High Command and the SS offices. A frantic effort was underway to destroy valuable intelligence archives, documents, and other materials that might fall into Allied hands. My enduring memory is of the smell of burning paper. Some days the air was so thick with smoke you might have thought the city had already fallen.

"Around that time, a single planeload of material deemed too valuable to be destroyed was boxed up in metal crates to be flown back to Germany. Among the haul, was a considerable amount of Nazi war loot, gold and the like, silver bars, priceless antiques, that sort of thing. The plane, a converted Junkers long-range bomber, crashed in a sandstorm sometime after takeoff.

"I had the distinct impression that the professor believed he knew where it went down."

49

Alex was finding it hard to sit still. Hesse had piqued his curiosity and his mind was racing. The Smith he knew inhabited the obscure, bookish world of New Testament scholarship. He was an academic, an expert in early Christian literature, not Indiana Jones.

"So, it was the Nazi treasure the professor was interested in?"

"That is what I assumed at first. Many expeditions have been mounted since the end of the war, but ultimately they have all failed to find any trace of the wreckage," Hesse said.

"The flight was actually a scheme dreamed up by the SS. At the Abwehr, we had very little to do with it. But we were aware of the plan. They offered a small amount of space to rescue any documents we deemed vital to the security of the Reich. Naturally, given the level of distrust between the two intelligence services, we were reluctant to place anything of true value in the hands of our Nazi colleagues."

Hesse explained that as a relatively junior officer, he was assigned the task of boxing up a few old files and loading them into a snub-nosed Kubelwagen for delivery to the SS. To Alex's annoyance, he went into some detail describing the vehicle, Germany's equivalent of the American Jeep, a simplified Volkswagen Beetle with square lines and a rear-mounted engine. He could see that when it came to military hardware this man was a true enthusiast.

"Kubel means bathtub in German, by the way. Given this name because it looked very much like a bathtub with wheels, but, again, I digress."

As instructed, Hesse drove the tub to a desert airstrip just outside Tunis, where the Ju-88 was parked up inside a steel hangar. The aircraft's distinctive bulbous nose protruded from the sliding doors, its armored-glass bubble-like cockpit draped with a tarpaulin to keep out the sun.

The twin-engined aircraft was painted in desert camouflage, Luftwaffe markings erased. Hesse waited several hours before the Abwehr boxes were ready to be loaded into the hold. More than a dozen guards, armed to the teeth, milled around the hangar, and during the course of the afternoon several SS staff cars, black steel pennants with silver runes unmoving in the dry breeze, arrived with metal crates. The soldiers stacked them near the plane's bomb bay.

During that wait, Hesse smoked and chatted with the guards and drivers. He gleaned sufficient information to form a rough idea of the contents of at least some of the chests. During loading, one chest actually broke open, its lid coming loose to reveal what appeared to be a gold-encrusted screen from a church or synagogue. As it turned out, there was not enough room for all of the crates in the hold of the bomber. The pilot, an agitated regular air force man, insisted on weighing each one before loading. Not surprisingly, the first cargo to be bumped from the flight was Hesse's.

Since the Abwehr chests contained little of real value, he did not argue. Instead, he took a seat in the shadows and observed the process. Tempers flared when it turned out at least half a dozen of the SS boxes looked as if they would also have to be left behind. After being informed politely by the Luftwaffe pilot that he could "go fuck himself," the safety margins of the aircraft would not be exceeded, the irate corporal in charge sped off in his staff car to report the insolence to his masters.

About an hour later, another vehicle, a black Mercedes saloon, ground to a halt outside the hangar. The three men who emerged from the passenger doors were dressed in civilian clothes. They did not remonstrate with the pilot as Hesse expected but instead proceeded to prioritize the cargo, unloading some of the boxes already in the hold and peering through their contents before deciding which would remain on the flight.

The entire process of loading and unloading took hours, during which Hesse sat on one of his crates. The civilians appeared to be interested in ensuring that three of the smaller boxes were safely on board. Hesse could tell they were not military men. They sounded more like academics. To his astonishment, one spoke English. Hesse had no idea whether the accent was British or American, and he didn't understand what was said. From the German parts of their mumbled conversation that drifted across the hangar, he learned the boxes contained books, rare books, and manuscripts.

■ ■ ■

"It was this part of my story that the professor seemed to be captivated by," said Hesse.

Alex's watch showed 11:00 p.m., and he hoped Bairstow had not given up waiting at the restaurant. But he was too engrossed by the former German spy's story to end the conversation just yet.

"At the time, I had no idea what these books were, except that someone obviously believed they were extremely valuable. The fall of Tunis was a time of great upheaval, a real turning point in the war. Up until then, I think Hitler and many of the top Nazis really believed Germany would prevail, win the war. After the disasters at El-Alemain and then Tunis, the tide turned, both literally and psychologically."

Alex was on the edge of his seat, willing Hesse to continue. But he seemed to have lost the thread of his thoughts and fell silent. Although he was staring at the cabinets of medals, helmets, and other military paraphernalia lining the walls, Alex could see his eyes were focused beyond the walls of the small study.

"You said at the time you had no idea what the books were. Did you find out later?" Alex prompted.

There was urgency in his voice, and he forced himself to remain calm. *Things are beginning to fall into place.* But large pieces were still missing. Hesse did not continue immediately. More than a minute passed, the silence between them filling with the ticking of a grandfather clock in the living room next door.

Finally, his host picked up the story again.

"North Africa at the beginning of 1943 was swirling with rumors, and, needless to say, in the intelligence community we heard them all. To be honest, to this day, I have no idea what books were in those crates.

"But there was one story in particular which sticks in my mind. It involved a specially formed unit within the Sicherheitsdienst, or SD, the primary intelligence service of the SS and the Nazi Party. This unit consisted of civilians and officers. The civilians were mostly academics, archaeologists, and linguists."

Hesse fixed Alex with an intent gaze.

"My knowledge here is hazy at best and, as I said before, I was relatively junior, but the rumor was that this special antiquities unit had close connections with Section D3, you might know it as the Jewish Desk, of the Abteilung Deutschland in Berlin, the German Foreign Office."

Connections were forming in Alex's mind. He thanked his host and stood to leave. Hesse led him out into the hall and opened the front door.

As he said good night to the old man, a thought struck him. He and Hesse had not been the only people Smith planned to see in Cairo. He paused in the hallway, trying to recall the wording of the letter from his friend.

The German looked at him inquiringly.

Then it came to him. *There is a gentleman I want to visit, one of the country's finest modern-day explorers. Many would say the finest.*

"One more thing, Mr. Hesse. Who would you say is Egypt's finest modern-day explorer? Living, I mean."

If the question seemed an odd one, Alex's host did not show it. His reply was immediate and unequivocal.

"No contest there. There are only a handful, really, and one stands head and shoulders above the rest, a fellow by the name of Ahmed El-Mestekawi. A former colonel in the Egyptian Army, he makes a living as a desert guide. Calls his outfit Zarzora Tours, if memory serves me correctly."

Alex said, "Is there any reason you can think of why the professor might have planned to visit him while in Cairo? In his letter he mentioned that he hoped to visit someone he described as Egypt's greatest modern-day explorer."

Hesse thought for a moment, frowning in concentration. Then, gesturing for Alex to wait, he turned and disappeared into his study, reappearing after less than a minute, carrying a book.

"To be honest, I can't think of any. If he was looking for the downed plane, he'd be interested in Tunisia. That's separated from Egypt's Western Desert by a rather large expanse of barren sand and rock known as Libya. I've got the colonel's latest book here, first published in English last year."

Alex took the paperback tome. It was mundanely titled *The Ancient Rock Art of Al-Gilf Al-Kebir*. He turned it over, read the back cover, and then flicked through the pages. An account of an expedition in 2002, during which El-Mestekawi stumbled on a cave while seeking shelter from a vicious sandstorm. It contained prehistoric rock paintings, among the best preserved found in the region. The paintings helped prove that the now-barren expanse of desert once teemed with forests and wildlife.

The colonel was a good writer and the account read easily, the text peppered with beautiful hand-drawn sketches of rocky outcrops and desert plants. Occasionally, locations were recorded with geographic coordinates.

He turned to the index and found a list of them.

Something was pricking his subconscious as he stared at the strings of numbers representing longitude and latitude. After a few seconds, it hit him. He had literally stopped breathing. He looked up to see if Hesse noticed his reaction, but the old man seemed oblivious.

Alex took a deep breath and closed the book, handing it back to his host.

"Thank you so much for your time. Given the late hour, you've been most gracious."

"Not at all. Please feel free to stop by again."

He assured the German that he most certainly would.

On the street, he pulled out his phone. He flipped it open and scrolled through the dialed numbers.

He was sure about what he'd seen, but he needed to check.

50

Forty minutes after Alex left the Heliopolis mansion, two figures turned on to Sharia Cleopatra from the direction of the presidential palace. The tallest of the pair wore a threadbare brown business suit and grubby skullcap. His younger partner sported more youthful attire: Levis and an imitation-leather jacket. There were no streetlights and they picked their way up the road through darkness, skirting potholes and an open sewer. The younger man occasionally flicked on a flashlight to illuminate the numbers on the gate posts.

They stopped outside No. 23. No lights burned in the windows of the old house. The man with the flashlight leaned into his companion. Speaking in a whisper, he said, "Are you sure this is wise, Brother?"

The reply was gruff. "We must know what the journalist plans to do. Think of it as insurance."

Earlier in the night, Alex had presumed that he and Bairstow were not followed to the restaurant. In a manner of speaking, he was right. The Islamic Army had not put a tail on them. There was no need. A taxi driver and committed member of the Muslim Brotherhood loitered outside Bairstow's Gezira apartment. He put in a call from his cell phone soon after dropping them off at the Palmyra. Another operative later tailed Alex the short distance to Hesse's home and then left so as not to attract attention.

The men now outside No. 23 waited a further twenty minutes, watching for movement within. There was none. Silently, they opened the gate and moved through the darkened garden to the back of the residence. With a steel blade, the younger man forced a lock on the doors to the verandah. Inside, they removed their shoes and climbed the stairs in stockinged feet.

The old German was asleep in the bedroom. He woke with a start when the sheet was pulled roughly from his body. He cried out in surprise, curling up to cover his nakedness. But if his assailants had expected to see fear in his pale-blue eyes, they were disappointed.

It took just over an hour to beat the information out of Hesse. He was a surprisingly tough nut to crack. When the job was done, there was a considerable amount of blood on the wall next to the bed and on the sheets and pillows. The men went downstairs and rifled through drawers in the study and living room, ensuring that the scene looked like a burglary.

It was still dark when they left through the front door.

Once they reached the end of the street, the taller fellow took a cell phone from his suit jacket and keyed in a number. Across town, the call was answered in the small motorcycle workshop off Shari Al-Azhar.

He kept it brief. "As-salaam Alaikum, Hatim." Peace be unto you.

"Wa 'Alaykum As-Salam," and on you be peace, came the reply.

"We have finished with the German. He was most helpful. Prepare the girl for a journey."

51

Wednesday, 15 July 2009

When Alex returned to the Palmyra it was after midnight, but the place was still packed. Cairenes habitually didn't start dinner until after 9:00 p.m., and restaurants were usually still open and crowded in the early hours of the morning.

Bairstow appeared not to have moved, the only evidence of activity a large mound of cigarette buts in the ashtray at his elbow and a collection of empty Stella beer bottles. Alex related to his friend his conversation with the retired German intelligence officer: the professor's interest in the fall of Tunis, the crashed Luftwaffe long-range bomber flown by a disgruntled pilot, the Nazi loot and the collection of ancient books and manuscripts it carried.

As he'd sat listening to Hesse, it dawned on Alex that several pieces of the puzzle about Smith's discovery of the Secret Gospel of Mark may have just fallen into place.

"I have a theory."

"I'm all ears." Bairstow was slightly drunk.

"Do you remember what Father Julian said about the manuscript? Since Smith photographed it, no other scholar has been able to subject it to a careful examination."

Bairstow nodded and took another gulp from the bottle he was nursing.

Alex continued.

"I can appreciate what Father Julian said about the difficulty other scholars would have experienced gaining access to Clement's letter at Mar Saba. After all, it is an isolated monastery and the monks don't just let anyone in, right? But this is what troubles me: Smith had contacts there. He knew he had not properly examined the pages themselves under a magnifying glass or a microscope, only photographed them. So why would he spend the next twelve years of his life verifying the text without taking the most important step?"

Bairstow raised a hand, signaling for a waiter.

"Beer?" The question was rhetorical. Alex waited until he had a bottle in his hand before continuing.

"After our chat with the librarian up at St. Catherine's, I thought the reason he never went back was because he knew he faked it, the whole thing was a hoax. But what if he never went back because he knew damn well the book wasn't there?"

Bairstow signaled for Alex to stop.

"Hang on a minute, old man, Father Julian said there was never any doubt the book of St. Ignatious's writings existed, or that the letter attributed to Clement of Alexandria was penned into the back of it."

"I'm not saying that it never existed. I'm just saying perhaps it did not remain in the library at Mar Saba."

"You think Smith took it?"

"In a manner of speaking."

"Don't be cryptic, Alex. It's too late and I've had a lot to drink."

"Ok, I'm saying what if Smith took the book and gave it to the Nazis?"

Bairstow spat beer down the front of his shirt, drawing stares from the other diners. He peered at his friend, looking for a sign he was joking, but found none.

"Okay, now I really think I'm losing you. How strong is this stuff?" He gave the label on the bottle and exaggerated glance. "Listen to yourself, you're sounding like a nutter. We are talking 1958. For fuck's sake, the war was thirteen years ago. This is post-Nuremberg we are talking about. The Nazis were either all hanged, in jail or living in South America."

"But what if we have the whole timeframe wrong here, Aubrey? What if Smith didn't actually discover the manuscript at Mar Saba in 1958, but seventeen years earlier, in 1941. Remember, he spent most of the war in Palestine. He got stuck there by the closure of the Mediterranean. He always was quite open about the fact it wasn't his first time at Mar Saba.

Bairstow looked skeptical, but held his tongue. He motioned for Alex to continue.

Alex shook his head.

"There's somewhere we need to go first."

52

The curb outside the restaurant was crowded with taxis and saloon cars. Cabbies and the chauffeurs of wealthy Cairenes squatted or sat on low stools smoking cigarettes. Others sipped hot tea from a clutter of nearby street stalls, playing backgammon and gossiping as they waited for the patrons of the Palmyra to call it quits and drift off to their beds around the city.

When the two men emerged into the darkened street from the entrance of the restaurant, they were swamped with offers of service. Bairstow stepped toward the throng and was about start negotiating a fare when Alex took his arm at the elbow and pulled him back. A mutter of disappointment rippled through the all-male crowd. He took out his cell phone and punched in a number. After a brief conversation in Arabic, he ended the call and dialed another number, waiting for a time before hanging up.

Bairstow raised an inquiring eyebrow.

"Emad will be here in a few minutes."

Alex paused before continuing with the explanation. "Look, if someone is monitoring our movements, I don't think we can be too careful. There are lots of ways to be followed."

The young English diplomat did not argue.

"So where are we going?"

"To see an old friend."

Due to the late hour, the journey took less than twenty minutes. They pulled up outside the walls of the old Roman fort at 2:00 a.m. A settlement existed here as early as the sixth century BC. The Romans built their fortress later. Known today as "Babylon" by the locals, it formed the foundation for the Coptic quarter and gave it its distinctive character. After the spread of Christianity in Egypt, the area of about one square mile became a Christian stronghold, home to some twenty churches and the world's oldest surviving Christian community. Now, many centuries later, it sat at the heart of a Muslim nation. Only five of the original churches remained, but the enclave was a time warp that also preserved the country's earliest mosque and its oldest synagogue.

They left Emad parked down a side street and followed the age-worn wall to one of the quarter's several gates. Two black-clad policemen stood guard. Wearing Kevlar vests and armed with AK-47s, they sat behind movable, welded-steel barriers. An aging patrol car was parked nearby. Alex could just distinguish the forms of two more men slumbering in the front seats, caps pulled down low over their eyes. The officers greeted the nocturnal visitors gruffly. The younger of the two checked their identification papers and recorded their names in a tattered ledger before waving them through.

Street levels inside the ancient quarter were considerably lower than the modern level outside, and it felt to Alex like they were descending into a darkened pit. In the maze of narrow, cobbled streets there was little light. The moon's glow bled into the narrow canyons formed by the old buildings, casting viscous shadows like pools of blood. No dogs barked, and there were none of the communal sounds that a visitor might expect to find in a vast Middle Eastern metropolis. The hush was eerie, and their shoes echoed loudly off the stone walls as they picked their way toward St. Sergius.

Alex slowed his pace. He was reminded of his experience at the monastery the night before. His head still ached from the blow, and a lump the size of a pigeon's egg sat at the base of his skull. As old as they were, the surroundings here reminded him that most of the truly ancient churches in Egypt were the ones found in the isolated monasteries of the Eastern Desert. He knew Father Boutros would be awake, even though the call he put through from outside the Heliopolis restaurant went unanswered. The man only slept a few hours each night, usually between about 3:00 a.m. and dawn. He always maintained that the early hours of the morning were his most productive when it came to prayer and study of the ancient texts of his faith.

Alex's conversation with Gunther Hesse played on his mind: the rumor about a special SD antiquities unit with connections to the Jewish Desk of the German Foreign Office. The video message from the Islamic Army, with its references to warming ties between Israel and the Vatican, must fit with it somehow. He needed to know more about that wartime period in the Vatican and felt sure his friend the priest would be able to point him in the right direction.

A light burned in the north-facing upstairs window of a squat apartment block opposite the old basilica. They found the entrance off a cramped alleyway running along the south side of the church. Alex was shown the wooden door by Father Boutros early on in their friendship and told it was never locked. The stairwell was musty and narrow, requiring that the pair climb it single file, guided by the light a bulb on the landing above.

Standing outside Emil's door, Alex knocked softly and listened. There was no sound from within, and he waited about a minute before knocking again, this time a little more loudly. Having seen from the street that the light was on in his rooms, he felt sure the old priest was here.

A third knock elicited a rattling of locks from farther down the landing. A door opened, and a bearded and bespectacled face squinted out at them.

"Hello, can I help you?"

"Sorry to disturb you. I'm a friend of Father Emil Boutros."

"Ah, indeed. I think he's in his office, in the church. Do you know where that is?"

"I do. Thank you. Many apologies again for disturbing you at this hour."

They made to leave.

"It is no problem. None of us sleep much around here. Emil seems to be having a busy night."

Alex was surprised. "He has visitors?" he said, turning back to face the priest.

"Several, I think. Foreigners. But that was some hours ago."

They made their way back down the alley and crossed to the entrance of the ancient church. A flight of steps took them below street level to the heavy exterior doors, which opened onto the south aisle of the basilica. The interior of St. Sergius was several degrees cooler than the warm night outside and almost completely devoid of light. Four large candles burned on the high altar some distance to their right, creating a small circle of light that only served to make the rest of the nave seem darker.

A sliver of light spilled from the partially open door of Father Boutros's office next to a deep niche known as the Chapel of St. Michael, about twenty-five meters across the nave. They picked their way between the rows of wooden pews, past the tall stone pulpit, and through the wooden iconostasis screens, to the north aisle.

Alex cleared his throat and knocked lightly on the door.

"Emil, it's Alex."

No response.

"Father Boutros?"

Bairstow pushed the door of the vestibule wider. Ancient hinges complained noisily. The two men took in the small, windowless space. A half-empty pitcher of water sat on a side table next to the open-fronted wardrobe, in which ornate priestly vestments hung. Schools of fish swam lazily across the screensaver on Father Boutros's computer atop the desk. Otherwise, the room was empty.

Alex looked back to the darkened church, scanning the space. All quiet. Nothing moved. Stepping into the study, something crunched beneath his shoes. A smashed glass lay on the floor.

He crouched to examine the mess.

Bairstow was the first to speak. "I don't like this at all. It gives me the creeps."

Alex breathed heavily. "You and me both." Something on the ground had caught his attention. His breath caught.

"Aubrey, take a look at this."

Flecks of a dark, sticky substance were clearly visible on the worn flagstones.

Bairstow moaned. "Oh God, is that what I think it is?"

53

Large spots of blood led from the vestry into the nave. Panic constricted his throat as he called out his friend's name.

"Emil, are you in here?"

Silence.

"Father Boutros?" Bairstow joined him. Their voices boomed through the cavernous interior of the basilica.

It was a vast space, impossible to search properly in the darkness. They needed light, but Alex had no idea where the switch box was. In an old building like this, a modern-day electrician could have installed it in any of a hundred places. He hurried over to the high altar and pulled two of the large candles from their brass stems.

He handed one to Bairstow, and they began a closer examination of the flagstones. The blood trail led toward the center of the church and petered out. Just looking at the red-brown splashes seeping into the cracks between the dark stone filled him with fear for the priest. Was it finally time to bring in the authorities? He thought of the two policemen at the gate, asleep in their patrol car. *There isn't time, mate. Sadie's life is in your hands.*

Although there was no evidence of it, he was sure that whatever happened to Emil must be connected, somehow, to his own quest for the manuscript and the strange events in recent days. *Emil seems to be having a busy night,* the priest's neighbor said. He'd also said there were visitors, foreigners who left some time ago.

A cold sensation tingled down his spine. He wished he'd probed the neighbor further. His mind flashed back to the library at the American University the day he'd received the letter. The fellow who stole his bag was also a foreigner, unlike the man in the galabaya that accosted him at the monastery. Was it stretching credulity to make a link?

Probably.

His thoughts were interrupted by a sudden crashing sound from the center of the nave, followed by a moan.

He spun to face the commotion.

"Aubrey?"

Silence. His whole body tensed.

"Aubrey, you all right?"

The question was greeted by a howl from the darkness.

"Jesus Christ! Who put these fucking things here?"

Alex could tell from the tone, and inappropriate choice of words given their surroundings, that Aubrey was more frightened than hurt.

"You gave me a hell of a fright, mate. Where are you?" Alex moved toward the sound of his friend's voice.

"Down here. I can see your candle. I've dropped mine somewhere."

Bairstow was lying at the bottom of a narrow, stone staircase. It descended into the floor of the sanctuary about five meters from the vestry, in front and slightly to the left of the high alter. Alex crouched at the top to retrieve the dropped candle and immediately saw the blood trail. Passing the area earlier, he'd failed to notice the steps in the darkness.

He'd completely forgotten about the crypt, which contained the remains of the original church where tradition had it that the Holy Family sheltered on its flight into Egypt nearly two thousand years ago. It had been a draw card for Christian pilgrims since medieval times. Below the level of the Nile, it was often inaccessible due to flooding.

Alex said, "The blood trail starts again at the top of the stairs. It's smeared, as if he was being dragged."

He relit Bairstow's candle and clambered down to where his friend was brushing himself off. They were standing in about six inches of dirty, greenish water that gave off a rotten stench.

"Nothing broken?"

"Just a bit of a fright..."

An animal-like moan cut Bairstow off abruptly in midsentence, sending a chill through both men.

They faced the noise, feet sloshing in the filthy water.

Alex shot his companion a glance. Bairstow shook his head, confirming he had not made the sound. Directly below the sanctuary of St. Sergius, this space had itself once been the sanctuary of a much smaller and older church. It measured about six meters long by five meters wide, and had a low ceiling supported by two rows of slender pillars, dividing the room into a nave with two aisles.

Alex held his candle higher, casting its unsteady light farther into the crypt. The glow danced off the surface of the water. Within the north, south, and east facing walls, he could just make out the black shapes of narrow horizontal recesses. To his horror, something moved in one of them.

"Aubrey, there's something in the burial niche on the south wall," he hissed.

Bairstow grabbed his arm, fingers gouging painfully.

"Who's there?" Alex heard the fear in his own voice.

Another moan filled the sanctuary, this time distinctly human. He recognized it as the sound of someone in extreme pain, and he waded quickly over to the niche.

Father Emil Boutros was lying on his back in the cleft, as if laid out for burial. Blood and spittle dribbled from the corners of his broken lips and bubbled out his nose. He opened his puckered eyes, and Alex saw recognition and surprise in them as he placed his arm gently underneath the old man's head. His beard and hair were crusted with dried blood and vomit.

"Emil, what's happened to you? We've got to get you to a doctor," Alex croaked.

The old man shook his head weakly, but Alex had already pulled out his cell phone with his free hand and was dialing a number.

Father Boutros's voice was barely a whisper. "No, Alex. If it is my time, I'd prefer to die here than in a hospital. This is a holy place."

Alex examined the glowing screen of his phone. They were surrounded by rock. This far underground, there was no reception.

"You're not going to die, Emil." Hot tears began to flow as he cradled his friend's head. He knew he was wrong. Emil was dying. There was not much time left. With all the commotion in the basilica, someone was bound to eventually call the police in from the gates. They did not have time to explain their presence here to the authorities.

He whispered, "Who did this to you?"

No response, just gurgling as the old man struggled for air. Alex kept talking softly. Doing his best to keep his emotions in check, he told Father Boutros about the fire in his apartment, Sadie's disappearance, and the video message from the Islamic Army, with its references to the warming ties between Israel and the Vatican.

"Who did this to you, Emil? Was it them, the Islamic Army?"

The priest shook his head. His lips trembled as they moved haltingly. Blood continued to bubble from his nose. Alex leaned closer. The words were barely discernible.

"They wanted to know what I'd told you…"

Father Boutros's words trailed off. Alex thought he heard "crates," or something like it, and "California." It made no sense. Silence descended for several long seconds, broken only by the priest's labored breathing.

His eyes cleared fleetingly. Air hissed from his throat.

"Call Father Moretti."

The priest's body stiffened and then went limp. His friend was dead.

54

Bairstow gripped Alex's shoulder as he leaned abruptly forward and blew out both their candles.

"What the…"

"Shhhh!"

Muffled police sirens and the screech of tires drifted down the stairs into the crypt. Somebody shouted in Arabic, barking orders. Doors slammed and feet thudded through the nave of the church.

"Let's just hope they don't know about this place. The last thing we need is to explain what we're doing here with a murdered Coptic priest."

Bairstow whispered his agreement. "Even with my diplomatic status, it would take days to sort out."

In the pitch darkness, Alex gently laid Father Boutros's head on the cold stone, brushing his fingers across the old man's eyelids to close them. Indicating for Bairstow to wait, he made his way through the flooded room to the stairs that led up to the sanctuary.

At the top, he peered carefully over the lip.

Flashlight beams danced off the frescoed walls. At least three officers went through the motions of searching the nave. A minute or so later, a fourth police-man emerged from the vestibule, having satisfied himself it was empty. He was followed from the small room by Father Boutros's elderly neighbor.

They crossed to the south aisle and exited through the large doors leading onto the street.

A few minutes later, one of the officers returned and made himself comfortable on a seat inside the door. The chair creaked as he stretched out, crossed his ankles, and pulled his cap low. A pump-action shotgun rested on his lap.

Alex's heart sank. He quietly returned to the crypt.

"They've put a bloody guard on the place," he reported.

"Shit! We need to get out of here. It won't be long before they bring in reinforcements to look for Father Boutros."

"With any luck, they'll wait until morning for that."

Alex thought for a moment, running a mental picture of the interior of the church through his mind. He'd visited on several occasions in the past and had seen at least two other doors, one at the west end of the nave and the other off the north aisle, about twenty meters from where the guard was seated.

He said, "I reckon it should be possible to slip out the door off the north aisle without being spotted."

"If it's not locked." Bairstow sounded doubtful, but they were running out of time and options.

"There's something I've got to do first, though. Emil said something before he died. He said to call Father Moretti. I've no idea who that is, or how to reach him, but the only place to find out is in Emil's office."

Bairstow groaned. "Are you crazy?"

"Quite possibly."

They climbed the stairs and paused at the top while Alex checked on the status of the police guard. They were in luck. His head lolled forward on his chest.

"Looks like he's dozing, let's give him a few minutes."

They sat on the stairs just below the level of the floor. Within a quarter of an hour snoring was clearly audible.

The few seconds it took to cross the five meters of exposed ground between the entrance to the crypt and the vestibule felt like an eternity. The squelch of wet shoes sounded unnaturally loud. Once inside the office, Alex quietly pushed the door to without closing it, fearing the click of the lock would wake the guard. They stood still for a full minute, listening. The policeman's snores were long and even.

The glow of the computer monitor was enough to allow him to search the desk. Bairstow used his cigarette lighter to examine the drawers of the bureau to the left of the door, where Father Boutros stored his priestly robes and a selection of ornately carved crooks.

After five minutes of searching the computer's hard drive, it was clear to Alex that his friend kept his contacts elsewhere. He was on the verge of quitting when Bairstow whistled softly.

"Bingo!"

"Got it?"

"Yep, let's get out of here."

In the gloom, Alex could see he held an address book in his hand.

A sound from outside the office caught their attention. Footsteps crossed the nave, coming closer. It was only then that Alex noticed the absence of snoring. He looked around frantically. Bairstow, still to the left of the door, raised a hand to his lips and flattened himself against the wall. He extinguished the lighter and the room was once again lit only by the bluish glow of the simulated aquarium on Father Boutros's screensaver.

Alex stood rooted to the spot. His heart hammered wildly, making a loud thumping noise in his ears as the door slowly opened.

Colored fish swam slowly across the computer screen.

"Stop what you are doing." The policeman was speaking in Arabic.

He leveled the shotgun at Alex with one hand and used the other to play the beam of his flashlight over the scene. Alex slowly raised his hands in the universal gesture of surrender.

There was a flurry of movement behind the door.

The policeman opened his mouth and closed it again, an expression that reminded Alex of a cartoon goldfish. His eyes widened in shock as Bairstow brought the heavy wooden crook down on the back of his skull with a sickening crack.

The policeman crumpled to the floor.

"Go!" Alex yelled. They exited the vestry and sprinted down the northern aisle of the basilica.

"That diplomatic immunity is sure going to come in handy now." Bairstow was breathing heavily.

Once on the street, they took a different route out of the Coptic quarter, scaling the old Roman wall where it abutted an office block and was low enough to clamber over without too much difficulty.

Within ten minutes, they were seated in the back of Emad's taxi, speeding back to the apartment on Gezira.

55

"This is not something I would normally discuss with a stranger, let alone a journalist…"

The frailty of the man's American-accented voice was exaggerated by the twelve thousand kilometers separating Egypt and South America. Alex struggled to make out Father Giulio Moretti's words over the hiss and crackle on the line. He fumbled with the tiny volume control on the side of the cell phone and returned it to his ear.

"Anyway, you say you know Emil, and hell, if Emil gave you this number, well, that's good enough for me."

It was nearly 3:30 a.m. when Alex put through the call from the backseat of Emad's taxi as they hurtled toward the apartment. The number he dialed was in Buenos Aires. Cairo was four hours ahead of the Argentine capital, and it was nearing 12:30 a.m. local time when Father Moretti picked up the phone. Alex quickly resolved that now was not the time to inform him of Emil Boutros's brutal murder.

After brief introductions, he explained what he discovered about the Nazis' collecting books and ancient manuscripts, and his own quest to find out what happened to one in particular, a letter from Clement of Alexandria containing fragments of a secret Gospel that challenged the accepted accounts of Jesus's life, traditional sexual mores, and the authority of the Church. As he related the story, he realized just how fantastic it all sounded. He half expected Father

Moretti to burst out laughing, or simply hang up, but there was only a thought-ful silence. When the old man's voice came back on the line, a note of relief was detectable, as if he had been waiting to get something off his chest for a long time. Alex took a spiral bound notebook from the side pocket of his cargo pants and began to scribble.

Moretti worked on the Germany Desk at the Secretariat of State, the Vatican's foreign ministry, for much of the war. There was no need to ask him how he now came to live in South America. The stories of priests working the so-called "Rat Lines" in 1945, helping prominent Nazi war criminals escape Germany and the occupied countries, as the Allies closed in on Berlin, were well known. The es-cape routes mostly ended in South America, but other destinations included the United States, Canada, and the Middle East.

Often in return for money or treasure looted from wealthy Jewish families, priests provided papers, including identity documents issued by the Vatican refu-gee organization, the Commissione Pontificia d'Assistenza. Those papers were not in themselves enough to travel internationally, but they were the first step in a paper trail that eventually qualified the holder to obtain a displaced person's passport from the International Committee of the Red Cross.

■ ■ ■

By the time Alex ended the call, things were becoming much clearer. Despite the lack of sleep, he was wide-awake. He reached up and switched on the overhead light, its dull glow enough to illuminate the scrawl-filled notebook in his lap. He flicked back through the pages. Bairstow had listened in on much of the conver-sation. It lasted only twenty minutes, and dawn was still several hours away as Alex filled him in on the rest.

One government, other than neutral Switzerland, had maintained diplo-matic relations with both the Allies and Nazi Germany throughout the war—the Vatican. It had diplomatic envoys and local priests in all the countries, cities, and towns where the Jews were rounded up before being sent to concentration camps. Those representatives had contacts and influence that ran deep within the fabric of society, which could have made Hitler's murderous plans much more difficult, perhaps even impossible, if they'd chosen to intercede. Yet history bore witness to the fact that Pope Pius XII did not denounce the Nazis, nor did he protest Hitler's Final Solution for the Jews as it unfolded, despite his being one of the first leaders outside German-controlled Europe to become aware of its staggering scale.

On October 16, 1943, more than twelve hundred Jews were arrested by German soldiers in the Jewish district of Rome, at the foot of the Vatican Hill, a stone's throw from the Pope's offices. Within a week, nearly all were transported to Auschwitz and gassed. It was a fact that Pius XII never used the word Jew in any wartime pronouncement, or the word anti-Semitism.

Since the war ended, critics of the Pope accused him of cowardice and even being a closet Nazi. Yet that was not the case. His contempt for Hitler was amply demonstrated early in his pontificate. In 1939, Pius XII became deeply involved in a plot to overthrow the Fuhrer, serving as the link between a group of anti-Hitler German army officers and London via Britain's envoy to the Vatican.

So why, all of a sudden, had he rolled over and played dead? What happened between 1939 and 1943 to change his mind?

Hitler desperately feared that if Pius XII ordered priests to preach against the extermination of the Jews from pulpits across Germany and occupied Europe, people might rise up against the Third Reich. He was so concerned about keeping the Vatican on his side that he dispatched the second highest-ranking official in his foreign office as his ambassador—Baron Ernst von Weizsacker, a personal friend of Heinrich Himmler, and the first and last SS Officer to have served as German ambassador to the Holy See. According to Moretti, Hitler's envoy managed to convince high-ranking officials in the Secretariat of State that papal condemnation of the Holocaust was not in line with the Vatican's best interests.

"After all, over the past two millennia the Church, by and large, had a monopoly on the persecution of Jewish communities. It didn't take much persuading," said Alex, the sarcasm audible in his voice.

"To a certain extent, Baron von Weizsacker was preaching to the converted. The Pope had already seen the writing on the wall. The exodus of German and European Jews to Palestine was well underway in the 1930s. He became convinced that condemnation of the Holocaust would only hasten things, create a greater international appetite for a Jewish state in Palestine and, consequently, Jewish control over Christendom's holiest sites. Better to remain silent and let the Nazis get on with it."

Bairstow was astounded. "Could they really have been that venal?"

Alex said, "You have to remember, Aubrey, we are talking about the Vatican, here. That venerable institution, riddled as it is with secret societies and factions, has been involved in plots and intrigues for nearly two thousand years. Remember the Crusades. When it comes to politics, they play the game harder and better than anyone. You've got to admit, history shows religious fervor, and battles over doctrine have seen priests and cardinals, the princes of the Holy Roman Church, stoop to shedding blood with some regularity."

Bairstow seemed unconvinced. "But why the Nazi archive, why was the SD unit tasked with tracking down ancient manuscripts if the Pope was already persuaded?"

"Insurance. A little incentive, in case Pius XII got cold feet. We're talking about the greatest mass murder in history, after all."

"What do you mean, insurance?"

"Moretti described it as Hitler's insurance policy, another layer of the complex diplomatic game he was playing with the Vatican. The Nazis amassed an archive of ancient documents, many of them early Gnostic writings, that threatened the very foundation of the Catholic Church, and which for centuries the Church had sought to destroy."

"Jesus!" Bairstow whispered.

"Yeah, literally."

They sat for several minutes without talking. Alex stared out the window. They were close to the river, and the taxi was soon on the 6 October Bridge and descending onto the island.

Bairstow broke the silence. "What happened to this fellow Weizsacker? I mean, did he make it to South America, or wherever?"

"No, thankfully. From what Moretti told me, after the liberation of Rome in June 1944, he used his diplomatic immunity and holed up in the Campo Santo hospice on the south side of St. Peter's, avoiding the first round of Nazi war crimes trials at Nuremberg. But he was eventually arrested in 1947 and put in the dock. He served just three years before being released in a general amnesty. He died of a stroke a year later, in 1951, taking whatever he knew of all this to the grave."

56

Back at the apartment, Bairstow made a pot of strong Arabic coffee and poured two cups of the dark brew.

Alex lit a cigarette and threw the pack to his friend. Inhaling deeply, he flopped onto the couch and stared thoughtfully out at the dark swath of the Nile. His encounter with the German, Gunther Hesse, was playing on his mind.

"Do you remember those strings of numbers Smith wrote in the corner of the envelope?"

"Yep."

"Remember I tried to dial them, but they weren't phone numbers. I've worked out what they are."

Bairstow cocked an eyebrow.

Alex pulled out his cell phone and scrolled through until he found the numbers again.

"The most common way to locate points on the surface of the Earth is by standard geographic coordinates called latitude and longitude. These coordinates represent distances calculated from the center of the Earth. I think what the professor scribbled on the envelope were coordinates."

Bairstow interjected. "I thought longitude and latitude had degrees, minutes, and seconds north and south of the Equator, or east and west of the meridian line running through Greenwich. The prime meridian, or whatever it's called."

"Exactly. They do." Alex breathed deeply, willing himself to stay calm. If he was right, and it was a big *if*, they could be closer to discovering the location of the manuscript and saving Sadie than he'd ever believed possible. He took a gulp of coffee and explained to Bairstow what had happened as he prepared to leave Hesse's home in Heliopolis the previous evening.

"The plus signs at the start of the strings of digits got me thinking. Especially since Hesse said he suspected that Smith believed he knew where the plane went down. Then I recognized the same sequence in the book by the Egyptian explorer, Ahmed El-Mestekawi."

Alex pulled the crumpled envelope from the pile of papers lying on the coffee table next to Smith's vinyl suitcase. He smoothed it out and stared at the numbers for several minutes. A plus sign followed by eight numbers in the first series, and then another plus and seven digits.

+29132174, +2532360

He took a pen and began to rewrite the first string of numbers, dividing it up with the appropriate symbols for degrees, minutes, and seconds.

He explained what he was doing to Bairstow as he went.

"All lines of latitude are parallel to the Equator. They are sometimes also referred to as parallels. There are 90 degrees of latitude going north from the Equator, and the North Pole is at 90 degrees N. Likewise, there are 90 degrees to the south of the Equator, and the South Pole is at 90 degrees S. When the directional designators are omitted, northern latitudes are given positive values and southern latitudes are given negative values.

"We know from what Hesse said that the plane went down some time after takeoff. It was heading for Germany and so would logically have headed north from Tunis, which is in the northern hemisphere, anyway."

Alex leaned back, allowing Bairstow to see his handiwork: 29°13'21.74"N.

"Now, lines of longitude, called meridians, run perpendicular to lines of latitude, and all pass through both poles. Longitude values indicate the angular distance between the prime meridian, which, as you correctly point out, runs through Greenwich, England, and points east or west of it on the surface of the Earth.

"The Earth is divided equally into 360 degrees of longitude. There are 180 degrees of longitude to the east of the prime meridian. Once again, when the directional designator is omitted, these longitudes are given positive values. There are also 180 degrees of longitude to the west of the prime meridian. When the directional designator is omitted, these longitudes are given negative values.

"Tunis is east of the UK, so let's make this east."

They both stared at what he had written: 29°13'21.74"N, 25°32'3.60E"

Bairstow whistled softly.

"What's the bet that is somewhere in Tunisia, on the route taken by the German plane in 1943?" said Bairstow triumphantly, jabbing the envelope with a forefinger.

"That's where it gets confusing," said Alex. "I'm not sure that it is."

57

Alex powered up his laptop and logged on to the Internet. Within a couple of minutes, he was on the Mapquest site.

He punched in the coordinates deciphered from the two strings of numbers Smith scribbled on the envelope and waited for the search engine to do its work. It took only fifteen seconds for a box to pop up on the screen and the outlines and contours of a map to begin to emerge.

Alex immediately recognized the shape of the North African coast. He waited for place names to appear.

"Just as I thought."

"What?" Bairstow came from the kitchen and sat two fresh glasses of steaming black coffee on the table. He looked over Alex's shoulder.

A red star flashed at the center of the map, marking the coordinates.

"Siwa?"

"Yeah, Siwa. It's in Egypt, an oasis in the Western Desert, near the Libyan border."

"But how could the plane have gone down in Egypt? It would have been at least two thousand kilometers off course. That must have been one hell of a sandstorm, old boy."

Alex thought for a moment, replaying in his mind the story of the plane Hesse told him. He couldn't think of any good reason. Perhaps the professor had not discovered the crash site after all.

"Beats me, but these coordinates represent something the professor regarded as important."

The morning call to prayer at the local mosque across from the Indian ambassador's residence drifted in through the balcony doors. Sunrise bathed the sky in pale orange.

Alex picked up the phone and dialed Hesse's number, written on a pad next to the phone. He let it ring fifteen times before giving up.

"No answer. He must be asleep."

"Can't say I blame him." Bairstow yawned. "I think Hesse knew more than he was letting on. I guess for an old spy, old habits die hard."

Bairstow stretched and yawned a second time. "In a way, it would fit. All this business of Nazis, the Vatican, and ancient documents, I mean. Something has been bothering me since watching that video. Why on earth would a bunch of Muslim terrorists want to get their hands on the writings of an early Christian leader?"

This time it was Alex's turn to be surprised. "I was thinking the same thing," he said. "They used the word inheritance. How could the Secret Gospel or Clement's writings be part of their inheritance?"

Bairstow said, "As I said, in a way it would fit. I think I know the answer."

"I'm all ears."

"I didn't mention this before because I didn't make the connection myself. But it stands to reason that a group supporting Palestinian statehood, like the Muslim Brotherhood, or its offshoot the Islamic Army, would want to influence the Vatican against the modern state of Israel in the same way as the Nazis wanted to sway it against the Jews."

"Go on." More pieces of the puzzle were slotting into place.

"Well, the links between the Nazis and Islamic terrorists are more than ideological. After World War I, the European powers were vying for control over the Middle East's oil fields and trade routes, with France and Britain holding mandates through most of the region. These days, add the United States to the mix, and in many ways little has changed." Bairstow shook his head sadly.

"In the 1930s, the fascist regimes that arose in Italy and Germany decided they wanted in on the action and began courting Arab leaders to revolt against the Brits and the French. Not surprisingly, close collaboration between fascist agents and a range of Muslim leaders ensued. During the 1936–39 Arab Revolt in Palestine, Admiral Wilhelm Canaris, the head of the very same Abwehr our friend Hesse worked for, sent agents and money to support the Palestine uprising against the British, as did Muslim Brotherhood founder Hassan al-Banna."

A prickle of excitement raced down Alex's spine. Bairstow had Alex's full attention.

A key individual in the fascist-Islamist nexus and a go-between for the Nazis and al-Banna was the Grand Mufti of Jerusalem, Haj Amin el-Husseini, himself a senior member of the Brotherhood. Having fled from Palestine to Iraq, the Mufti assisted there in the short-lived 1941 Nazi-financed coup to topple the British administration. But by June of that year British forces reasserted control in Baghdad, and the Mufti was on the run yet again. This time he fled via Tehran and Rome to Berlin, where he received a hero's welcome. He remained in Germany as an honored guest of Hitler.

"The Mufti and the Fuhrer shared a hatred of the Jews, although for very different reasons," said Bairstow. "Throughout the war, the Mufti appeared regularly on German radio broadcasts to the Middle East, preaching a pro-Nazi, anti-Semitic message to the Arab masses back home."

Bairstow wrapped things up with a story that saw the chronology vault into the more recent past.

"Incidentally, in 1951, a close relative of the Mufti named Rahman Abdul Rauf el-Qudwa el-Husseini began study at the University of Cairo. The student decided to conceal his true identity and enlisted under the invented name—Yasser Arafat."

Alex, stunned by what he was hearing, finished the story. "Who went on to found the Palestine Liberation Organization, the PLO. Fucking hell, mate, this is starting to make some sense. Not much, but some."

■ ■ ■

Alex's head buzzed with information overload. He was dizzy from the effects of a night without sleep, as he tried to piece together what he'd learned from Hesse, and now Bairstow.

Could Smith, the man he'd met in Southeast Asia and grown to respect, could that same man possibly have been mixed up with the Nazis, recruited as an academic into a top-secret project to influence the Vatican? It seemed absurd.

Yet the evidence was there.

It would help to explain the medal, the Order of the German Eagle, awarded to foreign civilians for services to the Third Reich. The date engraved on the back certainly fit: 1941, the year Smith first visited Mar Saba. Alex knew such medals were rare and could fetch huge sums from collectors at auction. There would be little reason for Smith to have been carrying it with him unless he planned to trade it with Hesse, perhaps for information.

Had Smith, in the course of his research, discovered the final resting place of a treasure trove of early Christian writings hoarded by the Nazis? Did those ancient documents, long believed by the Catholic Church to have been lost or destroyed, include fragments of the Secret Gospel of Mark?

If it were true, it did nothing to clarify whether the Secret Gospel was a hoax or not. But Alex thought perhaps there was a clue to that riddle in the fact that in 1958, Smith returned to Mar Saba and subsequently announced to the world he'd found the Clementine letter. The photos he produced of it were black and white and could easily have been taken during his earlier visit. With the war over, had he felt that the early Christian material he handed to the Nazis was of such scholarly importance that he had to find a way to make it public?

Smith certainly would not have done that if he forged the manuscript in the first place. Neither, Alex now realized, would he have spent his life engaged in researching the kind of religious rituals he witnessed all those years ago as he crouched in a garbage-strewn alley in Phnom Penh.

But why had Smith worked with the Nazis? Had he been a willing recruit? Nothing the professor ever said to him indicated leanings in that direction.

One thing was clear. If Smith believed the manuscript was on that bomber flight out of Tunis in 1943, then he and Bairstow must find the crash site. Finding the manuscript was their only hope of saving Sadie, and the only clues they had to go on were the coordinates.

58

The angry buzzing of his cell phone woke Alex from deep sleep. He ignored it at first, until the vibrating gadget slowly migrated across the top of the nightstand and hurled itself off the edge, landing with a clatter on the tile floor.

Amazingly, the phone kept ringing.

He was dreaming again, the same disturbing yet frustratingly elusive dream as on the morning they left St. Catherine's. Once again, on awaking he could not recall the details of the dream. But he had the distinct feeling he'd missed something, something important in the DVD made by Sadie's captors.

He reached over and scooped up the cell phone.

"Hello."

"Hi, Alex. Can you talk?"

His head felt stuffed with cotton, and he could barely open his eyes, even in the diffused light that bled through partly drawn curtains. Pressing the phone firmly to his ear, he heard Noora's softly accented voice. Instead of being glad to hear her, his heart sank.

His mind flashed back to their encounter on Mt. Sinai. It seemed a long time ago.

"Noora!" Alex said hoarsely.

"Are you okay, Alex? You sound strange."

He squinted at his watch. Just after 9:00 a.m. He'd been asleep for about three hours.

"Yeah, sure, everything's fine." A lie.

"I just called to say hello. It would be great to see you. Somehow we missed each other at the monastery." She paused, as if sensing something was wrong. "Are you okay?"

Alex did not reply. So much had happened since they last spoke. Sadie was alive, and at the moment he could not think of anything else. He drew a deep breath, mind still on the dream and the feeling that an important clue from the DVD was hovering just beyond his grasp.

The voice on the phone pulled him back to the present. "I'm not interrupting anything, am I, Alex?"

"No, of course not. I'm sorry Noora, I've just woken up. My head is still a bit fuzzy."

Alex liked Noora. She was fun, intelligent, and undeniably sexy. Under other circumstances, he would be actively pursuing the relationship. *I owe this woman some kind of explanation.* He climbed out of bed and padded through to the kitchen, where he set about making a pot of coffee while he talked.

"Look, Noora, a lot has happened since we last saw each other. Stuff I can't go into right now. But I'm finding it hard to take it all in, to think straight."

"Oh."

Noora sounded defensive, hurt. Guilt like a physical weight balled in Alex's chest. *Shit, you idiot.*

"Noora, it's not what you think, seriously. I've just got a lot on my mind. I'm glad you woke me. I've got to go drive to Siwa today. It's just for a couple of days. There is something there I need to check out for a story, but we can talk as soon as I'm back. I promise."

"Sure, okay Alex, I understand."

There was a click and the line went dead. *Damn.*

He was just placing the cell phone down on the bench when he realized what it was about the DVD that tapped his subconscious. Adrenaline surged through his body. He was wide-awake now.

"It's probably nothing," he whispered to himself. *Don't get your hopes up.*

Heart pounding, he poured two cups of coffee and went to wake Bairstow. A long day lay ahead, but first they needed to watch the hostage video again.

59

Alex slid the DVD into the player in the cabinet below Bairstow's large flat-screen television.

He pressed play as Bairstow took a seat on the couch beside him.

The familiar black-and-white graphic appeared on the screen, the circle on which was superimposed the jambiya and pistol above an open Koran, flanked by text in Arabic.

He gripped the arm of the couch, knuckles white, bracing for what was to come.

After a few seconds, the second graphic, with more Arabic text, appeared with the Muslim funeral scene: two men carrying a dead body on a stretcher as relatives, women clad head to toe in long, black robes, wailed an ululation, a high-pitched keening common at Muslim funerals.

On the larger screen, the images were much clearer than the laptop they used to view the recording for the first few times at the monastery. The sound quality was also better, although still poor.

The image on the screen cut to a medium shot. Sadie faced the lens, eyes lowered, hair tied back under a blue headscarf. Alex's hold on the remote tightened.

"Steady, old man, steady." Bairstow placed a hand on his shoulder.

Other than the scarf given to her by her captors, Sadie still wore the same clothing as the last time Alex saw her, on the morning he left to go to the university, a long skirt and loose-fitting white blouse. There were blankets hanging behind her. He assumed they were soundproofing. The muzzles of the AK-47 assault rifles were visible at head height on either side of the screen. To the left side, part of a figure dressed in olive-green battle fatigues could be seen.

Sadie began to speak, delivery wooden.

"I am Sadie Cooper, a citizen of the United Kingdom…"

"There! Did you catch that?" Alex pressed pause. The image of Sadie, mouth open, face wet with tears was frozen on the screen.

"I'm sorry. What am I looking for?"

"Listen carefully."

Alex backed up the image to the start of Sadie's monologue and pressed play. Sadie began speaking again.

"…citizen of the United Kingdom…and I think this is possibly my last chance to speak to you."

Alex let the recording run a little longer this time.

"There! Hear that? That sound in the background."

Despite the poor quality, muffled metallic, clanking noises were clearly audible in the background. The camera panned jerkily to the left. A man, visible from the chest down, stood directly behind Sadie, who was still kneeling.

Alex stopped the DVD, rewound and played it again.

"That sounds a lot like the metalworkers quarter down at Khan el-Khalili."

Bairstow was skeptical. "Don't get your hopes up, Alex. There must be countless places in Cairo, or Egypt for that matter, where you can hear sounds like that."

On his feet now, he ignored the doubt in his friend's voice.

"I was down there just before we drove up to Mt. Sinai. I walked through the metalworkers' quarter on the way to buy clothes. It sounded just like that, I swear."

"Even if you are right, the district covers several city blocks, Alex. It's a rabbit's warren. We'd never find her in there, not without the help of the police, and we can't go to them. You know that. We would be signing her death warrant."

Alex slumped back onto the couch. His morale crumbled. Bairstow was right. It would be hopeless trying to locate Sadie in the old Turkish bazaar, even if they could narrow down the search area to just a few streets.

He was probably mistaken anyway. For a moment, he'd let himself believe they were on to something. He stared at the ceiling, rubbing his face with the palms of his hands.

"You're right, of course."

"Come on, we'd better get cracking. It's a long way to Siwa, and we've got to sign the Land Rover out of the embassy car pool."

Alex nodded but remained where he was. Sullen.

"Up and at 'em, tiger." There was forced jollity in Bairstow's voice. "We can do a drive by, a recce of sorts on the way out of town. Just to see the lay of the land, old boy. It might help put your mind at rest."

60

Rough hands shook Sadie awake. A glimpse of a bearded face, and then the hood was pulled over her head, reducing her world to shadows, vague outlines in light and dark.

The usual sounds of the workshop, the ear-splitting clank of metal striking metal, were absent. Her breathing was the only noise, loud and ragged inside the coarse material. Tugging at her feet, the jangling of keys in the padlock as the chain was removed.

Panic, a tightness in her chest that made breathing even more difficult.

The time has come, they are going to kill me. I must remain calm, think clearly.

Barked commands in Arabic from the hallway. A new voice. Richer, more educated. Sadie's heart beat wildly, her breath came in short gasps.

The chain rattled as it dropped to the floor. Shoes scraped the concrete, retreating, and the door thudded closed again. The click of the lock was followed by the staccato sound of the bolt being slammed home. She was alone again.

Sadie remained still for several long minutes, ears straining. There were voices in the hall, urgent whispering so low it was impossible to make out individual words. Slowly, she drew her knees up to her chin. With a trembling hand, she gently inspected her ankles, wincing. The flesh was puffy and swollen, raw under her fingers, skin rubbed away by the constant chafing of the shackles.

Since making the video, Sadie's faith in eventual rescue had deserted her. She was worried for herself, friends and family, Alex. She was fatigued by the need for constant alertness. She had never felt so utterly alone.

Her anxiety was heightened by the knowledge that her captors were mistaken, and Alex did not have the book they wanted so desperately. The three men had also become less concerned about protecting their identities, no longer always forcing her to wear the hood in their presence. This worried her deeply. It could only mean one thing. They planned to kill her, whether or not they got what they wanted.

After about ten minutes, footsteps approached the door again. The bolt slammed back and she was pulled to her feet. Unused to standing, she staggered and her head swam. It took all her strength to put one foot in front on the other as she was manhandled through the door. She sensed a narrow hallway, the bodies of her captors pressing up against hers as they moved forward. The rank stench of feces filled her nostrils as they passed the lavatory with its wet floor and squat toilet.

The roller doors connecting the workshop to the street outside were closed, but windows high in the wall let in white light. The air was fresher, and Sadie drew it into her lungs through the hood in deep breaths. Car doors opened, and she heard the rumble of a van door. A hand pushed her head down as she was thrust onto the floor of a vehicle. Damp, gritty carpet. The legs of two of her captors pressed in painfully on either side.

Doors slammed and the engine started.

A heavy blanket settled over her, blocking out the light. She lay curled in a fetal position, using her arms and elbows to create breathing space around her face, lifting the hood just enough to clear her mouth. Despite the dehydration, she felt an urgent need to urinate and willed herself to concentrate on her surroundings. *I must not wet myself, I still have my pride.*

Metal screeched as the roller door to the workshop rose and the gearbox shunted into reverse. A second car engine started and the van began to back out onto the road.

It jerked to a halt as the driver slammed on the brakes. There was a screeching of tires from a vehicle outside and the driver of the van swore loudly in Arabic.

"Ya hamar!" You donkey.

"Bloody foreigners," muttered one of the men pinning Sadie to the floor.

Collision averted, the driver finished backing the vehicle out of the work-shop and threw it into first with a loud grinding of gears.

From her position on the floor, Sadie felt every bump in the road. She tried to visualize the streets outside, building a mental map of their route. Even though she had no idea of their starting point, she used the mental exercise to occupy her mind. The van slowed for an intersection and took a right, bouncing over the broken and rutted macadam and splashing through an open sewer. Water drummed against the metal floor.

Horns honked as they joined the main flow of a larger road. The rumble of trucks and buses mingled with the higher-pitched whine of motorcycle engines. Moving in a straight line, the van picked up speed and then slowed again and turned left. She had the sensation of rising and realized they must be on a bridge. Images of the Nile filled her mind as she tried desperately to remember the location of the city's major river crossings. One of her captors had said something about foreigners as they had backed onto the street. Could they be near Gezira Island, near Alex and Aubrey's apartments?

After a few minutes of waiting for the descent, Sadie realized she must be mistaken. They were on one of the city's many expressways. She was being taken out of Cairo.

The thought filled with a renewed sense of dread.

61

The collision occurred without warning and with such jarring force that she was knocked unconscious. When she came to, after just a few seconds, she was still under the blanket in the back of the van. Urgent voices sounded outside, people yelled. Nearby, someone sobbed. Sadie checked herself gingerly for broken bones and realized her lower half was soaked. She'd lost control of her bladder.

She lay still for a few seconds, taking in the sounds of the street, and then she shrugged off the blanket and cautiously removed the hood. No sign of the two men either side of her. Tiny cubes of broken glass glittered on the van's gray vinyl seats, stinging her hands and knees as she hoisted herself into an upright position. After days spent in darkness, her eyes ached.

The man called Hatim was wedged in behind the steering wheel, head covered in blood, blank eyes staring to infinity. Sadie knew instantly he was dead. The windshield was gone. The two men who had pinned her down had passed through it. Scrambling out the door, Sadie could see Abdul-Aziz and Dhul Fiqar lying on the road.

A crowd was quickly forming. Onlookers milled around the driver of the other vehicle, a black-and-white Cairo taxi. He whimpered on the pavement next to his open door.

With his neck bent and limbs protruding at odd angles, Sadie could tell that Dhul Fiqar was very dead. But Abdul-Aziz was moving. Within a few seconds, he staggered to his feet and looked around blearily. His face was covered in blood from a broken nose and smashed top lip.

Sirens wailed in the distance, coming closer.

Sadie assessed the situation in a split second. In the mayhem, nobody noticed her stumble from the van. *This is my chance.* It was now or never. The second car in the convoy, the one she heard starting up as they pulled away from the workshop, would not be far behind.

She ran.

Gasping for air, muscles burning, she willed her legs to keep pumping. Curious residents peered from doorways as the wild-haired foreign woman charged barefoot down the street. She ran swiftly, not daring to look over her shoulder. The distance to the van widened and elation coursed through her. *I'm going to make it.*

As she neared the intersection at the end of the street, a dirty white Fiat 124 fishtailed onto it at the other end, tires clawing tarmac. The driver scanned the road as his passenger barked orders. The Fiat screeched to a halt beside the wreckage. After a pause of a second or two, it accelerated again, bearing down on the fleeing woman.

About five meters separated them. The car pulled to a stop, skidding sideways.

A man leaped from the front passenger door, pulling something from the waistband of his pants. He leveled the pistol at Sadie, now about ten meters on, running flat out and approaching the corner.

A second, then two, ticked by as the man took aim. The black compact weapon barked once. Fire spat from its short barrel.

A woman screamed. Heads disappeared from windows and doorways, and mothers grabbed their children and slammed shutters.

Sadie lurched forward into the gutter, face down, unmoving. A red stain spread across the back of her blouse.

62

Northern Egypt
Wednesday, 15 July 2009

Mersa Matrouh was a riot of activity as the crowds of travelers jostled for places on the next leg of their journey to Siwa oasis, or across the border into Libya. Horns blared as taxis competed with donkey carts and buses for the attention of potential customers.

The central square seethed with activity. But, with the exception of the occasional huddle of veiled women, it was mostly turbaned men and grim-faced Egyptian soldiers in ill-fitting uniforms and scuffed boots, casually munching sunflower seeds and spitting the shells on the cracked concrete.

The town itself was a grid of mold-poured, low-rise apartment blocks. Housing forty thousand people, it spread up from the rubbish-strewn coast toward a ridge festooned with radar dishes. Whatever the Egyptian tourist board liked to claim about the place being a beach resort founded by Alexander the Great, it had definitely seen better days.

Alex climbed out of the British embassy Land Rover. He was thankful they were able to borrow the vehicle, equipped with GPS satellite navigation that would help them find the coordinates of the downed German bomber. It would have taken two local buses and a full day to get to the town of Siwa, about forty kilometers from Egypt's desert border with Libya, on the ancient Saharan caravan route. The oasis had once been the easternmost extent of the ancient Berber civilization, which stretched all the way from Morocco, until conquered by the Arabs.

As it was, the drive to the coast from Cairo in the air-conditioned comfort of the four-wheel drive took nearly six hours. At least forty minutes of that had been spent maneuvering through the narrow streets of Khan el-Khalili. Although he knew the feeling was not rational, Alex was assailed by the sensation that they were close to Sadie. But neither man spotted anything promising.

We were lucky not to have been stuck in the old bazaar for longer. He recalled their near miss. Not far from Al-Azhar mosque a van backed out of a workshop straight into their path. Bairstow slammed on the brakes. Even with diplomatic plates, had there been a collision, they could have been stuck there for hours haggling over damages, although there was little doubt the reversing vehicle was at fault, and the Land Rover, with its steel bull bars, would have come out of it relatively unscathed.

"God bless the British taxpayer," he murmured appreciatively, patting the hot metal of the hood. "Come on Aubrey, let's stretch our legs and find a café. I need caffeine and I'm famished."

"Hang on, old man. I'm right behind you." Bairstow eased himself out of the driver's seat and stamped his feet on the dusty pavement. The thin layer of sunflower seed shells crunched and popped under his boots.

Elsewhere in the square, another all-terrain vehicle and a van pulled to the curb and disgorged their passengers. Neither group was aware of the other, yet both had followed the Land Rover from Cairo.

After leaving the clogged streets of the Egyptian capital, Alex and Bairstow had made rapid progress north toward the Mediterranean. The swirling chaos of the city was quickly replaced by a barren landscape of flat desert and brown scrub. *Blink in Cairo and you miss a dozen vibrant scenes of daily life,* Alex thought as he trudged across the square. *Sleep on the desert highway, and you wake up pretty much where you left off.* They'd passed El Alamein in the early afternoon, with its war memorials and neat cemetery, where the Allies put a stop to Germany's dreams of controlling the Suez Canal and oil supplies of the Persian Gulf.

The two friends pushed their way through the throng of taxi drivers toward one of several watering holes at the edge of the square that doubled as the town's bus terminal.

"Taxi to Siwa only one hundred and fifty pounds!" bellowed one of the younger drivers, correctly picking them for English speakers.

"La' shukran." No, thanks. Alex shook his head and smiled. It never ceased to amaze him the optimism of these people. The man had been eyeing them since they exited the Land Rover. They obviously didn't need a ride, but he figured there was no harm in asking anyway. Don't ask, don't get.

As the two men sipped scalding coffee from tiny glasses, they discussed their plans, which were basic at best. Nearing Siwa, they would punch Smith's map coordinates into the GPS on the dashboard of the Land Rover and see where it led them. From what Alex could make out from Mapquest, the crash site must be some distance southwest of the oasis town.

"Let's hope the readings are accurate. A single degree of latitude is one hundred and eleven kilometers, that's about sixty-eight miles."

"That is a lot of desert," was the only reply Bairstow could muster.

Alex pulled out his phone and called Hesse again. There was no answer.

They sat in silence for a while, before Bairstow said, "If the wreck is out there, can it really have lain undisturbed in the desert for more than sixty years?"

"For sure. People were looking in the wrong place, and it is pretty hostile terrain. An accidental discovery would be highly unlikely. We're talking about the Great Sand Sea, an unbroken mass of dunes the size of the UK on the frontiers of Libya and Egypt. There's not a single well or water source in more than fifty thousand square kilometers. That's extreme."

"Sounds pleasant, old boy."

Alex explained that until the 1930s, the region had not been entered, let alone explored, since ancient, possibly prehistoric times. During the war, clandestine German and British desert patrols probed the area, sometimes disguised as archaeological expeditions, spying on each other's movements. Hesse himself was involved here, infiltrating German agents into Allied-occupied Egypt.

"Since then, the region has been neglected. I've heard in some parts that sixty-year-old tire tracks are still visible. The ancient Greek historian Herodotus reported that in about 500 BC a fifty-thousand-strong invading army completely disappeared in there."

Bairstow contemplated this last snippet of information, shaking his head slowly. "In the modern an age of satellites, it seems incredible that some parts of our own planet are less well charted than the surface of the moon."

Alex agreed. "If the plane carrying the Nazi archive and loot crashed in a sandstorm, it may even have been covered up immediately. And we are talking about North Africa here. There are parts of the United States where literally dozens of planes have gone down, and the crash sites have never been discovered, like in the Sierra Nevada. I read somewhere that missing-aircraft reports indicate there are nearly two hundred uncharted crash sites in that mountain range. Some go back sixty years or more."

Bairstow grimaced. "Thanks for the encouragement old man. If a Nazi bomber and a fifty-thousand-strong army can disappear in there, the odds are stacked against the likes of you and me."

They finished their coffees. None of the food at the café appealed, and they were on the road again within thirty minutes.

■ ■ ■

For the next few hours, nothing changed on the desert highway, its two lanes of pale, cracked macadam stretched out endlessly before them. In places the road was obscured by soft flurries of sand.

Alex, who took over driving duties at Mersa Matrouh, recalled a conversation he'd had with Private Jemma Harris a week and a half ago, while visiting the peacekeepers in the Sinai. It seemed like a lifetime had passed. The young Kiwi army driver told him that sand drifts sometimes shifted war-era minefields onto roads, adding to the already considerable perils of desert travel. The thought did wonders for his concentration.

About twenty kilometers outside of Siwa, the desert reared up into mounds, gullies, and hills. Alex switched on the GPS and entered the coordinates. The road made a sudden descent through a scattering of patchwork vegetable plots and mud brick houses and they were there, Siwa oasis—an island of water, palm trees, and low dwellings amid a vast, dry ocean of sand.

This was somewhere Alex and Sadie talked of visiting, an alternative to the tourist-thronged Sharm El-Sheikh and the Nile Delta. He'd looked forward to exploring this area with her, sleeping under the dense star-studded sky and soaking in the natural hot springs.

The thought made his heart sink.

As expected, the satnav system showed they needed to continue on south and west of the main town into the Great Sand Sea.

Evening settled over the dunes, and the sun was low in the sky as Siwa disappeared in the rearview mirror. The Land Rover crested a rise in the road and pulled to a halt.

Both men stared out the windshield. A stunning vista lay before them, endless parallel rows of dunes like giant waves stretched to the horizon. It was easy to see how a downed World War II bomber might remain hidden in such terrain forever.

63

The Western Desert
Wednesday, 15 July 2009

Rivers once flowed in these bone-dry valleys, gushing into lakes surrounded by great forests. Thousands of years ago, onyx, gazelle, even giraffes grazed here. But this vast range where early man hunted and gathered was now a wasteland, without even a glimmer of life.

Alex jumped out and skirted the vehicle, chuckling at the alarm on Bairstow's face as he bent down to release air from the tires. His friend's concern lessened when he explained that softer tires found a better grip on the silky, white sand. It returned as raw fear when he climbed back in and hauled the wheel left.

For an instant, empty sky floated dizzyingly in front of the hood.

Then the vehicle slowly began to tip forward. Yet still the slope in front of them was worryingly absent from their line of sight.

"Jesus fucking Christ!" Bairstow bellowed, fingernails embedded in the dash as Alex threw the truck into second gear and floored the accelerator.

The Land Rover's four-liter V8 roared as it careened wildly down the dune, sliding at a seemingly impossible angle. Its two occupants jerked violently forward and then back, restrained by their seat belts.

■ ■ ■

They approached the eastern ridge of a large raised plateau of dark sandstone just as the sun's tangerine orb touched the thin blue line of the horizon, turning the dunes shades of indigo and apricot. The GPS showed about fifteen kilometers to the crash site. With the slow progress they were making over the sand, Alex declared they should camp for the night.

The temperature had fallen sharply, and a cool breeze came with the onset of darkness. He pulled on a light jacket and wrapped a cotton scarf around his neck. Soft sand hissed beneath his boots as he set out for a high dune about a hundred meters from their campsite. At the top he found a spot from which to watch the stars as they slowly began to appear. The sky was crystal clear, and the absence of the moon meant he was able to pick out distinct constellations.

Except for Venus glowing on the horizon, Alex recognized none of them.

He thought about the last week and a half, about the unpredictability of it all. Growing up, he was never good at sitting still. He craved action. He often told friends, only half joking, that going to high school and university in New Zealand was like being waterboarded. No individual part was particularly bad, but the sum total was pure torture. His parents' version of a sensible life plan—marriage, kids, and a mortgage—he tossed out the window at the earliest opportunity.

Most of the friends he went to university with spent only a couple of years traveling before settling back home, marrying young, starting careers and families. Alex found over time they had less and less in common. When they did catch up, he felt claustrophobic. He couldn't wait to get away again, as if their condition might be contagious.

Now, looking up at the unfamiliar night sky, he wondered if he had played it all wrong. He was in his midthirties, unmarried, alone, and without faith. Was he missing out on something, a vital part of the human condition? Did he really have any more answers to the big questions in life as a result of his wanderings?

Alex rubbed his face and was surprised to find tears there. He wiped his nose with a sleeve. The last week and a half was a nightmare from which he could not wake.

"What am I doing out here in the desert?" he wondered aloud. "Do I really think I'll find a plane that crashed more than fifty years ago filled with Nazi treasure?"

His voice sounded small in the vast space that surrounded him. "Mate, you're fucking kidding yourself."

An almost-full moon appeared over the horizon, turning the desert to pure silver. He lay back on the sand, its residual warmth radiating through the thin material of his jacket, and then he did something he had not done in a very long time. He prayed.

He prayed he would find the manuscript and that Sadie would be okay. Somehow, the mumbled words made him feel better, restoring a sense of order.

64

Thursday, 16 July 2009

The hours before dawn are the coldest in the desert.

Alex woke with the first rays of light. He shivered and pulled his sleeping bag tightly around his shoulders. After several attempts with freezing fingers, the gas camping stove fired up. Hurriedly he made a pot of hot coffee and used it to rouse a grumpy Bairstow. Neither man spoke as they lingered over steaming mugs. After coming this far, there was little left to say.

Following breakfast, they packed up. According to the GPS, the imposing ridge in the distance was Al-Gilf Al-Kebir, meaning Great Barrier. It was an apt name for a plateau roughly the size of Switzerland rising three hundred meters from the desert floor. Alex was introduced to it years earlier by the novel *The English Patient*, a book that helped inspire him to come to Egypt in the first place. The author, Michael Ondaatje, used the region as a backdrop for his wartime love story.

Under any other circumstances, Alex would be excited by the prospect of visiting an area containing some of the world's oldest artistic sites. Thousands of years ago, hunter-gatherers roamed the region. In the caves where they sheltered, they painted some of the most spectacular rock art to survive into the modern age. The Cave of Swimmers was discovered by Hungarian explorer-turned-spy László Almásy in 1933, Shaw's Cave not long after. Another site, El-Mestekawi Cave, was found only as recently as 2002, a testament to the inaccessibility of the region. It was named after its Egyptian discoverer, the ex–army colonel whose book Hesse mentioned, and whose writings contained the coordinates that piqued the interest of Professor Smith.

Just the previous year, Alex wrote a story about a particularly intriguing discovery near Al-Gilf Al-Kebir. It was picked up by all the main papers in Britain. A kit bag lost during World War II by a dispatch rider attached to the Long Range Desert Group, a mobile commando unit of the British Army specializing in sabotage and harrying the Germans, was found sitting in plain view on the desert floor. It contained the complete personal belongings of a British soldier: clothes, letters, photographs, signals log, and a number of other items. The letters and photographs in the bag were somewhat damaged by weather, but otherwise well preserved. A touch of comedy was provided by the highly personal nature of some of the correspondence. It appeared that the owner of the bag had had two girlfriends on the go. The satchel was eventually returned to relatives, the soldier having died just a year earlier. Sadie had loved that story. Alex pushed the thought painfully aside.

He forced his mind back to the present. Daydreaming would get them nowhere. It was early Thursday morning, the deadline set by Sadie's captors nearly upon them.

After again climbing the dune he'd sat atop the night before to watch the stars, it was clear they'd have to proceed on foot. Closer to the limestone escarpment, the ground became riddled with crevasses and deep gullies, making it impassable to vehicles. The news upset Bairstow, and Alex literally dragged him to the edge of a crevasse to make his point. The young diplomat trudged back to the Land Rover with a defeated stoop.

Before setting out, they unclipped the GPS from the dashboard and filled packs with everything they thought they might need: flashlights, a compass, rope, a shovel, food, water, and warm clothes. They set off in the direction of the black escarpment, walking slowly. It was still early. By Alex's estimation, they should be able to cover the fifteen kilometers to the crash site in four or five hours, if they were lucky. In the desert, landmarks can disappear. Sand dunes move. Distance is hard to judge.

He had heard about the ancient form of desert navigation known as detouring. The Arab proverb, "By three sides is the quickest way across a square," made perfect sense when you had a large obstacle in your way. A ninety-degree departure from your planned route, followed by measured distances and two subsequent ninety-degree turns would bring you back on course. Not for the first time, he was grateful for the satnav slung around his neck. He checked their progress regularly.

The morning wore on and a stifling wind began to blow, tugging at their shirts and pants. As the sun rose in the sky, the breeze grew stronger, turning the atmosphere into a blast furnace. By noon, it blew into a half gale, so dry the two men felt their lips shrivel and crack. Bairstow's face was chapped and windburned, and he was blinking rapidly. Alex's own eyelids had gone granular, seeming to creep back and expose his shrinking eyeballs. He cursed himself for not thinking to bring goggles or even sunglasses. They stopped to wrap shirts around their heads Bedouin style, pulled tightly across their noses with brow folds forward like visors and only a narrow slit of vision.

This part of the Sahara was made up of kilometer upon kilometer of shifting dunes, many more than two hundred meters high. The world's highest dunes were in the Algerian part of the Sahara, soaring over four hundred and seventy meters, taller than the Empire State Building in New York. Twice, as they trudged over the higher drifts, he scanned the horizon in the direction from which they had come and thought he caught a glimpse of another traveling party.

On the first occasion, he wrote it off as a trick of the desert light, a mirage. The second time, he was sure it was not his imagination. Far in the distance, three, maybe four figures, stretched, impossibly tall, shimmering and ephemeral in the heat haze rising off the sand. Between them, he could make out the taller, swaying outlines of camels. The traveling party were dressed in local fashion, loose-fitting tunics, sleeveless cloaks and distinctive *kufiya* wrapped round their faces and necks, cinched at the forehead with *agal*, heavy woolen rope coils.

Alex admired the Bedouin. They traveled with such ease over the same terrain he and Bairstow now traversed, without the help of modern tools like satnav. He observed their progress a moment longer and then scanned the horizon ahead.

The black escarpment in the distance did not seem to be getting much closer.

65

They stood on the edge of an ancient watercourse. A deep rift carved into the uneven surface of the desert. Above them, the dark sandstone plateau reared up like an ocean wave.

It was after 1:00 p.m., and the sun had passed its zenith when the satnav gave off a series of short burps heralding their arrival. They'd finally reached the precise longitude and latitude the professor wrote on the envelope.

Alex surveyed their surroundings as Bairstow slid his pack to the ground and took several gulps from his water bottle.

"Careful, that's got to last until we get back to the vehicle," Alex cautioned, taking a small sip from his own flask.

Bairstow ignored the admonition and took another long slurp, scanning the area doubtfully.

"This place looks pretty empty to me. If a German bomber went down on this spot, it's not here anymore. You sure about those readings, old boy?"

Alex recalled his own comment at the café in Mersa Matrouh. *A single degree of latitude is one hundred and eleven kilometers; that's about sixty-eight miles.*

They were at the edge of a deep wadi. It ran westward, away from the dark mass of Al-Gilf Al-Kebir. As they'd approached the massive escarpment, the dunes had given away to a rocky plane. The wind, which grew stronger as the day wore on, now tugged fiercely at their clothes. Alex swore under his breath and adjusted the shirt more tightly around his head. He hated wind, let alone wind mixed with sand, and he cursed the turn of events that brought him to this godforsaken place. A sudden vision of Sadie, tear-stained face staring into the camera, made the irritation at his own discomfort vanish in a flash.

The place seemed to be completely bare of vegetation, although he knew some forms of life would be present, mostly species of scrub, snakes, scorpions, and lizards. *And a Kiwi and a Brit.* But if there was a crashed plane here, its location was not obvious.

While Bairstow smoked a cigarette, he scrambled down to the floor of the wadi. Stones dislodged by his boots clattered and echoed off the rock walls. The flapping of his shirt in the wind was the only other sound to break the eerie quiet. The area at the bottom was half in shadow and about a quarter the width of a football field. Other than several piles of boulders, it was empty.

He lit a cigarette and approached the far rock face. On the valley floor, the wind died away, and the tobacco smoke drifted lazily in the still air. Ahead, he could see a rift in the ground about ten meters wide and several meters deep. It was half filled with soft sand and bathed in deeper shadow.

He stared for several seconds before he realized what he was looking at.

The outline of a tail fin rose out of the gloom, its shape unmistakable.

The plane was broken into three sections by the force of its impact with the earth. Most of the checkerboard of armored glass from the nose cone was gone. The bomber's wings, mangled engines, and landing gear lay farther down the rift. He immediately recognized the wreckage as that of a Junkers-88, a distinctive shape, clumsy and out of proportion. Painted in desert camouflage and with no other markings, the crumpled contours were hard to pick out in the shadowy half-light. *This would be completely invisible from the air.*

Other than the damage from impact, the plane was well preserved. Lying belly down, the bomb doors were buried in sand, but access to the hold could be gained from any of the gaping holes in the broken fuselage.

He called to Bairstow, "Hey Aubrey! Get down here—and bring those packs, would you?"

Echoes rumbled off the sandstone walls for several seconds, doubling up on themselves before fading to silence.

"Coming, sir." The sarcasm was undiminished as the reply bounced back. A clatter of rocks followed and then a yelp and a string of obscenities. Within a few minutes, Bairstow stood panting by his side, a pack slung over each shoulder.

"Bloody hell, would you look at that!" Bairstow flung his load on the ground. Alex retrieved the flashlights. He handed one to his friend and grabbed the bundle of nylon rope.

"It seems so well preserved, other than the crash damage," Bairstow said, whispering as if on hallowed ground. "Think there's a body in there?"

Alex shrugged. "Only one way to find out, mate. The dry air of the desert does amazing things. East of Wadi Dayyiq, on the other side of Al-Gilf Al-Kebir, a fully loaded ammunition truck from the Long Range Desert Group was found by tourists in 1992, almost fifty years after the end of the war. It was a Bedford and held several tons of high explosives. When the Egyptian authorities were notified and found the truck, they filled it with petrol and it started. It's now in the museum at Alexandria."

Bairstow stood speechless for a few seconds. "I'll stop worrying about leaving the embassy Land Rover back there then."

"Care to join me?" Alex gestured toward the plane.

"Ladies first."

■ ■ ■

Alex had no idea what more than half a century in the North African desert would do to a corpse. He braced himself for whatever might remain of the ill-fated pilot. But, once on the floor of the rift, it took only a few minutes for them to discover that the cockpit was empty.

"Where the hell is the pilot? Surely he can't have survived the impact."

Bairstow looked relieved. "Maybe he bailed out."

They scrambled along the fuselage to the hold by the buried bomb doors, entering it through a section peeled back like a sardine can by the impact with the desert. It, too, was empty. Not even a single packing case remained.

"Looks like we aren't the first to find this place." Alex's voice was flat, disappointment written all over his dirt-streaked features.

Someone beat them to it, probably local Bedouin tribesmen with no understanding of the cargo's significance. There was no way of knowing when that might have happened. It could have been just yesterday, or years, even decades, earlier.

It didn't really matter. The trail had gone cold and the thought made him sick. *Things can't get any worse.*

66

Drawing back and releasing the bolt catch on an AK-47 makes a distinctive sound, a kind of metallic double click. Alex recognized it instantly. He'd heard it many times in Cambodia. It never failed to chill his blood.

The sound of several of the deadly Russian assault rifles being cocked at the same time was a terrifying one. It was the sound of defeat and precisely what he and Bairstow heard behind them as they squatted in the sand facing the wrecked aircraft.

And I thought things couldn't get any worse.

Despite the intense heat, the sweat on his back had turned cold.

"No rapid movements, gentlemen. Where is the book?"

The language was English, but the accent Egyptian. *No fucking around, no pleasantries, straight to the point.*

He was not sure he could move quickly even if he wanted to. His legs were weak, seemingly incapable of lifting his body. A pounding like wings beating in his ears made it difficult to hear.

They rose to their feet in slow motion, limbs heavy, as if caught in quicksand.

"Turn around."

They obeyed, slowly.

Alex tried to speak. Throat dry, the only sound to leave it was the hiss of expelled air. Four men stood at the lip of the rift, each with an automatic rifle pointed downward, directly at them. He recognized the traveling party he'd seen from atop the dunes. Not local tribesmen after all.

He was in no doubt now who they were. These men and their associates blew up his apartment in Cairo and kidnapped Sadie. They were his only hope of finding her, and they were the men who believed the manuscript was their inheritance, a tool with which to gain leverage over their enemies.

"Well?"

Alex did not know how to answer, or what to think. But if it was over, he wasn't going to give these assholes the pleasure of seeing him simper.

"Where is Sadie?" He was surprised to find his voice sounded stronger than he felt.

"You are in no position to make demands. Now, where is it? The German told you where to find it, no? He indicated as much before we killed him."

The last sentence hit him like a punch. *No wonder Hesse hasn't been answering my calls.*

"It's not here." He gestured at the mangled carcass of the German bomber.

"That is not a good answer. Perhaps you need some persuading." Without unlocking his eyes from Alex's, the man turned a fraction and addressed two of the others standing behind him.

"Bashir, Qasim, get the whore."

The pair lowered their weapons and disappeared from view.

After about a minute—which felt like hours—they returned, dragging a limp, hooded figure between them. They let go of Sadie's arms and she collapsed onto the rocks, unmoving. Dried blood stained her blouse and skirt, and her left arm was bandaged from elbow to shoulder.

Alex gasped, an involuntary spasm that left him temporarily breathless. The leader crouched down and roughly removed the hood, revealing matted hair and a pale, unconscious face.

Without thinking, he lunged forward and began scrabbling up the slope toward Sadie, clawing at the loose rock.

"Stop! If you come any closer, she won't look as pretty as she does now."

Alex shook violently, his voice barely a whisper. "What have you done? What the fuck have you bastards done to her?"

"Perhaps she will live to tell you about it." The man grinned, revealing to-bacco-stained teeth.

The men behind him sniggered.

The last of his energy reserves seemed to drain from his body. His knees began to buckle and then Bairstow's hand was on his elbow.

"Steady, old man," he whispered.

Then, as the pair stared upward, rooted to the spot, a strange thing happened. The leader's facial expressions went through a rapid series of contortions that would have been comic had the situation not been so deadly.

Smug self-assurance gave way to mild alarm and then, finally, wide-eyed panic. Alex read the man's lips as he silently mouthed, "El Khara Dah?" Roughly translated, it meant what the fuck? The man directly to the leader's left, whispered "Ebn el metnakah!" Son of a motherfucker!

Bashir and Qasim mouthed similar obscenities. Had anyone been watching their faces, they would have recognized the words "Gahba!" and "Sharmoota!" Both were versions of the Arabic word for whore.

From above and behind Alex, a familiar voice rang out. Its tone was cool, cutting through the stifling air like a whetted blade.

"Put down the weapons, gentlemen."

Alex was having difficulty believing his ears. He didn't need to turn around to know who was there. That same voice had whispered to him as dawn broke over Mt. Sinai. He'd heard it again only yesterday morning in a brief, awkward telephone call. *What the hell is she doing here?*

"Do as she says." This time it was a male voice, one he hadn't heard before. He swiveled his head.

Noora stood on the lip of the wadi. Next to her was a tall, blond man. Even at that distance, Alex could make out his terrible facial scarring. Two other very young, European-looking men stood nearby.

All four shouldered SWAT-style Heckler & Koch MP5 submachine guns. Alex could see Noora also had a pistol stuffed into the front of her shorts. Absurdly, he noticed they were the same shorts she wore when they climbed toward the point where Moses had his rendezvous with God. He felt confused.

He turned back to the Arabs, now reluctantly lowering their weapons.

Then, in a single, fluid motion, the lead man raised his AK-47 again. The Arab's trigger-finger tensed.

From Alex's perspective, the world went into slow motion. A loud crack, and then a pressure wave passed his right ear. The gunman's head exploded backward and outward, spraying blood and chunks of wet flesh onto the surrounding sand and rocks.

As if from very far away, he heard himself scream, "No!"

More shots rang out in rapid succession and the other Arabs collapsed, heads like split watermelons. A warm mist sprayed Alex's face and neck, coating his lips and tongue in a metallic taste. Fleetingly he thought about Sadie. Had she been hit? He lurched forward, hands on knees, and vomited powerfully down his own legs.

67

The wind had risen to gale force, full of so much grit it was hard to breathe without gagging. The sun was just visible, a burning disc in the dense orange gloom.

Alex and Bairstow were bound together, seated back to back, at the top of the wadi. Sadie, unconscious, lay next to them. She, too, was bound at the wrists and ankles. Fully alert to the impending danger, the two men stared up in awe at the storm blurring the horizon. A giant tsunami of wind and sand at least a thousand meters high bore down on them, dwarfing even the dark mass of the escarpment.

Alex had experienced dust storms, but nothing like this. They could be among nature's most violent and spectacular phenomena. As high winds passed over loosely packed grains of soil or sand, those particles started to vibrate and then to bounce. As they struck the ground repeatedly, they loosened more particles, which began to travel in suspension, aided by a static electric field created through friction.

He felt panic rising, constricting his throat. It was storms like this one that had buried armies, cities even.

After the shootout, they'd been dragged up the side of the canyon to a spot where five camels were tethered using Arab-style rope hobbles. The brief hope Alex nursed that Noora and the scar-faced man were their saviors quickly faded. Under the watchful gaze of her companions, Noora questioned him roughly on the whereabouts of the manuscript. There was no trace of warmth in her eyes or voice, no indication of the past intimacy. The thought of what happened between them on the summit of Mt. Sinai sickened him. He had no idea who she was, or what outfit she was with, but one thing was for sure, they were not on his side.

When Alex insisted he had no idea where the book was, the blond man, whom Noora addressed as Cyrus, flew into a rage, striking him hard across the face. The force of the blow made his nose bleed and his vision blur.

His attacker ranted about something called "the Communion" and someone called "the Heart Master."

"The professor's detractors were fools! Savages!" he screamed, veins pulsing in his forehead.

Alex was growing more confused by the second. His head pounded and he stared hard at the man, willing his brain to function clearly. He had seen him somewhere before. Then it struck him, almost as powerfully as the blow he received a few moments earlier.

It was at the café near my apartment, nearly two weeks ago, when I first opened the letter from Professor Smith. The blond man was sitting at a table nearby, drinking Coke and reading.

Cyrus continued to rant, the tendons in his scarred neck taut like steel cable. "The Communion follows the true path to salvation! It is God's will that the manuscript be in the possession of His children. It shows we are right, the true Church, persecuted and suppressed through the centuries."

He waved the submachine gun wildly.

Once Alex slotted home that piece of the jigsaw, the rest began falling into place. It was Noora and her associates who stole his bag from the library. He recalled the blond foreigner running through the foyer. Smith's words returned to him with renewed force. *I sometimes feel that I am being watched, but perhaps that is just the foolishness of an old man.*

Alex blanched at the thought of what happened between him and Noora. His betrayal of Sadie was greater than he'd imagined. This woman was using him, and he'd been foolish enough to imagine some bond, some attraction.

Once the blond man was convinced Alex had not yet found the manuscript, he took his foot soldiers down to search the wreckage of the bomber.

Alex and Noora were alone.

"Who are you?" Alex forced his voice to remain level. "Please, why are you doing this? Can't you see she needs a doctor?" he said, gesturing with his head to where Sadie lay bound a few meters away, next to Bairstow in the lee of one of the camels.

Her response seemed to take an eternity. Finally, she looked at him.

"This is not what you imagine, Alex. Nothing is as it seems."

There was still something hard in her eyes, a cold professionalism, but he thought he detected a softening. He remained silent.

"I need you to trust me. Can you do that?"

"Trust you?" Alex was incredulous. His voice had risen to a shout and the look on his face must have been enough to persuade her.

"Okay, okay." She raised her hands in a defensive motion.

"Have you heard of Metsada?"

He shook his head.

What Noora said next took his breath away.

"Metsada is the Special Operations unit of Mossad. I work for the Israeli foreign intelligence service."

"You've got to be kidding! You expect me to believe that?"

"That is entirely up to you, Alex." Her face remained expressionless, but something in her eyes was enough to tell him she was being truthful. His mind was working in overdrive. Things were beginning to fit together, as he recalled the night he almost bumped into this woman and a stranger on the banks of the Nile, by the bridge across from the Egyptian Museum.

What he mistook for a nighttime tryst was something else entirely. Their conversation, begun in Hebrew, made more sense now. The man asked whether the others knew where she was. Alex cursed himself for not lingering behind the planter for longer, eavesdropping.

"Why on earth would Mossad be interested in Morton Smith's manuscript?"

As soon as the words were out of his mouth, he knew the answer. He recalled the research he'd done online in his room at the monastery guesthouse, the warming relations between the Vatican and Israel. What Father Moretti told him about the wartime silence of the Roman Catholic Church as Hitler murdered European Jews. The visit by the Pope to Jerusalem, planned for next month.

A pitched battle was raging for the affections of the Church and its millions of members around the globe. What's more, it had been going on for some time. Mossad's interest in the Secret Gospel of Mark was obvious, similar to that of the Islamic Army and the Nazis before them. Leverage.

"All right, all right. But you don't expect me to believe they are Mossad," Alex said, gesturing toward the wreckage, the direction in which Cyrus and the two other men disappeared.

"No, they are something else entirely. But there are synergies between their interests and ours, inasmuch as we both want the same thing—the manuscript. It was only natural we would infiltrate them, use them. Their search for the Secret Gospel has been going on far longer than ours."

"I'm confused, who are *they*?"

"Does the name Franklin Jones mean anything to you?"

"Possibly, it rings a bell."

"Franklin Jones is a fanatic, also known as the Heart Master. He founded a California-based Christian sect—the Communion. We want the Vatican on our side in our fight against Palestinian terrorists. But for the Communion this is about true belief, the historical Jesus, correcting two thousand years of persecution."

More pieces of the puzzle slotted into place. Alex had heard the name Franklin Jones. The sex trials in California over the cult's strange communal practices made international headlines when he was in high school. He and his friends sniggered over the more shocking practices that came to light.

The parallels between the Communion and the libertine Christian rituals practiced by the Carpocratians, the sect described in Smith's manuscript, were obvious. Jones believed he was a modern-day Carpocrates.

Alex's anger was building.

Was that what Emil tried to tell me as he lay dying in the crypt? The words that gurgled through his smashed lips sounded like "crates" and "California." The image of his friend as he lay dying was etched in his mind.

"How could you?" he whispered. "How the fuck could you? Father Boutros was an old man, harmless, a man of God."

The expression on Noora's face softened. She shook her head.

"I'm sorry, Alex. I wasn't there when they did that. It was needless. But I'm not sure I could have stopped what happened even had I been present. This is bigger than you or I, bigger than individuals."

"What about Professor Smith on the ferry? Was that your work?" Acid was in his voice. "The Islamic Army and the Communion needed him. I can't see them eliminating their only link to the manuscript. They wanted him to find it. Following him, keeping him alive, was their best chance."

Noora's response was matter of fact. The hard edge returned to her voice. "Relations between Israel and the Vatican are on the mend. When we first started this operation, our goal was to ensure that warming continued. Preventing the original manuscript of the Secret Gospel of Mark from surfacing, by whatever means, was the priority. We did not anticipate the professor would write to you. But for now, Alex, you are going to have to trust me. I am your only hope here. Do you understand that? As far as they are concerned, I'm one of them. If you cooperate, I'll do everything I can to protect the three of you, make sure she gets to the hospital."

Noora stood, shouldered her weapon and shuffled Alex over to where Bairstow was sitting. After tying them together, she marched off in the direction of the crash site.

That was several hours ago. Now, as the sandstorm raged, Alex struggled to clarify matters in his mind. It all seemed so fantastic. Sometime near the start of World War II, at an isolated monastery in the Judean desert, a young graduate student named Morton Smith discovered a copy of a letter penned by an early church father. That letter contained fragments of an account of Jesus's life that was older than any in existence. It painted a picture of the Son of God that was markedly different from the one accepted today. The young scholar handed his find to the Nazis, who used it in a scheme to buy the silence of the Catholic Church as Hitler orchestrated the biggest mass murder in history. Seventeen years later, after the war, Smith, now a respected professor, returned to the hermitage and "rediscovered" the letter, feeling its contents were too important to be allowed to disappear forever.

Jump forward half a century. A group of Arab terrorists were now intent on getting their hands on the manuscript, hoping to use it as leverage in their fight against the Jewish state of Israel. Meanwhile, Israeli spies were seeking the same manuscript to use against their enemies. To that end, they infiltrated a bizarre Christian sect that was willing to commit murder to gain control of the Secret Gospel, believing it validated their own dubious communal activities.

Such brutal power play, it was beyond anything Alex had ever encountered. A sense of hopelessness settled on him. Lying there, with Bairstow pressed tightly against his back and Sadie beside them, he realized there was still a question he needed to answer. Why had Smith done it? Why had he worked for the Nazis? It didn't fit with the man he knew as a good friend.

Just like in North Africa during the war, Palestine was crawling with German agents. So it was not difficult to see how a brilliant young British graduate student might have come to the attention of German intelligence recruiters. It was easy to understand what their interest in him would be, given his close ties to the Greek Orthodox community and access to an ancient library of Christian texts.

Yet why did Smith came under their sway?

A confusing picture was emerging. But one thing was clear to him. The bloody battle for orthodoxy, for the heart and soul of Christianity, did not end with the fixing of the modern canon of scripture hundreds of years ago. It was still raging.

There is one lead I still have to follow, if I ever get out of here alive.

Smith stayed at a hotel in Haifa, making payments into a bank account there. He suspected the answer to his final question, about his old friend's motivation, lay in that Israeli city, with a woman named Avigail Stern.

68

A loud groan from one of the camels brought Alex out of his reverie. Desperately thirsty, his throat ached. The sour taste of vomit lingered in his mouth.

He looked over at Sadie. A sense of hopelessness sat heavily in the pit of his stomach. Still no sign of Noora and her three associates, yet the sandstorm was abating. They'd gone down to the wreck with shovels to dig in the sand for anything from the cargo that might remain. If they did not return soon, Sadie would not survive for long. If they did, it seemed unlikely that Cyrus, or Noora for that matter, would free any witnesses to their killing spree. Neither prospect was a reassuring one.

"Aubrey, you okay?"

Bairstow moved against his back.

"I'm not sure I'd put it that way, Alex, but yes, I'm alive. I can tell that much because I'm dying for a pee."

Alex smiled. He was thankful for the presence of his friend, and his sense of humor. "We've got to get free, and not just so you can take a leak, but to get those rifles. They're with the bodies on the other side of the wadi."

"I'm open to suggestions."

Bound to Bairstow at the chest, waist, and elbows, Alex had little freedom of movement in his arms pinned against his sides. But the bonds securing his left arm were loose. He wriggled his left hand into his pocket and felt the plastic grip of his cigarette lighter. It took about twenty minutes, and several painful burns, to melt through the nylon rope.

Alex went straight to Sadie, freeing her hands and feet, and smoothing the hair off her face. Bairstow pulled him away.

"Come on, Alex. We're fucked if we don't get those guns."

From the lip of the wadi, the plane wreck was invisible. Leaving Sadie where she lay, they scrambled down the canyon, clambered across and up the far side. The clattering of rocks as they climbed was masked by the remains of the sandstorm as it blew itself out.

Sure enough, the assault rifles lay next to the corpses of the gunmen. A few meters away, beside a rocky outcrop, four camels stared impassively. Alex tried not to look at the men's hideous wounds as he picked up a weapon and made to hand it to his friend.

Bairstow shook his head.

"Wouldn't know where to start, old boy."

Alex had used an AK-47 on several occasions at a Cambodian army firing range on the outskirts of Phnom Penh. It was a popular tourist attraction. For a dollar a round, you could shoot almost any weapon. For twenty bucks, you could fire a rocket-propelled grenade at a cow. But after the initial adrenaline rush of target practice with a real-life assault weapon, he was filled with remorse. He knew the Cambodian military was using tourist dollars as just another way of funding the country's long-running civil war.

He removed the ammunition clip by depressing the catch between the magazine and the trigger guard. A quick inspection revealed it was full. The Arabs had not fired a single shot. He blew into the magazine to clear it of sand and slotted it back in place with a satisfying click. There was a selector switch on the right side of the rifle, a thin piece of metal protruding from the receiver. He slipped it into the downward position. Grasping the bolt catch, he pulled firmly backward until it would go no farther and released, producing a double click.

The piece was loaded.

"Where the hell did you learn to do that?"

"Don't ask."

He handed the rifle to Bairstow, who took it reluctantly.

Alex picked up a second weapon and repeated the process, before gathering up several spare clips. Moving over to one of the camels, he crouched to rummage through its saddlebags. Food, hurricane lanterns, more ammunition, and a boxy, lightweight Uzi submachine gun. Alex left them where they were and quickly found what he was looking for, a large plastic bottle of water.

"Don't move."

Alex jumped. The voice was calm, and carried clearly across the wadi. The sandstorm had finally petered out and the air was brittle and still.

"Lower your weapon and place it on the ground."

A trickle of sweat rolled from his hairline into his right eye, blurring his vision. He blinked rapidly. Shielded by the rocky protrusion from the speaker's line of sight, Alex recognized the voice. He carefully peered around the outcrop. Cyrus was standing on the far side of the wadi, an MP5 pointing directly across the chasm at Bairstow.

"Where is your friend?"

Bairstow did not answer. The man's grip tightened on the submachine gun.

At a distance of thirty to forty meters, Alex knew that as an inexperienced marksman he would be lucky to place a shot anywhere near the blond man. But it was a gamble he had to take. He raised his weapon carefully, steadying the barrel on the rock, blinking the sweat from his eyes.

With his focus on Bairstow, Cyrus hadn't seen Alex pop up.

Alex's heart thundered in his ears and his vision narrowed. He would go for the chest. It was a bigger target than the head. It seemed like he was staring through a tunnel as he drew a bead on his target.

A female figure appeared beside Cyrus. Then two more figures, the foot soldiers. It was obvious from the direction of Noora's aim that she had spotted Alex. There was no stopping what was about to happen.

The following seconds seemed to last an eternity.

Alex was first to squeeze the trigger. Nothing happened. The gun was jammed. *Fuck!* Ducking behind the rock, he hastily reloaded. His hands shook so badly he failed to get the magazine in the slot.

Then the silence of the desert erupted. The crackle and pop of gunfire lasted about five seconds.

Chest heaving, gasping for air, it took Alex a few seconds more to notice the silence. He rolled over and peered cautiously around the base of the rock. Across the void four bodies lay sprawled on the sand.

Sadie stood about three meters away, the Uzi from the saddlebags outstretched. Her shoulders shook. Spent brass casings glittered in the sand around her feet. Even at that distance, Alex could tell Noora and the others were dead.

His gaze snapped around to where Bairstow had been standing.

His friend lay prone, on his stomach, face to the side. Blood seeped across the dirty white fabric of his shirt. Wisps of smoke rose from the muzzle of the assault rifle at his side.

69

Sadie dropped her weapon and scrambled down the far side of the wadi. She picked her way unsteadily across the bottom and climbed the near slope to where Alex was attending to Bairstow.

The Englishman groaned loudly. The bullet had passed under his left arm-pit, grazing the ample flesh covering his ribs. An inch to the right and it would have been game over. Alex dressed the wound as best he could, using the first aid kit removed from the Land Rover that morning.

Once Bairstow was comfortable, they left him resting in the shade of the rocks and climbed down into the canyon. Sadie was shaken, but surprisingly strong given the bullet wound in her own arm. Within a few seconds they were at the bottom.

Alex took her in his arms.

"I thought you were dead."

For a long time, they stood there, holding each other, saying nothing.

Eventually they disentangled themselves and approached the cleft. Alex was shocked to find the German bomber completely buried by sand.

It will probably lie there for another fifty years before it is uncovered by another sandstorm. He wondered if Smith's manuscript had even been on the plane in the first place.

They sat on a boulder and stared at the sandstone slope on the far side. With the adrenaline no longer coursing through his veins, he was spent. He stared at his hands. They no longer trembled. But the knot in his stomach, pulled tight for days, was still there.

He retrieved a crushed pack of cigarettes from his pants and found one that was still intact.

"Alex?"

"I'm sorry, Sadie." They were the only words he could think of. He lit the cigarette, drew in a lungful of smoke.

"For what?"

"For not finding you sooner, for thinking you were gone, for…for everything."

Sadie gently adjusted his scarf and forced him to look at her.

"It's okay, Alex, we're okay. Tell me what else is wrong?"

"I dunno." Alex sighed deeply. "I guess I'm wondering if it really matters whether what the professor discovered was genuine, or if he was the scribe. I certainly think he was capable of either."

Wincing at the pain in her arm, Sadie took the cigarette and inhaled before replying. She pulled a face and handed it back.

"I'm not sure Smith's manuscript, if it was not a hoax, would change much for the two billion or so Christians around the world," she said. "What it might do, though, is create a big problem for a Church that has taken some liberties with scriptural interpretations over the centuries."

"Yup," said Alex. "As the wise man said: 'Faith is to believe what you do not see; the reward of this faith is to see what you believe.'"

"Mark Twain?"

"Saint Augustine."

"Didn't Mark Twain say something similar?"

"Yeah. 'Your faith is what you believe, not what you know.'"

"Alex?"

"Yeah?"

"I believed in you, and us, that we'd come out the other side of this. Maybe belief is more powerful than our cynicism lets us grasp."

■ ■ ■

They sat on the boulder in silence for nearly twenty minutes, when Alex realized something was different on the far wall of the wadi. His eyes were sandblasted and he rubbed them hard with the heels of his hands. The patch of deep shadow about ten meters up the sandy slope was still there.

He stood for a better view.

"Hey Sadie, wait here."

He scrambled up to the camels, returning a few minutes later with one of the hurricane lanterns from the saddlebags.

They squinted up at the rock wall. About halfway to the top was a darker patch in the shade, an opening. The surface around it appeared mottled, a deeper reddish-brown than the surrounding stone. Handprints were just visible. They reminded him of the aboriginal art he'd seen in Australia, as if hundreds of children had used their palms as cutouts.

He knew this part of the desert was riddled with caves. They appeared and disappeared with the storms. The caves were famous for their rock art dating back to the last Ice Age.

Alex shot Sadie a glance.

"You game?"

"You bet."

70

Alex heard the breath catch in Sadie's throat.

The depictions of human figures, animals and hunting scenes daubed on the rough surface of the walls flickered in the glow of their lantern. Crudely drawn in rust-colored ink, the animals looked like giraffes and buffalo. There was even something that resembled a hippo, and, in one place, a large a headless bull.

But it wasn't the painted figures decorating the interior of the cave that held their attention.

It was the real body lying on the sandy floor.

The skin of his face was stretched tight, blackened and barely distinguishable from the leather of the flying helmet. Mummification in the desert occurred quickly, the drying process depriving bacteria of fluid, preventing decomposition. Alex read somewhere that before they began to embalm their dead, ancient Egyptians buried them in shallow pits. Nitrate salts in the sand leached out every drop of moisture.

The man lay on his side, knees drawn up, eyes tightly closed. Scorch marks darkened the earth near his feet where he'd built a fire. With no cloud cover or vegetation, nighttime temperatures in the desert routinely dropped below zero. Alex bent down to examine the blackened earth, running his hand through the ashes.

It took a few seconds for him to recognize what he was looking at—the charred remains of books.

Dozens and dozens of brittle pages littered the ground.

He poked at some of the tiny fragments with a finger, turning them to dust. Here and there a few words were still discernible. Most were in languages he did not recognize, but some were in Greek.

He raised his arm. The unsteady flame illuminated empty steel packing crates nearby. Taking in the scene, Alex experienced a wave of sorrow.

This was a lonely death. I'm intruding on a still life undisturbed for more than half a century.

It occurred to him that by the time Smith returned to the monastery in 1958 and announced the Secret Gospel to the world two years later, the ancient manuscript that was to become his enduring legacy had probably already been destroyed, here in this cave.

"Who is he?" Sadie whispered.

Alex did not reply.

He gently pulled open the front of the mummy's pale-blue tunic. The lace around the man's neck securing the small oval plate broke at his touch. Three wooden beads dropped silently to the sandy floor of the cave. He held the plate to the flame: a standard-issue German military identification tag. It looked like zinc, perforated in the middle and stamped with identical information above and below the dotted line. Had this man been found by his comrades, the lower half of the tag would have been used for grave registration and notification of the family, the upper part left with the body.

There was no name, just a number and blood type.

Alex unbuttoned the man's breast pocket. The fabric broke apart in his hand and he removed a light-blue booklet. Stamped in black ink across the cover was the word *Soldbuch*, above which was an embossed German eagle in flight, swastika gripped in its talons, the basic pay and identity document for all active-duty German soldiers.

He lifted the cover gently. A handsome face, thick eyebrows, and square jaw, stared out from a black-and-white photo above a scrawled signature and typed name: Hans Otto, Hauptmann.

He closed the booklet and gently replaced it in the man's pocket. It caught on something. He slid his fingers deeper into the pocket and removed a square of paper. He carefully unfolded it, working slowly so as not to damage the brittle parchment. A single sheet of paper, a letter written in German.

The hand was large and messy. Probably penned here in the cave, in the flickering firelight by a man who knew he was dying of thirst, of starvation. The moniker scrawled at the bottom was just legible. Hans.

He refolded the page and slipped it into his own shirt pocket.

A gust of wind passed through the cave, and the burned remains of the books on the sandy floor disintegrated and scattered. Alex wondered, against his reason, whether Hans Otto's spirit had been waiting to be found, and could now travel away with the last of the pages that surrounded him as he died.

71

Avigail Stern knew the numbers were part of an effort by the SS guards to dehumanize her, but she wore them with pride. They were testament to the resilience of those who bore them and reminded her daily of those who had not survived.

She explained to her three visitors that she'd received hers as a young woman interred at Auschwitz before being transferred to Ravensbrueck, the Nazi concentration camp almost exclusively for women.

"That was where I met Rebekah," she said softly, stroking the faded blue ink on her forearm. "I can't look at these without being reminded of her. Given the circumstances, we became so close. Like sisters." Avigail paused to pour three cups of tea and then a fourth for herself, from the porcelain pot on the garden table. "We'll leave Rachel's in the pot until she gets here. It is busy down at the hospital today."

The sun was shining, the sky perfectly clear. It was a good day to sit outside, as long as there was shade. Much to her satisfaction, the flowers were doing wonderfully. A profusion of scarlet, crimson, blue, purple, and white surrounded them.

She continued with her story. Alex noticed her eyes. They were unfocussed, staring into the past.

The final pieces of the puzzle lie here, with this woman.

"The Nazis began construction of the camp in November 1938, at a site near the village of Ravensbrueck in northern Germany, about fifty miles north of Berlin," Avigail explained. "The first inmates were approximately nine hundred women. They were Jews, gypsies, communists, and criminals. By the end of 1942, the prisoner population had expanded to nearly ten thousand. By the beginning of 1945, the camp had more than forty-five thousand prisoners and was bursting at the seams."

Among them were Avigail Stern, daughter of a rabbi, and Rebekah Weizmann, whose crime against the Reich was to have a father that was a prominent Jewish industrialist. They became firm friends in a place where friendship inevitably meant pain and loss.

Avigail said, "In the camp infirmary, the SS doctors subjected the prisoners to medical experiments, causing terrible wounds that imitated those sustained by soldiers on the battlefield. They treated us with various experimental medicines to prevent infections. Some worked, some did not. Testing was also done on amputation techniques and setting and transplanting bones. Most of the women died."

Avigail, however, did not. Like the few other survivors, she'd suffered permanent internal damage and almost constantly felt pain. But in this, she also regarded herself as lucky. The SS doctors carried out sterilization experiments on some of the women.

"When Rebekah arrived at the camp, she had a daughter, just a year old. I'm not sure why the guards let her keep the child. Rebekah was strikingly beautiful and from the start, she was treated differently. The things they made her do..."

Avigail's voice cracked, "The only reason she did not end it all herself was the child."

Periodically, the camp guards subjected their charges to selections, isolating those prisoners considered too weak or injured to work, and killed them. At first, those selected were shot. When that became a waste of precious bullets needed in the war effort, the women were transferred to killing centers and to the Auschwitz-Birkenau extermination camp. There, they were gassed, a far cheaper and more efficient process.

Finally, in the autumn of 1944, the SS constructed a gas chamber at the women's prison camp. They gassed several thousand before the liberation by

Soviet forces in April 1945. Rebekah Weizmann made it all the way through to February of that year. Then, one day, she just disappeared.

"It was often the way at Ravensbrueck. One day, someone was there, another, they were gone," said Avigail. "I was heartbroken, of course, but I don't recall crying. There were no tears left by that stage, and I had her daughter to protect." Her words trailed off and Alex gently touched her arm. His hand settled on the tattoo and he wondered if he should be touching it, but Avigail smiled kindly and continued.

"It was one night early on in our time at the camp that Rebekah told me about the boy she'd met at boarding school in England, just before the war. It was a strange name, and I never forgot it. Morton. Morton Smith."

Alex swallowed, throat dry. He realized he had goose bumps. Finally they were getting to the truth. He took a sip of his tea and nodded for the old woman to continue.

"He was a little older than she was and his mother was Sri Lankan, father English, I remember that, too. They fell madly in love. The love of her life, Rebekah always called him. She was only sixteen, perhaps seventeen, but she was a very physical girl." Avigail chuckled.

"It was the memory of him, and his likeness in their child, that kept her sane through those years in the camp. She talked about finding him again after the war, marrying and having more children, a house, white picket fence, the works. You know, it seems strange in hindsight, but we always believed we would survive. Both of us did. It was not until Rebekah was murdered that I think I truly lost faith."

The final pieces of the story just slotted into place. Alex had a clearer picture of his friend.

He said, "After the war, you adopted the girl?"

"Yes. Her name is Rachel. Like me, she is an old woman now."

"And you found him, tracked him down?"

"It wasn't hard. When Rebekah's father learned of the pregnancy, she was abruptly pulled out of boarding school and returned to Germany. She and Morton corresponded until the letters stopped getting through. It was about a year after that that the family was rounded up and sent east to the camps.

"Rebekah knew Morton was studying at Cambridge. He was easy for me to find from there. I was fairly sure he had not fought in the war, even though he would have been of the correct age. Did you know he'd had polio as a child, he was a cripple?"

Alex did not, but recalled that evening at the riverside mansion in Phnom Penh when he'd first noticed Smith's slight limp. It seemed a lifetime ago.

"And you've been in touch ever since?"

"Yes. The early days in Israel were difficult ones. He would send money to help out, still does, even though we don't need it anymore."

"Does it upset you that Morton worked for the Nazis?" Alex couldn't think of a way of putting it gently.

The reply was immediate, without hesitation.

"Not in the slightest. In fact he told me about it very soon after we first met. I think it weighed heavily on his conscience. He needed to get it off his chest. He told me he would have done anything to save Rebekah. But it always puzzled him how the SS made the connection between the two of them, one an English graduate student stranded in Palestine and the other the daughter of a wealthy Jewish businessman. We never did manage to figure it out.

"But really, it is no surprise, the Nazis were cunning. In those days, it seemed they knew everything. They had eyes and ears everywhere. Nobody was safe or beneath suspicion. Neighbors turned on each other, families were divided. Morton said they approached him in the lobby of his guesthouse in Jerusalem. No beating about the bush, very matter of fact. They said he would work for them and Rebekah and his daughter would receive favorable treatment in the camp. He was stunned, of course. This was the first he knew of the child. Morton had no choice, he loved her desperately, and would do whatever it took to preserve her life, and that of the daughter he had not yet met..."

Alex interjected, "And he kept his side of the bargain. The Nazis did not keep theirs."

"Yes."

They sat in silence for a few minutes. Bairstow shifted noisily in his seat and reached for another of the sweet pastries.

The old woman was the first to speak. She cleared her throat and removed a square of folded paper from the pocket of her apron. "Now this letter in German, you say it was written by the pilot?"

"Yes. It was in his breast pocket."

Alex had faxed a copy to Avigail, after telling her the story of what transpired over the past few weeks. Back in Cairo after their experience in the Great Sand Sea, he first went to visit Gunther Hesse. He found the house in Heliopolis locked, police tape stretched across the gate and front door. A few journalistic inquiries and a call to a police contact, and he learned the old man was robbed and brutally murdered. Case closed. Alex left it at that. The Arabs were truthful in saying they killed the old man.

Avigail handed him the folded paper. "Here is my translation. I don't get to use my German often these days. It's not perfect," she said.

"Thank you."

He opened it out, smoothing the folds on the garden table.

The letter was addressed to "My Dearest Mary." Alex read it aloud. It was a love letter of sorts and chronicled the gradual disillusionment of a young German officer fighting a war he no longer believed in. Hans Otto told his young bride of the treatment of Tunisian Jews by the Nazi occupiers, his own feelings of shame and impotence. He explained his loss of faith in the Fatherland that his family long served. Then came the approach in early 1943 by an agent of British Intelligence and his decision to betray his country, defecting with the plane carrying the secret archive.

The story was moving. Alex swallowed hard to relieve the tightness in his throat. It was now clear why the aircraft was so far off course when it went down.

He continued staring at the translation. The British agent who recruited Otto was not named, yet Alex easily recognized his friend from the description. He was dumbfounded. Morton Smith must have gone to the Brits soon after being recruited by the Nazis, told them his story, and offered his services. He had been working for both sides, a double agent.

But what he read next literally took his breath away. He inhaled deeply, unable to utter a sound. He read it again silently and then a third time before looking up at Avigail.

She smiled.

72

Alex folded the translation and pushed it into the pocket of his shirt. He looked over at Sadie. Several weeks had passed since the kidnapping and subsequent shootout in the desert, but he was still struggling to believe she was actually there, alive.

Before, life had seemed so uncomplicated, yet also somehow bland. Now everything had a sharper focus, even the color of the sky seemed more vivid. He swallowed back the rising emotion, feeling foolish.

We are bound together by something invisible. Is it suffering? Alex didn't know. He wasn't sure it had a name.

A few days after they'd emerged from the desert, he used contacts at the *Jerusalem Post* to track down Avigail Stern. With her name and bank details, it was not difficult. She was shocked to hear of Smith's death and sad at having missed his funeral. They talked on the telephone several times, and as soon as Sadie and Bairstow were well enough to travel they'd booked flights on El Al to Haifa.

Deep in thought, Alex was startled by the clink of the garden gate opening and closing again. Avigail's face brightened as she replaced her teacup on its saucer and stood.

"Ah, there you are. You look exhausted!"

In her sixties, the woman walking up the garden path was tall and olive skinned, hair white as snow.

The likeness to the professor is remarkable, Alex thought as he shook her hand. *She even moves like him.*

"Dr. Stern, I'm Alex. I knew your father. I'm so sorry." It was all he could think to say.

■ ■ ■

It was midafternoon by the time they said their good-byes, promising to stop by on the way to the airport in the morning. The flight to Cairo was at 11:00 a.m. Rachel offered to drive them back to their guesthouse, but Alex insisted a walk down to the waterfront was what they all needed.

Nobody talked until they reached the esplanade, when Sadie broke the silence.

"So, are you going to write your story, about Smith?"

Alex pondered the question for several seconds. "It's too fantastic. Who would believe it?"

They fell silent again.

"What would I write? I haven't a shred of evidence. Can you imagine the uproar if I accused Israeli agents of murdering Smith to hide such a terrible yet inconvenient secret, the truth of the Vatican's complicity in the Holocaust? No editor in his right mind would touch it! Let alone the subplots of the Islamic Army and a communal Christian cult. I know I wouldn't buy it."

Sadie considered this.

"Perhaps, then, there's another story to be told, a story about the dangers of allowing the obsession with texts and interpretations to cloud the profound simplicity of faith. We may never know with any real certainty if the manuscript, or the Secret Gospel it quoted, was genuine. But we don't have the original text of any of the Gospels, do we? Seen in that light, at best the lack of academic inquiry into the professor's find represents a stubborn refusal to deal with information that might challenge deeply held personal convictions. At worst, it's about power and preserving it. I mean, think of all the volumes written about the Dead Sea Scrolls. Everyone is entitled to their perspective, and historical texts should be examined with academic rigor. Yet if we lose faith, or belief, or our common humanity in the process, haven't we lost what is essential?"

Alex grinned. *Good old Sadie, always seeing things a little more clearly than the rest of us.* He glanced at her again, allowing his gaze to rest on her face. She was pale and there were dark circles around her eyes. He wondered what scars her ordeal would leave.

Bairstow was walking a few meters ahead, munching on a bag of salted nuts purchased from a street vendor. The cries of hawkers selling pistachios and ice cream mingled with the chatter of weekend strollers as they passed the Port Inn Guesthouse. A rusty ferry made slow passage across the sea. There was no wind, and the sky formed a perfect blue dome over the Mediterranean. It struck Alex that this would have been the view Smith saw as he wrote the letter to him that changed everything.

He'd told Rachel he'd known her father.

But how well do we ever know anyone? Human beings are like dark continents with only the edges explored. The middle remains uncharted territory.

He turned to Sadie again.

"What was it they used to write in those blank spaces on old maps?"

"Here be monsters."

They were quiet for a while.

Sadie broke the silence. "So, Alex, I think you owe me an explanation."

"Of what?"

"The look that passed between you and the Stern woman. What did the final part of the letter say?"

Alex pondered the question for a moment.

"It was a map of sorts, a written set of directions."

Sadie spun to face him, eyes wide.

"It seems Morton told Hans Otto about the importance of the Secret Gospel. After the crash, he buried it."

"Jesus Christ, Alex! We've got to go back and find it."

"You think?"

They stared at each other for a long moment and then resumed their stroll along the waterfront. Alex took Sadie's hand and squeezed it. She pulled him closer and their shadows merged on the cracked and potholed footpath, human continents colliding.

AUTHOR'S NOTE

This novel contains a seed of truth. But most of it is purely the product of the author's imagination. The story borrows from the real-life discovery of the so-called Secret Gospel of Mark at Mar Saba in Israel by the renowned American scholar Dr. Morton Smith in 1958. It was a find that sparked a furious debate in the popular press and among scholars over the manuscript's authenticity, with some suggesting Smith was the perpetrator of one of history's most brilliantly executed hoaxes. That debate continues today. Since Smith's death in 1991, the speculation has only increased.

Where I cite excerpts from the Secret Gospel of Mark, these draw on translations from Morton Smith's work. For the analysis of Smith's work by the character Professor Tarb Herman, I rely heavily on the scholarly writings of Bart D. Ehrman, particularly his book *Lost Christianities*, published in 2003 by the Oxford University Press. For anyone wanting a good summary of scholarship on the Secret Gospel, it would be hard to go past "The Strange Case of the Secret Gospel According to Mark," an article by Shawn Eyer originally published in 1995 in *Alexandria: The Journal for the Western Cosmological Traditions*, volume 3.

The Muslim Brotherhood was founded in 1928 in Egypt. In 1941, a senior member turned up in Berlin, where he spent much of the war and met Hitler. For most of its history, the Brotherhood has been outlawed.

The Carpocratians were a libertine Christian sect in second-century Egypt. The Free Daist Communion, a California-based Eastern religious sect founded by Franklin Albert Jones during the 1960s, carries on some of its traditions today. Their practices have attracted a number of criminal lawsuits. When Morton Smith's book on his discovery went out of print, the Communion's publishing house, Dawn Horse Press, bought the rights and republished it. Franklin Jones died in 2008.

The news articles used in this story as the protagonist Alex Fisher researches the warming relations between the Roman Catholic Church and the state of Israel are based on real stories.

The Holocaust remains a historical thorn in the side of the Vatican.

CPSIA information can be obtained at www.ICGtesting.com
Printed in the USA
BVOW02s0123080915

416995BV00011B/92/P

9 781507 891308